THE GIRL WHO WAS TRAFFICKED

ADELINA THRILLER 1

KATHLEEN GUIRE

PRAISE FOR THE GIRL WHO WAS TRAFFICKED

By the look of the cover the book, you already know, "Okay, kids, strap yourself in, this is going to be good!"

A true eye opener!

-Rebekah Schoonover, teen from pre-read team

The Girl Who Was Trafficked is not only a compelling fiction story but a timely resource to bring awareness to the social justice issue of human trafficking. As an adoptive mom of 4 children from Eastern Europe I was wrecked several years ago when I learned that orphans are prime targets of human traffickers overseas. This dark disturbing industry is right under our noses here in the U.S. with foster youth being targeted as well. This book will help awaken the Church to the evil of this issue and how we must be a voice for the voiceless.

Sandra Flach,

Exec. Director of Justice For Orphans

The Girl Who Was Trafficked takes you through the twists, turns, and turmoils of life as an orphan who's trying to get adopted and also protecting her best friend. Kathleen draws you in from the beginning and takes you on an emotional roller coaster ride as you fall in love with and root for the main characters.

Lori Shaffer @ighomeschool.moms

Told from the voice of a Polish orphan, *The Girl Who Was Trafficked* brings to light the horrors of the sex trafficking industry while also hitting important nuances in older child adoption. The characters are endearing and the plot keeps you on your toes. ~Melissa Corkum, adoption blogger at The Cork Board (www.thecorkums.com)

"DISCOMBOBULATE-TO CONFUSE OR DISCONCERT; UPSET; FRUSTRATE," **I said to myself.**

"Where is the pink sweater?" I yelled. I needed the pink sweater.

"Calm down, Adelina, we will find something for you to wear. Stop throwing stuff. The littles are watching!" Daria answered as she picked up the clothes I had thrown on the floor. She gave me a warning look as she hastily folded them.

"I have to look perfect! This is my first meeting with my prospective parents."

"It's okay, you know how these meetings go!" She smiled.

"No, I don't. I've never had one."

"Oh yeah, that's right. Sorry."

"Hey, don't, Daria. I didn't mean to rain on your parade. Smile. You just have one more hoop to jump through before your adoption. Our dream come true!"

Then I saw it. Out of the corner of my eye, the pink sweater walked by on a blonde-haired girl. I stuck my head out in the hallway.

"Hey, I need that sweater!"

Blonde girl did a one-eighty and walked toward me. "What?" She smiled and showed a row of perfectly white, straight teeth. Her blue eyes glowed. Her hair shone. She tucked a strand of her shoulder-length bob behind her ear and tilted her head to the side. Who was this girl?

"Oh, I see you met the new girl. This is Cecylia, girls," Sabilia, our caregiver, said as she passed us, "She's interning here this semester. And hurry it up. Breakfast and then, Adelina, you have an important meeting, right?" And she kept marching down the hall.

Meeting-a coming together of two or more people, by chance or arrangement.

The definition popped into my head.

"Redheads shouldn't wear pink," Cecylia said. "Try the green one," she added as she thrust a sweater at me. "It will bring out your freckles." And she was gone.

"We need to get the littles ready," I said as I shoved the sweater over my head. "I love this sweater. It's so soft." I glanced in the mirror, licked my hands and tried to flatten my frizz. It wasn't working. But, the sweater really made my eyes look blue. I'd have to thank Cecylia later. Communal closets were the way of the Children's Home. First come, first served was the rule.

I ran across the hallway into the closet full of cubbies and clothes and grabbed some outfits. "How doth the little crocodile improve his shining tail," I quoted, and the littles squealed in their beds.

Daria joined me, "And pour the waters of the Nile on every golden scale." She yelled the last verse and four five-year-olds shot out of bed and ran in all directions.

We were just warming up…. Together we yelled the last stanza, "How cheerfully he seems to grin, How neatly spreads his claws," as we spread our arms. "And welcomes little fishes in With gently smiling jaws."

Daria and I each caught a little and wrestled clothes on

them while they laughed. After chasing and clothing every-one, we headed down to the cafeteria for breakfast.

Daria and I had been through a lot together. I was glad to see her laughing and helping with the littles. Lately, she had been acting so strangely. She had a boyfriend, and she was sneaking out to see him at night, which wasn't like her at all. She didn't seem focused on her own adoption. It seemed as if all her efforts were going towards this guy. And why? When I came to the orphanage as a little myself, she took me under her wing and we became inseparable. Today was the begin-ning of our dreams. I had prospective adoptive parents and she had parents ready to sign on the dotted line. Why wasn't she more excited about that?

My reverie was broken by a spoonful of oatmeal splatting right in the middle of my sweater. Could this day not behave? I needed to go clean up. I had half an hour before my prospective parents came. Prospective Parents- or PPs- were always a big deal for everyone in the orphanage. Even the staff dressed up. The cleaning women worked long hours the day before with the windows open to blow out the harsh chemical smells. On those days, it was always frigid in the Children's Home.

It did feel fresh and clean with the wind rushing through the huge glass doors. The floors shone. We all put on our best faces. However faded our clothes were, they were clean. Today was extra special. Not only were there PPs here, but they were from the United States, a first for our small rural orphanage. I wiped away the glob and forced a smile and swallowed my irritation.

"It's okay. It's just food," I reassured her. She smiled and went back to eating.

"What is on your sweater? That's a new look for meeting PPs!" Cecylia appeared with a wet wipe and scrubbed the oatmeal off. "There you go," she said.

"Hey, Kasia! You're late for breakfast," I said.

"I lost something important."

"What did you lose this time?"

"I'll tell you later. You'd better get to your meeting."

"I promise I will help you find it, after my meeting!"

Kasia was always losing things. She lost T-shirts, toys, and trinkets, all in an institution where essentially there was no ownership. Once a resident hit the teen years, she could squirrel away some money or a few belongings. It was never much or valuable or it disappeared. It seemed like my full-time job to help her find whatever she lost, but I didn't mind. It gave my brain a challenge. I think that sometimes, she didn't lose things at all, but rather just wanted to make sure I knew she existed.

With a fresh, clean, and slightly wet sweater, I headed to the common room to wait for the American couple.

Parent-a father or a mother. A protector or guardian.

Another definition. I could see it on the dictionary page in my mind's eye.

The room was empty. I headed toward the long bank of windows at the front of the orphanage to watch and wait. The leaves swirled around in small circles as the school bus pulled up and the kids filed out the front door to go to the village school.

"In rough October, Earth must disrobe her," I recited. I held my breath and clenched my fists until I felt dizzy. I exhaled and sucked in a long, slow breath. Waiting sucked.

What if they took one look at me and bolted? I took another breath and looked around. They could be my ticket out of here. I hope they live in New York City. The best place in the world. No village school where I stuck out like a sore thumb. A school where everyone was an individual. My art would be an accepted gift, not a curse. My red hair and freckles wouldn't be weird among a sea of blonde beauties like it was here.

"Your parents are here. They will have coffee with

Director Josef before they come up," Sabilia informed me as she joined me at the window. "See there?" She pointed towards a car. Four people got out. "They have with them a lawyer, an interpreter and oh! There they are! Remember your English!"

A thin average-looking woman, wearing a chartreuse pea coat and matching hat and scarf, walked toward the building. Her long red hair scraped her shoulders. A tall brawny man with wide shoulders wrapped his tan coat around himself more tightly and took long strides towards the door. They were talking to each other, but I couldn't hear them.

"She has red hair," I said quietly. Was it a sign?

"Yes, she does. They look like a lovely couple. Come away from the window. We don't want them to think we are spying on them."

Sabilia and I sat at the table on the farthest side of the room from the windows. She poured me tea, and I tried to drink it. My hands were shaking. This could be it. All of my dreams could be coming true. I could be adopted. There was a giant lump in my throat I couldn't swallow. I could go live in New York and have my own room. My own things.

"Sabilia, I'm super nervous! What do I say?"

"You just be yourself."

Nervous-highly excitable; unnaturally or acutely uneasy or apprehensive, I recited in my head.

No, myself was the worst person to be. I needed a few minutes to think. I needed to be someone else. Someone nice and lovable. Someone like Daria.

Just then, the door opened and Director Josef stepped in with the couple and two men in suits. She had taken her hat off and her red hair cascaded down to her shoulders. She smiled at me.

"Hi. I'm Marge. You must be Adelina."

"Hi. I'm Jim. We're the Hunters. Nice to meet you, Adelina."

They looked at the interpreter and waited. "That won't be necessary," Sabilia interjected. "Adelina speaks English well. Hello. I am Sabilia, a social worker here at the orphanage and her legal guardian."

What?! Why did she say that? I had only spoken English with the professor and at school. I practiced with partial books in the library like *Favorite Poems Old and New*. Suddenly, my head was reciting *"The Months"* by Christina Rossetti. *January cold and desolate. February dripping wet..*

My mouth took over and I heard myself say,"Hello, it is nice to meet you, " I thrust my hand out towards them and Marge took it. "Would you like some tea?" I pointed toward the tea and we sat down. I felt detached from myself, as if someone else had taken over my body. Someone polite with steady, calm nerves. It was as if I were an observer, watching another girl interacting with the Hunters.

It took a few minutes for me to loosen up and ask some real questions. I finally got the guts to do it when I saw a blonde head peeking in the doorway, then another, then another. The littles and Kasia.

"I haven't found that thing I lost, yet," she mouthed.

"Excuse me." I walked over to the entourage. "What are you doing here? You are supposed to be in school! And where is the littles' caregiver?"

"She wasn't feeling well. I told her I could handle them. I couldn't go to school. You had this meeting thing. I needed to make sure it went okay and besides, I lost something." I bit my lip and pasted on a smile.

The kids pushed their way into the common room and wandered over to Marge and Jim. This wasn't going well at all. I didn't want them to see the littles, then they might want one. They were all so curly-haired and cute. Next thing I knew, Marge was holding one on her lap and laughing. I looked towards Sabilia for some help, but she was laughing too.

disaster-a calamitous event, especially one occurring suddenly and causing great loss of life, damage, or hardship, as a flood, airplane crash, or business failure.

"What's this one's name?" Jim said. I knew it. It was all over.

"Ania," Sabilia offered. And I thought she was on my team.

"Kasia, get these kids out of here!" I hissed. I felt like a snake chasing the littles out of the garden of Eden, but this was my chance, my last chance. Not theirs.

"Hey, are you mad at me?" Kasia whispered.

"No. Sorry, kid. I just need to finish this meeting so I can help you find that important thing you lost." I was mad at her. Mad as a rabid fox in a hen-house. I couldn't stay mad, though. It would pass in a few minutes. It had to. I couldn't show the angry side of me. Not during this first meeting.

She rounded up the littles, and she was gone.

I walked back over to Marge and Jim. The two suits were at another table, drinking coffee and talking. Finally, I had them all to myself.

"Where were we? Oh yes, where do you live, Mr. and Mrs. Hunter?"

"Oh, didn't we tell you? We live in West Virginia. You will love it. The four seasons are beautiful."

"I think the weather is similar to here," Jim added.

West Virginia. Where was that? I wasn't super solid on the unimportant states. I knew the big ones -Texas, California, New York, and of course the Polish capital, Chicago, Illinois.

"Yes, we have a bit of acreage. You will love it!" Jim pulled out his phone and scrolled through some pictures of a suburban-looking home with white columns, a wooded back yard and a pool.

Not…. New York City. Not…

I smiled and said the right things. At least I think I did. I just wanted to get out of the meeting and think. Did I want this? Did I want to go to West Virginia?

"Adelina, they're leaving. The Hunters are leaving. You need to walk to the front door with them and say goodbye," Sabilia said as she took me by the elbow.

"Of course."

I walked down the stairs and we chatted about our plans for the next day.

"Would you show us around the village, Adelina? Would you like to see the castle we are staying in?"

"Oh, yes, sure. That would be nice. Goodbye!"

"Goodbye!"

"What is going on with you, Adelina? You should be on cloud nine. Those are wonderful people. Did you even hear a word they said?" Sabilia asked.

"Oh, I'm sorry. They are just not what I expected."

"They are a dream come true for a girl your age, or any age. She is an author and he is a business owner. You will live in a nice house and have siblings."

"Siblings? They already have children?" Boy, I wasn't paying attention. How did I miss that? That wasn't part of my plan.

"Yes, they have three children - sixteen, eighteen, and twenty-five. Rob, Anne and Laura. You need to get your head in the game. Get some rest before your next meeting. That's an order."

I trudged back up the stairs. My bubble burst. Siblings. No traipsing on the subway around New York City and going to art school by myself. I probably wouldn't even have my own room. Did West Virginia have art schools? Did it have schools at all? And who was Sabilia to tell me what to do? She had only been here a month. She probably had some fancy degree and …

"Adelina! You said you would help me!" Kasia yelled from the top of the stairs.

"I'm coming. I'm coming. What did you lose?"

"I lost my stuffed Teddy, the one my dad gave me."

"Again?" Kasia's dad hadn't given her anything.

It was a game that Kasia played with herself. Every time there was a new shipment of toys to the orphanage from some well-meaning church organization, Kasia attached herself to one of the stuffed animals and spread the rumor that her dad had given it to her. This month, it was a scruffy teddy bear. Last month it had been a bright red Elmo plush doll that laughed. I played along with her because I knew the pain of being abandoned.

I had fuzzy memories of my parents. They were noisy and angry most of the time. Noise meant someone was going to get hurt. My dad threw me across the room once, breaking my arm. Mom stuffed me in a moldy closet for hours on end. I peeled the paint off the walls to pass the time. I found a pencil in the closet and started drawing on the walls. By the time I was removed from the home, I had covered every inch of the closet walls with my sketches. I had flashbacks that showed up at the most inconvenient times. Kasia didn't seem to have any. She was an infant when placed in an orphanage in Piotrkow. So, she made up memories, and I played along.

"Here it is! I found it!" It was stuffed under one of the littles' pillows.

"Oh, so glad you found it. My dad would have been so disappointed if he knew I lost it."

Her items were never hard to find. Sometimes I think she hid them herself.

"Let's get the littles and go to dinner. I'm starving!"

Kasia and I walked back down the stairs to the main foyer with the littles following us like ducks in a row. The foyer was bursting at the seams with the rest of the kids fresh home from school, noisy and hungry. I held a child's hand on either side of me. Kasia did the same, and I scanned the crowd for Daria.

"Hey!" I shouted her way, but she didn't respond. Her eyes looked red and puffy, like she had been crying. What's going on with her? The only time I really got to see Daria anymore was on Sundays. We'd meet after church and talk for an hour over coffee, and then she made excuses. She had to go see this new guy in her life. Everything was so secretive. He was great, she said, good looking, and he really understood her.

All the while, she was edgy one minute. Euphoric another. Weepy the next. I couldn't read her anymore. Why was she pushing me away? Because the adoption was going to be final? She'd be leaving the orphanage for good. Maybe that was it. We pushed our way through the crowd and to our table. Daria will join us, I thought. I was too busy handling the littles, getting them food and thinking about my dreams going down the tubes. I hadn't even noticed until halfway through the meal that she wasn't there.

"Where's Daria?" I asked Kasia.

"I don't know!"

"I'll tell you where she is," Cecylia said from the next table. "She is upstairs crying. She wouldn't tell me what the deal was. Maybe she would tell you."

I couldn't leave the littles. I would catch up with her later.

After the littles were in bed, I joined Daria in our room. She was under the covers, head and all.

"Hey, you!" I said.

"Oh, Adelina. How did your meeting go?"

"It was great. Fine. Good. I don't know. They don't live in New York. They live in some place called West Virginia. And, get this, they already have three kids. Bummer. I'm not sure what I want to do."

"What?!" she yelled. "I mean, what?" she said, softer this time, "Adelina, this is your chance. Don't mess it up because of your perfect dream of living in New York City. It's not worth it." Then she sniffled and pulled the covers back over her head.

I pulled myself up on the top bunk and snuggled under the covers. "I am not sure. I want to give them a chance. This is our chance, remember. Hey, how did your psychologist meeting go today?"

"I don't want to talk about it. Goodnight, Adelina! Accept the parents. Don't mess this up!"

"I'm going to get a drink. Goodnight."

I padded to the teen kitchen and pulled the strawberry juice out of the fridge. I poured a glass and sat down. I needed to think. Was Daria right? Should I give up my dream and accept reality? I headed to my favorite spot in the orphanage, the library. The shelves weren't lined with books, but contained just a few donated from the States from well-meaning churches, all in English. All with multiple pages missing because the teens used them to make homemade cigarettes.

Today, the walnut shelves shone for my PPs. A massive ancient cassette tape player sat in the corner on a table with a small stack beside it. Vivaldi, Bach, Mozart, Handel. Most had whole songs recorded over. Another practice of the teens was to tape a rap song and play it until the tape wore out. I knew where the classical music still existed. I could fast forward past the rap by eyeing the tapes. This was my sanctuary. I pretended this room glistened like the library I had seen on TV.

It was the …

antithesis-opposition; contrast

(I found that word in the dictionary) of the rest of the orphanage. I could imagine it was homey, with rich woods and a colorful rug instead of stark and cold. I could listen to the few tapes, study my English, sketch on the few book covers or scraps of graph paper, and sometimes get a few minutes of peace. Not often. The other teens came in and scavenged for whatever they needed and taunted me. They called me bookworm and ripped pages out of the only poetry book.

It had been five years since Professor Wroblewski, a retired literature professor from Warsaw University,had started my English lessons here. He volunteered his time every afternoon to teach anyone willing to learn. I was the only one willing. Fueled by my dream of going to New York, I learned the English language with him. He had died suddenly last fall, leaving me. Just one more person in my life to leave. I blamed him for having a heart attack. Why did he die? I needed him. After he died, his granddaughter came to the orphanage and handed me a small leather bound dictionary. She cried, and I awkwardly patted her on the back.

"He would want you to have this," she said. "He spoke of you often. He was proud of you."

I thanked her and thought of his massive library, which I had borrowed books from. Gone. My source of literature and language was gone. I had offered her a weak smile and cried with her. I cried for the loss of books. She cried for the loss of a grandfather.

I plopped a tape in the player and switched it on. I could use some Vivaldi's *Four Seasons* right now. I made sure the volume was low before I sat down to study.

"Hey, too bad about your friend!"

I turned around to see Cecylia in all of her glory, wearing pink PJs and smiling. She had her hands on her hips like some sort of superhero. I was beginning to like her. She was too preppy and happy, which was annoying, but she was also kind. I needed some kindness and some counsel right now.

"Yeah, her PPs pulled out. Sad. But, I'm sure you knew that, being the best friend and all. I can't see her ever getting adopted, can you?" She sat down next to me and her shoulders slumped forwards as if she were sad. Was she? I couldn't read her.

"I didn't know that. She didn't tell me."

"Really, I thought she would have. Vivaldi, huh? My mom listens to that." She looked as if she had swallowed a sour apple when she said that. Tears pooled at the corners of her eyes. "Ignore me. Homesick college girl. Tell me about Daria."

"She's been acting weird. It's almost as if she wanted this adoption to fall through and now maybe she regrets it?"

"Why do you say that?" She picked up the dictionary and thumbed through it. I wanted to grab it. It was mine. As if she read my mind, she handed it to me.

"I don't know. She has this boyfriend. It's a secret. She sneaks off and meets him. She says he is amazing, but she seems so conflicted."

"That stinks. I'm so sorry. I wish I could help."

"Thanks for listening."

"Get back to your studying. Your English is impressive," she said in flawless English." I heard you today. Speaking English will get you places."

I started back to my room with a black cloud hanging over my head. How could I have been so stupid and selfish? BAM! I walked right into Sabilia because I wasn't paying attention. She looked down at me.

"Oh, Adelina, good meeting today. Nice parents." I guess she wasn't paying attention either.

Daria was asleep when I got back to the room and I didn't want to wake her. I would apologize in the morning. I had so much to think about. *I think that I shall never see A poem lovely as a tree....* *I fell asleep dreaming of apple trees and subways.

The next day dawned gray and cold. I looked out the window. The trees looked naked. All their leaves sat in wet mushy heaps in the yard, waiting for someone to burn them. No one would. They would sit in slimy piles, rotting, stinking and advertising the poverty of the orphans inside. At least I

---

* Joyce Kilmer, Trees

didn't have to go to school today. I got to show the Hunters around Sulejow.

"Hey, Daria, you awake?" I peered over the side of the bed at the rumpled pile of her under the covers. "Wake up. I'm sorry. I've been stupid. I will be nice to the Hunters. I heard about your PPs pulling out. I've been a jerk. Daria!" I jumped out of bed and onto her. Or not. She wasn't there. I pulled back the covers to find a pile of stuffed animals. "Daria's gone!" I yelled to anyone who would listen. Sabilia came running in. "What?"

"Daria. She's gone! I think she ran away and it's all my fault."

Gone- departed, left.

"DON'T OVERREACT, ADELINA," Cecylia said as she peeked her head around the corner. "Maybe she just needed some time to chill."

"Cecylia is right, Adelina," Sabilia agreed, "maybe she is taking an early walk to think about things."

Were they crazy? Daria, my Jiminy Cricket, play-by-the-rules girl. She didn't use to leave the premises without permission. First the secret boyfriend. Now this. Was something really wrong or was I freaking out about nothing? Daria did take long walks to clear her head. I needed to remain calm. I am just making a mountain out of a molehill.

Molehill- to exaggerate a minor difficulty. (Idiom)

"Adelina, your PPs are going to be here in half an hour! You need to get ready," Sabilia added as she walked out of the room.

I looked down at the pile of blankets. Gray pewter caught my eye. What was that? Under the fold? The bracelet with the home charm. She wouldn't have left that!

"The littles are waiting for you, "Cecylia said. I was beginning to like Cecylia, but at the same time, she irritated me. Always showing up. She seemed to be everywhere. What did a shadowing intern do anyway? It wasn't clear what her position was. Social worker? Computer specialist? Both? Suddenly, I heard Daria's voice in my head, "We help the littles because we were once them and no one helped us, remember?"

I picked up the charm and stuffed it in my pocket and breezed past Cecylia. She turned and followed. I could feel her breath on my neck.

"What was that? What did you pick up?"

"Nothing."

"It wasn't nothing. Let me see."

I showed her the charm. "Oh," she said quietly. She didn't get it. I could tell.

"Listen, Cecylia, I need to get the littles ready for breakfast. I have a PP meeting, remember? I know you're new here, but we like to stick to a schedule."

"Let me help," she said.

I really wanted to fill her in. She had been so kind, but I couldn't. Not yet.

We dressed the littles, and I threw on some clothes myself. We all headed to the cafeteria, with the littles chattering like baby chicks. Kasia joined us.

My stomach was in knots. I couldn't choke down any food. I sipped the *Kawa z mlekiem* (coffee and milk).

> *Sometimes with the Heart*
> *Seldom with the Soul*
> *Scarcer once with the Might*
> *Few — love at all.*

I had started defining words or reciting poetry in my head when I was little. I suffered from mutism for the first ten years of my life, but I taught myself to read. After the professor died, I recited a larger variety. He had become a part of my life in a way I had never known. He wasn't just a teacher. He was like a grandfather. I think. I didn't really know what a grandfather was like. The professor told me stories about his life, how his father fled Poland to the U.S. to escape the Nazis. When the Nazis came, his father had been in Switzerland at a Zionist convention for journalists. He was warned not to return home. Instead, he fled to the US. and started working on arrangements to get the rest of the family out. Why was I thinking about this now? I guess his stories had a calming effect.

Calm-not showing or feeling nervousness, anger, or other emotions.

"What's wrong, Adelina?" Kasia asked. "Are you nervous about your second meeting?"

"No, I'm worried about Daria."

"Daria? I thought she just went out for some air. That's what Sabilia said. Cecylia too."

"I'm not sure. I think there is more to it than that. Look!" I slid the bracelet out of my pocket.

"It's the home bracelet," she stated matter-of-factly.

"Right. And she wouldn't even go to breakfast without it. And where is she now? She didn't eat dinner last night. And now, no breakfast."

"She must be starving!"

"Right!"

"Looks like we have some*one* instead of some*thing* to find today."

"I have to go show my PPs around Sulejow. Can you keep your ears open today?"

"Yes, I can!"

We stood up and cleared the table. I ushered the littles back to the common room and walked back to the foyer to wait on my ride. A taxi pulled up and Marge waved through the rolled-down window. I opened the back door and slid in next to her.

"Are you ready to show us the sights?" she asked.

"I think so." Focus, focus, focus, I told myself. You blew it yesterday.

Focus-a central point, as of attraction, attention, or activity.

You need to do this not only for yourself, but for Daria, I told myself. She was right. I had an unrealistic dream. Truth is, I knew it could never come true. In fact, I didn't expect it to. I just knew it was something I could control. This daydream. I could add or subtract things from it as if I were writing a novel. I reworked my wardrobe, my hairstyles, my art supplies. I imagined every moment of every day of my future in New York. Who was I kidding? I didn't have a clue. I lived on the outskirts of a small village that was lined with apple orchards. I knew Daria was missing, and she was my best friend. She was the one dream that had come true in my life. A friend.

"Let's stop here first!" I pointed out the window at a small white building set back from the brick street. One window was covered with cardboard and secured with duct tape. The stucco was cracked and peeling. The owner met us at the door, dusting his flour-covered hands on his white apron. He wasn't only the owner, but the baker, custodial staff and bookkeeper all rolled into one. His small living quarters were connected to the building. I wasn't friends with the baker or any of the shopkeepers. The only adult friends I had were Josef, the director and the professor. Okay. Really, just the professor. Josef wasn't really my friend.

'What is this?" Marge asked.

"It's a bakery."

"I'm in," Jim exclaimed with enthusiasm. He had the door open and was three strides ahead before we were out of the car. "Do they have white rolls here? I am tired of this dark brown stuff. Marge loves it."

I opened the door and ran to catch up with Jim before he tried to order. Too late. I could hear him butchering the phrases. I didn't want the baker to be offended. They both laughed, and I was relieved. Jim seemed to have some super charm power. He had a dozen rolls in his hand and the baker gave me a price.

"What did he say?" Jim asked.

"A million American dollars," I said. Now Jim was going to be offended. How could I manage this day? I looked up, and he was smiling, then guffawing with giant belly laughs. He threw some money on the counter (three times the going rate) and yelled, "Keep the change!"

Whew! What a relief. If he kept throwing money around like that, the whole village would love him. I turned around when I realized that Marge hadn't said a word. She was standing silently behind me. She smiled at me. Her blue eyes sparkled.

"Yes, Adelina, he is like this everywhere we go. Everyone loves Jim. Everyone remembers Jim. He has a superpower. You'll get used to it."

She linked arms with me and we walked out onto the sidewalk. "How about we ask the taxi to wait while we browse a few more shops?"

Jim was on it before she could finish the sentence, as if he had read her mind. Is this what married couples were supposed to be like? My parents were never like this. Not two people complimenting each other and anticipating thoughts, but two animals at each other's throats like that poem in the book in the library. *The Duel*. I had memorized that poem because it reminded me of my family. I thought it was family. The last stanza came to mind.

Next morning where the two had sat
   They found no trace of dog or cat;
   And some folks think unto this day
   That burglars stole that pair away!
   But the truth about the cat and pup

Is this: they ate each other up!
Now what do you really think of that!

This was my bio parents. They ate each other up. But here were the Hunters, being kind to each other. They weren't fighting about every little thing. We walked into a shop with a LEGO emblem on the door. "Do you like LEGO kits? Our son likes them. Jim says sixteen is too old for LEGO sets, but I don't think so, do you?"

I had never owned a LEGO kit. The kids in the orphanage had been chased out of this shop over and over. Our mouths had watered over the kits. They were out of our reach. No one ever donated LEGO bricks or sets to the orphanage. There were broken, outdated toys in the common room and no end of stuffed animals. LEGOs were the Holy Grail.

"LEGO sets are okay," I said evenly. I looked at the shop owner. He hadn't even noticed me. I was tucked between two Americans. I doubt he remembered he had chased me out of the shop the week before with a bunch of the twelve-year-old boys. I picked up a kit and held it in my hand. It was amazing. I was browsing without the shouting that usually occurred about now.

"Why don't you help me pick out a kit for Robert?" Marge suggested.

"Okay. What does he like?" I pretended to know what I was doing. I pretended I had always shopped for LEGO sets and purchased them like these people did. It was nice to pretend.

"Oh, he likes building things. He is great with hands-on stuff. It has to be complicated though. Nothing too simple."

I picked up a kit and handed it to her. I had no clue. I waited, studying her face.

"Yes," she said, "this will be perfect." She smiled. Her eyes sparkled.

"Hey, you two! I found some art stuff. Adelina, what do

you think about this? You like art, right?" He was holding the kit of my dreams. At least the dreams were available to me in this small village, and even that was out of my reach.

"Yes, that's a nice kit." Don't act too excited, I told myself. Play it cool. Then I could hear Daria telling me not to blow it. Don't waste your chance. Be real. I took the kit from him; the wooden box felt wonderful. I read the content label even though I had read it a thousand times before. "Yes, Mr. Hunter, this is a super kit. I really like it."

With one swoop, it was out of my hands and on the counter. "Are you getting that Lego kit, Marge? Don't you think Robert is getting too old for LEGO sets?" But, there it was, on the counter and the shop owner was ringing it up and grinning from ear to ear.

Jim was out the door with a giant shopping bag on his arm and five steps up the sidewalk before I could process what had just happened. He just bought me an art kit. He just bought me an art kit. Maybe this adoption could work out after all.

"Ladies, let's get some food! I'm starving. I could really go for a burger. A real American burger. Where can we get one of those, Adelina?"

"We'll have to leave the village and go to Piotrków Trybunalski. Is that okay?"

"What about the castle, Jim? We were going to show her the castle, remember?"

"We can do that later. Let's go!" And he turned and headed back to the taxi.

Marge and I followed and slid into the back seat. I gave the driver some directions and we sped out of the village.

"How is it that you speak English so well?" Jim asked.

"Well, we have to learn it in school, " I said, a half truth, "and we had a tutor at the orphanage." None of the other kids became very proficient in it because they never believed they would have an opportunity to use it. I did because it was part of my dream. I thought if I could learn English, I could *will* myself to be in New York City. I didn't want to share too much about the professor. I don't know why; I guess I still got angry when I thought about him. Often, when I was falling asleep, I saw his face. Heard his stories. I dreamed of them. I saw him as a little boy in the ghetto. Hiding with his sister. He often reminded me to be thankful that I had shelter and food. The Nazis were full of rage. It consumed them.

"Don't let it consume you. It eats up your soul until you are an empty shell. Don't be an empty shell, Adelina," he had said.

As the taxi moved to the edge of the village, the castle, well, monastery, came into view. It was now a hotel. Beside it sat a church with a wall falling in.

"There it is," Marge said. "Isn't it amazing?"

I had never thought of it as amazing. It was just part of the landscape I saw every day. Now I was seeing it through fresh eyes as Marge related some of its history. The Cistercians Abbey, founded in 1176, housed the hotel the Hunters were currently staying at.

"The very picture of European charm," Marge said.

The taxi driver slowed; he must have sensed the history lesson. As we drove around in front of the castle before hopping back on the main road, I saw something. A blonde head, disheveled, peeking from behind the broken wall. Could it be? Was it Daria? I knew the shape of her head. I knew that hair. What should I do? Should I say something? Should I do something? I wrung my hands. I twisted and squeezed them. I set my jaw. What could I say? I think that's my best friend who ran away, or I think ran away, but I don't know for sure. She might just be taking a walk.....

Children of the future age,
  Reading this indignant page,
  Know that in a former time

Love, sweet love, was thought a crime.

"You're boring the girl, Marge. She knows all this!" Jim said. He looked at me and patted me on the head like a small child and said, "Let's get this girl a burger!"

And it was too late. I had missed my chance. I smiled. The Hunters were nice. I couldn't ruin this day for them. But what if it was Daria? I would run back and check later. Much later.

We pulled into the orphanage after dark, after snack and games.

"Wow! You have been gone all day! Did it go well?" Cecylia said from the other side of the lobby, smiling. I wanted to tell her the truth.

"It was okay, " I lied. "Any sign of Daria?"

"Nope," and she waltzed up the stairs.

I followed and checked on the littles. Good. Someone had helped them into their pajamas.

"Hey! You're back!" Kasia yelled from across the hall.

"Yep. Great day! How are you, kid?"

"I'm okay,"she said as she skipped toward me.

"Let me guess, you lost something."

"How did you know?"

"Good guesser."

"What is it?" I wanted to see if she had heard anything about Daria, but I knew Kasia. I had to play the game.

"I lost my favorite shirt. The one my mom gave me. The one with the heart."

"The one you wear every other day?"

"Yes, you know, it has a big purple heart in the middle! I can't find it anywhere!"

The purple hearted shirt. Kasia wore it constantly. Told everyone her mom sent it to her, even though everyone knew it came in a giant box from some church in Texas. I rifled through the cubicles attached to her section of rooms. Nothing. I went across the hall to the next suite. I began the methodical search. Kasia joined me. Her hands seemed to stop shaking when she was looking for something. The rest of the time she seemed to be in adrenaline overdrive. Something was always moving: her arms flapping, her knees knocking and/or her hands shaking. I wished I had some of her energy right now. I wanted to go to sleep, but I also wanted to sneak back into the village and look for Daria.

"Here it is!" I held it up, and she lunged for it.

"Thank you! Thank You! You're so good at finding things!"

"Welcome, kiddo. Hey, I have some snacks. Let's go in my room and eat them and you can tell me everything that happened here today."

Within minutes, my room was full of littles. I passed out squares of chocolate and Kasia talked and ate. "Well, after you left, I had to go to school. Daria didn't get on the bus. She didn't come to dinner or snack. She is just gone and none of the adults are saying or doing anything. Weird. So weird."

"Thanks, Kasia. I'm going to run up to the office and see if the director is still here. I'm going to see if he knows anything. Be right back. Don't give the littles too much chocolate." Ania reached for another square and chocolate dripped out of her mouth and down her chubby chin. Too late.

The door to the director's office was slightly ajar. I crept closer. I could smell the coffee. It smelled bold. I wished I could harness its boldness.

Bold-(of a person, action, or idea) showing an ability to take risks; confident and courageous.

"a bold attempt to solve the crisis"

I didn't feel bold. I could hear Cecylia laughing. She was leaning her head back, looking at the ceiling and laughing, crowing like a rooster on top of a hen house. The director was laughing too.

"Adelina, come in. What are you doing lurking in the

doorway? Come in. Come in. Have some coffee," he said with a chuckle.

He handed me a cup and poured some water over the grounds. I held the cup with both hands to keep my hands from shaking. I'm turning into Kasia, I thought. All a jumble of limbs.

"Cecylia was just telling me a funny joke!" He laughed again."Did you need something? Oh, I spoke with your prospective parents yesterday. You are a lucky girl." He smiled.

"Yes, a lucky girl," Cecylia echoed. She smiled a warm smile.

"Yes, I am. Thank you. I just came to ask if you had any news about Daria?"

"Ah, yes, Cecylia and I were just chatting about her. Too bad, I say."

I could feel my cheeks burning. They were red, I knew it. Chatting. They were chatting.

Chat-informal conversation.

What did that mean? He was the director. Shouldn't he be looking for her? Right now? Like the lost sheep? Isn't that what the shepherd types were supposed to do? He was always going on and on about that story in the Bible and calling us all his little lambs.

"I mean," I started slowly, carefully, "are we going to bring her back? Look for her? Find her?" I knew my voice was rising. I was squeaking by the end. I couldn't help it. I did a quick sideways glance at Cecylia.

The director put a hand on my knee and looked me straight in the eye. "Cecylia says she isn't anywhere to be found. She took a group to look for her earlier while you were away. She's gone, I'm afraid." He dropped his gaze. "That's the end of it. She has caused enough trouble. Just let it go. Let it go."

I couldn't tell them I had seen her, or I thought I had seen her. What if it had been her? And I hadn't said anything. I just sat there and let that moment slip away. Maybe it had been the only chance I had to help.

"Trouble?!" I squeaked. I really squeaked. I felt my fist ball up. The other hand gripped the mug and hot brown liquid sloshed on the floor. The director looked at me with compassion and patted my leg again.

Then I saw the folder on the desk. It had Daria's name on it. It was open. The words glared at me. Incidents of her stealing, lying, violence.

The director saw my intense gaze and quickly shut the folder, but not before I saw Cecylia's name. Why? What was going on? Why should her name be in the report. She had only been here a few days. And by whose authority?

"I'm sorry about Daria, but why don't you focus on your new family? You have your first court appointment this week, right? Exciting!" With that, he stood, and I knew I had been excused.

Then something caught my eye. Another folder on the desk. It had my name on it. What was going on? Why did the director have my case file out and why was Cecylia allowed to see it?

I had to find Daria. I had to go to the village and look for her myself. I walked back to my room and yawned a few times on the way, so as not to raise suspicions. Instead of putting my PJs on, I layered on more clothing and grabbed a flashlight. I didn't know what was going on. I didn't know whom to trust. I had to do this alone.

The woods were creepy at night, but I knew my way. I tripped on a few tree roots and bit my lip to keep from yelling. Pine trees loomed like giant guards, their boughs scraping me with pointed pine needle swords as I passed. The harvest moon hung low in the sky, yet in the dense forest, it helped little with lighting the path.I felt a presence. I felt as if someone was following me. Cecylia? I turned around quickly, waving the flashlight in an arc. No one. Just nerves.

> *THE GINGHAM dog and the calico cat*
> *Side by side on the table sat;*
> *'T was half-past twelve, and (what do you think!)*
> *Nor one nor t'other had slept a wink!*
> *The old Dutch clock and the Chinese plate*
> *Appeared to know as sure as fate*
> *There was going to be a terrible spat.*
> *(I wasn't there; I simply state*
> *What was told to me by the Chinese plate!)*

I quoted the poem aloud to calm myself. Then I did a sketch in my head. Cecylia's face with its perfect features. Her obedient hair. I ran my fingers through my unruly locks. I needed to focus on something else. The dead pine needles crunched beneath my feet. The scent of pine reminded me of Christmas when Director Josef brought a towering pine into the foyer. All of us had decorated it with homemade snowflakes. On St. Christopher Day we each got a candy bar. I had made Daria a hair ribbon. Huge. Blue gingham. Daria. Her kind face. Her blue eyes. Her blonde hair.

Wait. I remembered something. Her hair ribbon. I had seen her. She always tied her hair up in a ribbon. Always. And I had caught her hair bow out of the corner of my eye. Blue gingham. "Like Doris Day", she always said. I ran to the church yard. I called her name, quietly. I circled the church and went back to the broken wall where I thought I had seen her. I heard someone breathing.

"Daria, is that you?" I turned and tripped over a piece of broken wall and my flashlight glanced upwards into a face. "Kasia! What are you doing here?"

"I wanted to help! You always help me find things! I want to help you find Daria."

"Oh, sweetie, I need to get you back home." I stood and looked at my knee. My pants were ripped. Blood oozed out of the cut.

I couldn't look at it. I swung the flashlight around the area one last time. I wished I had said something. Why hadn't I asked Jim and Marge to stop? Was it too late?

A rock crashed and rolled in front of my feet. I jumped and swung the flashlight that direction and it landed on a face.

"What are you girls doing out here so late? Won't your parents be worried about you?"

He was handsome, fair-haired. He wasn't young. Time had etched lines around his eyes. His voice had concern, but the smile on his face seemed pasted on. I gripped Kasia's hand and dragged her away from him.

"Why don't you girls just come with me?" He asked as he advanced towards us.

I was running now. I ran through the narrow streets back towards the path to the orphanage, pulling Kasia along with me. "We just lost something, sir," Kasia was yelling. I didn't stop. I ran harder. Faster. Kasia tripped. I was flying her like a kite, her legs whipping behind her in the air. Was he following us? All I could hear was my labored breath. Was Kasia crying? Or was that sound coming from me? I couldn't tell.

THREE

THE ORPHANAGE WAS PITCH BLACK. Kasia had stopped crying and slumped against me.

"Was that man following us?"

"I don't know, Kasia. Let's get you to bed." I didn't know, but I was going to find out. Why was he lurking about the church where I had seen Daria? Did he have anything to do with her disappearance? I didn't know. Did he chase us? Was I imagining it? Maybe he really wanted to help. I imagined things. The professor said I had a vivid imagination that I let get the better of me. I let fear boss me around.

"I think I need some hot milk," Kasia whispered.

"And you deserve it, too. Let's go. Quietly. I went to the window of the supply closet and pried it open. All the teens knew this route and the staff seemed to ignore it.

Once in the teen kitchen, I warmed some milk and pulled out my sketch pad. Once the milk was warm, I poured some for both of us.

"You need to fix your knee, Adelina. It's bleeding," Kasia said.

"I will. I need to draw him first and you're going to help."

"Me? I can't draw!"

"I mean, you're going to tell me if I have it right or not."

"I'll try, but it was dark."

I had shone my flashlight on his face for just a few seconds, but it felt like an eternity. I sketched his blue eyes. Pale blue eyes. And the smile. White teeth. One missing off to the side. What were they called? I teeth? Eye teeth? Chiseled features. Blond hair, short, and well kept.

"Well?"

"Yeah, that's him. I don't like his eyes," Kasia answered as she slumped in her chair. "Can we go to bed now?"

"Yes. " and I led her to bed and tucked her in. "Don't tell anyone about this, okay? Our secret."

"About what?" she answered. Within seconds she fell asleep.

I went back to the kitchen and got out the small first aid kit and cleaned up my knee. No one would notice a pair of ripped pants. Most of the orphanage clothes were threadbare, but they would notice the blood. I stripped off the pants and rinsed them in the sink, cleaned up the dishes, and headed to my room.

I slept fitfully, with weird dreams of being chased by a giant gingham bow. I could see Daria in the distance huddled in a corner of the church, but I couldn't get to her. Finally, the night was over. I went through my normal morning routine with the littles. Kasia joined us for breakfast, groggy and sleepy-eyed. I didn't know if she was going to spill the beans or not. I couldn't risk being around when she did.

"Your PPs are here," Sabilia announced to my table. "Go get ready. I will see to the children."

"Okay, thanks," I mumbled. I was too busy formulating a plan in my head to answer coherently. Pack my bag. Get the sketch. Get emergency money out of the hiding place. I tiptoed past the common room where Marge and Jim were sipping coffee and laughing. I hated to miss this. To blow this whole deal. It wasn't exactly the way I thought it would be. No New York City or subways. I wasn't sure about art schools. They were nicer than I thought parents were.

Hope is the thing with feathers. Hope is the thing with feathers

I didn't have a lot to base my parenting picture on, and what I did have was negative. I turned back to the common room and stuck my head in.

"Adelina, hi, we're a bit early. We can wait if you're not ready," Marge said.

"I'm not. I need to gather some things." *Truth.* "I'll be back in a few minutes." *Lie.* "I just wanted to tell you I had a great time yesterday. It was cool." *Truth.* I could feel the red creep up my neck and settle on my cheeks.

"Oh my, that is wonderful, dear," Marge jumped up and hugged me. "We had a great time, too."

"We were thinking about a longer road trip today. The church of the Black Madonna. You ever been?"

"No. Sounds interesting."

I had learned from the dusty, torn and incomplete books donated to our library. I pored over the few art books and poetry books. I read the histories. I loved the story of the Black Madonna. Legend says St. Luke painted a portrait of St. Mary on a table Jesus himself had made. After the crucifixion, it had been taken to Jerusalem. After many adventures and miracles, it ended up in the forests of Belsk, in eastern Poland.

My favorite story was when the Hussites stole the picture and the horses of the invaders refused to move forward toward the village they intended to destroy. No amount of beating could persuade them. I felt like I could relate to the Black Madonna - tossed around, thrown in the mud, yet she had guts and determination and I would genuinely like to see her. I could look for Daria later. Maybe she would reappear. Maybe she was just hiding out, grieving. Then the scene from last night played over in my mind. Was the man chasing us or not? No, as much as I wanted to see the home of the Black Madonna, I wanted to find my Daria even more. I hoped for a miracle of the Black Madonna.

Miracle-a surprising and welcome event that is not explicable by natural or scientific laws and is therefore considered to be the work of a divine agency.

I'd never had a miracle in my life. I'd always had the opposite of a miracle. One of the antonyms of miracle is normality. Normal for me was negative. Any good that came my way seemed to be severed by negative things like fear, death, despair, and abandonment.

The professor had said I was a miracle to him. I had asked him why. "You give me purpose. In a way, you're a lot like me."

"How could I be like you? You went to America. Got an education. Had a life."

"The war took my parents from me. Just like you. My father never recovered from losing my mother. I was a social orphan. Like you are. On my own. Trying to sort out my grief and live life at the same time. I survived. I want you the thrive."

"I'll be right back." *Lie.*

"Oh, wait, I bought you a book," Jim said as he extended his hand with a thick, hard cover book.

Art of the Masters. I took it gingerly. I could feel tears. *Stop.* Don't cry. They trickled down my hot face. I wiped them away with my sleeve.

"This is great," I had only owned one book. Just one. The dictionary. I pretended I owned the books in the library. But, here was a book about art. I wanted to run back to my room and read it. A tiny miracle. Huge and bulky, I held it in my hand. I wanted to thrive. *I did.*

I sat down and skimmed the pages. I could feel Jim and Marge looking at me.

"We should get going, Adelina. Why don't you get your stuff?" Jim said after clearing his throat. He sounded like he had a cold. What was wrong with him?

I looked up and Marge was wiping a tear away. Her face was red and puffy around the eyes.

"Maybe you should hold on to this for me, Jim," I stated as calmly as I could. I knew my voice quavered.

"No, it's yours," he said, shoving the book back towards me.

"Umm, I don't want to lose it. Things seem to disappear around here." Just then, Kasia stuck her head in the door.

"There you are. I can't find my heart shirt and I have to get on the bus in a few minutes." A tear dripped down her cheek. This was my fault. She was too tired to be human today.

I glanced at the clock. "You still have twenty minutes."

"But my shirt," she yelled, "I need my shirt!"

"Go," said Marge, "go help her. We can wait and we will keep your book safe."

I marched Kasia to the cafeteria.

"My shirt isn't in here," she cried and slumped to the floor.

"I know. I know," I went to the window to the kitchen and called for Pani Gita, "Kasia is a little tired this morning. Can you mix her some *Kawa i mleko*?"

"Got some mixed up right here. What did she lose this time?"

"Her heart shirt," I stated.

"Ah, that one again, huh?"

"Yeah, could you give her the *Kawa i mleko* and keep an eye on her 'til I find it?"

"Sure. Go on then."

"Where are you going?" Kasia wailed.

"I'm going to find your heart shirt."

"I want to help!" she said while prostrate on the floor.

Pani Gita came out with the *Kawa i mleko* brew and propped her up. "Drink this, sweetie. Let Adelina find your shirt."

"But, I need to help you find it."

"Not this time. Sometimes I need to do things by myself." And I left. I could hear her crying as I took the stairs two at a time. She must have known there was a double meaning in that statement or she was having a delayed reaction to last night's events.

I passed the common room. Marge and Jim were chatting with Sabilia. Thanks, Sabilia, I thought. Talk for a long time, please. I found the heart shirt in a cubby off of Kasia's room. I had been right. This meltdown had nothing to do with the loss of the shirt. They never did. They were always a result of something else, for attention, for someone to tell her she existed. She mattered. That's what the professor had said. And I seemed to be that person, every time, no matter how inconvenient. I owed it to her today. I raced back down the stairs to the cafeteria. I couldn't bear to look in the common room again. I had made up my mind. I was going to look for Daria and Kasia was going to school.

Kasia had quieted down to a guttural sob. I helped her into the shirt and put a cardigan on top, then her coat. She stood up.

"You're going to school today, Kasia, No more skipping. I know you want to help me, but today, you can't." *No. No. No.* I wasn't taking her along this time. I wasn't changing my mind.

Pani Gita bustled back into the kitchen and soon we heard the clanging of pots and pans as she sang a Polish folk song.

We laughed as she danced a polka out into the cafeteria and back into the kitchen.

"There you go, Kasia. That smile is what I want to see!"

she said through the window from the kitchen and she went back to work, humming.

"Why can't I go with you today?"

"It's dangerous."

"Wait. You aren't going with your PPs?"

"No, I'm going to look for Daria. The best thing you can do is keep it quiet. Not a word to anyone. Got it?"

"Yes, I can do that."

With her shoulders slumped, she took off towards the door, giving me a pitiful glance every half second. The school bus pulled up and kids came from all directions into the foyer and headed out the door. Kasia was swept up in the crowd and onto the bus.

I ran back up the stairs and into my room. I packed my stuff quickly and ran down the stairs and went to the back hallway where the sick quarters were. Thankfully, they were empty today. I walked through them and out the back door.

"Where are you going?" I heard as the door whooshed shut.

Should I run? No. that would cause a stir. I turned and faced the voice. Cecylia.

"I'm going to look for Daria. I have to. Don't tell."

"I'll cover for you. Are you sure you want to do this?"

"Cecylia, do you have a family?"

"Yes."

"Would you do anything for them? To keep them safe?"

Her face fell, just for a microsecond, but I saw it. She had to understand. She was working as an intern. What degree was she working toward? Oh, yeah. Computer science and social work. Weird combination. It should give her some sort of understanding of us orphans. Sabilia had told me Cecylia was updating the files on our computer system. Some business had donated some boxy old computers with large towers and set up Wi-Fi as a favor to the teens. None of the teens had any technology to use the Wi-Fi. The director decided to use the computers to keep all of our files in, so they weren't wasted. Cecylia's sleek Apple laptop was a coveted item, and she kept it under lock and key. She couldn't risk it being stolen. Her parents must have paid for that.

"Yes," she said, "anything."

"Daria is my family."

She nodded.

"You PPs are waiting. Nice people. I went in for a little chat. I could go back and distract them."

"Would you?"

There is another Loneliness
*   That many die without -*
*   Not want of friend occasions it*
*   Or circumstances of Lot*

I walked out of the yard towards the wood. I didn't look back to see if she had retreated inside the building or not. I just kept going. I looped around the woods to the path that led to the village. I was running now. If I didn't run, I would turn back. An art book. Jim bought me an art book. I tasted my salty tears and ran faster. I was messing everything up. I was going to lose a family. I put Kasia in danger. Cecylia was probably going to go to the director, tell him some more jokes and spill the beans about my running away. He would write me off just like he wrote Daria off. I had to take that chance. I couldn't abandon Daria.

I started with the bakery on the edge of Sulejów, the one I had taken Jim and Marge to the day before.

"Have you seen this girl?"

"I don't know. Do you want to buy something?" Shop owners were always wary of orphans. They imagined us all being beggars and pickpockets, like out of the Dickens novel I had read from the professor's library. What was it called? *Oliver*. That's right. The professor understood this kind of treatment. The orphan had no value, just as the Jew's life had no value when Hitler took over. Sulejów had been completely destroyed during the war. Jews were rounded up and sent to the first ghetto in Poland, just 15 km away in Piotrków Trybunalski. After the Germans took control of Piotrków Trybunalski on September 1, 1939, the persecution of Jews began immediately.

"You should know your history," the professor had often said. "Those who cannot remember the past are doomed to repeat it."

I wasn't sure how I was repeating the past. Maybe he meant the village's treatment of orphans. I wasn't sure.

"Not today. I think my parents bought enough yesterday."

Jackpot. His face lit up.

"The Americans! Yes."

He looked at my sketch again.

"Yes, I see her sometimes with you, right? But, not lately."

I pulled out the sketch of the man. "How about him?"

"You need to stay away from that man. I have seen him. He likes little girls like you. Have a roll. Your parents would not like you asking about a man like that. Have a roll and go to school." He handed me two rolls and turned to go back to work.

"Americans," he said with his back turned. He laughed, "in my shop!"

I spent the rest of the day trudging from shop to shop. Most people just told me to go back to school. A few said they had seen Daria the same day I thought I had, but didn't know where she was now. My feet hurt. I sat down on a bench. I was hungry and not making any progress. School would be letting out and I decided to head back to the orphanage so I wouldn't blow everything. I still needed a place to live. I wasn't going to be adopted. I wasn't going to have a family, and I had lost Daria. I would go back out looking after everyone was in bed.

"Little Girl, little girl with the American parents! *Chodź tu*! (Come here!) It is I, Panie Piotr."

I turned to see the bakery owner running out of his shop. "I saw your friend. I saw your friend." He stopped and put his hands on his knees to catch his breath. "She was with the man I told you to stay away from. She got on the bus to Piotrków Trybunalski with him."

"What? When?"

"About an hour ago. I didn't know where you were. Then I look out my window and you are sitting on bench across from my bakery. You see, I was mailing a letter and I walk past the bus stop and I saw her with *him*," he pointed toward my backpack where I had the sketch.

"Is there another bus?"

"Yes, soon, if you go now, you can catch it."

"Thank you!"

I jumped up and jogged toward the bus station. I glanced over my shoulder.Piotr was still standing there.

"Bring your parents to the bakery, yes?"

"I will try!" I yelled back.

Who was I kidding? I had no parents. When would these lies end? When I found Daria.

The bus was waiting at the bus stop. I climbed on, paid the fare and found a seat in the back. I tried to formulate a plan. Where should I start? Nearest the bus station, I guess. I didn't have fare for taxis, so my range of research would be limited. At least I had the sketches. I heard a familiar voice and slumped down in my seat. I quickly peered around the aisle, only to see the back of Cecylia. She plopped down on the front seat. She was wearing all pink. Pink sweater. Pink plaid pants. Pink penny loafers and a shiny pink trench coat. She leaned toward the driver and struck up a conversation. Then she pulled out a cell phone and began texting.

My neck was getting tired, so I slumped back down in my seat. I couldn't focus on her right now. I was looking for

Daria. I would talk to Cecylia when we got off the bus. I thought that walking around in a ten or twenty block radius from the bus stop would be a great start. I could get a map. My head nodded. I could feel myself slipping into the seat. And then I woke up, my backpack stuck to the side of my face. The driver leaning over me. "You getting off here, girlie, or you just want to go back to Sulejow?" I sat up. The bus was empty.

"I'm getting off. I guess I dozed off. Thank you, Panie."

He chuckled and went back to the front of the bus. I gathered my stuff and limped off the bus. My foot was asleep. I shook it and stomped it on the stairs. I turned back to the bus driver.

"Do you know where I could get a map?"

"Try the post office."

I headed down the street in the direction he had pointed. I looked for Cecylia, but she had disappeared. The maps were easy to find. I sat on a bench and plotted out a route. I started out in the shopping district and looked in cafes, markets, and everything in between. Why would she be with him? Where would he be going? If his plans for her were wicked, it wouldn't be a public place he took her.

I headed down a residential street. Suddenly, I was surrounded by large narrow houses on a brick street. Stately. The kind of house an orphan only imagines she would live in. She wouldn't be here, I thought, but I kept walking slowly and daydreaming.

I thought of the house in the pictures that Jim had showed me with its large white columns. What had he called it? A colonial. And the huge windows in the front. The yard with Marge's flowers and the pool. I had never been in a pool. The water, clear and clean. I could stand that. Why was I thinking about them again? That was over. I had ruined it and for a good cause, for Daria.

Then I saw Cecylia. There she was again. I tried to hide

behind a tree. She walked up to a red front door and paused, straightening her hair, tucking a strand behind her ear. What was she doing here? Who would she know here? She reached for the knob and the door opened and the man from my sketch stood there. The man who had chased me. Cecylia kissed his cheeks and slipped inside.

CHAPTER
FOUR

I BLINKED and tried to focus. Were my eyes playing tricks on me? Why was Cecylia here? What did she have to do with the man Piotr the baker had seen Daria with? I felt dizzy, disoriented. My legs cramped from squatting and the cold. Think, I told myself. No matter what I thought, I couldn't come up with any positive scenario. Well, maybe. Was Cecylia just following the lead I was? Had she talked to the baker?

> *Yet if hope has flown away*
> *In a night, or in a day,*
> *In a vision, or in none,*
> *Is it therefore the less gone?*
> *All that we see or seem*
> *Is but a dream within a dream*

Or was this something entirely different? Like the time Muchiek told me he would give me his copy of Emily Dickinson poems if I kissed him on the lips. I agreed. I really wanted the book.

> *"Hope" is the thing with feathers -*

That perches in the soul

Those were the only two lines I knew. I so wanted to read the rest of the poem. I loved those lines. I repeated them often when I felt despair creep in. It had been torn out of the poetry book in the library.

He had grabbed me and kissed me hard for what seemed like forever. Then I had to fight him off. "Give me the book," I had said breathlessly. He had tasted stale, like cigarettes, which made me angry. He was wasting precious books to make cigarettes to smoke.

"There is no book, stupid. Can't wait to tell the guys how easy you are." He had shoved me to the ground and swooshed his long blond mane. He had spread the rumor that we had done stuff in his room. The next few weeks had been brutal. I had been badgered, chased, and tormented by the other teens who expected the same. Daria had told me to keep quiet and let it pass. I couldn't.

The professor had said, "Fight back with intelligence."

I wasn't sure what he meant. Hit Muchiek with a book? One night I had sneaked into Muchiek's room with some scissors and chopped off his prize possession. His golden locks. The guys calmed down then and gave me a wide berth.

berth-the distance maintained between a vessel and the shore, another vessel, or any object.

I read that in my dictionary, a wide berth- a nautical term.

What should I do? Knock on the door myself and demand an explanation? No. Too rash. Too impulsive. What would Daria do? She was the calm, rational one. Jiminy Cricket, what would you do? Memorize the house number. I could do better than that. I walked down the street a bit and crouched behind a large tree that lined the brick street and got out my sketch pad. I drew the house with the red door. I drew the scene I had just witnessed. My legs cramped. My fingers ached. I put away my supplies and gingerly got up. What next? Find help. That's what the professor would do. But who? Where? The director seemed to be under Cecylia's spell. Everyone was. I decided I'd better hightail it out of there before Cecylia came out. I packed up my stuff, rubbed my hands together for a minute to get the circulation going and took off towards the businesses. I headed for a cafe near the bus stop.

"Adelina, what are you doing here?" I turned quickly, an overreaction, and almost lost my balance. Sabilia grabbed my elbow to steady me.

"I, uh…."

"You missed your outing with your PPs," she said sternly.

"I know. I skipped it." I put my head down and waited for the familiar rush of red up my neck. I felt a tear at the corner of my eye. I tried to will it away. No luck.

"What's going on?" She put her arm around my shoulder.

How much did I tell her? Could she be trusted?

"I'm upset about Daria." That wasn't a lie.

"Let's get some coffee." She nudged me toward the cafe.

In the warmth of the cafe with my hands wrapped around a steaming mug of coffee, I begin to thaw. I looked at Sabilia. Could I trust her? Would she brush me off? I decided to take my usual approach.

"What are you doing here, Sabilia?"

"That's not important right now. I'm concerned about you. What's going on?"

She didn't take the bait. I relaxed my face to neutral and tested the waters.

"I'm looking for Daria on my own. Nobody seems to care. Nobody is doing anything. She was part of the orphanage family for ten years and she is gone. No one bats an eye. What's up with that?" I was red and angry again. Tears slipped hot and salty down my cheeks.

"Friendship is unnecessary, like philosophy, like art... It

has no survival value; rather it is one of those things that give value to survival."

The professor had written that quote down in the front of the dictionary. It wasn't the first time I had heard of C.S. Lewis. I had seen many of his books in the professor's library with neatly lined shelves, categorized by subject. I wanted to live in that library. When the professor died, I not only lost him but also access to his books. I hadn't understood the quote before. I think now I was beginning to grasp its meaning.

Friend- noun. a person attached to another by feelings of affection or personal regard.

"I do care," Sabilia said. "I can tell you why I am here. Same reason you are. I am looking for Daria."

"You?"

"Yes, me. The local police don't seem to be any help, so I struck out on my own. What kind of caregiver would I be if I didn't take care of my own?"

That statement sounded vaguely familiar, but I brushed it away. I decided to tell her everything. I told her about running off after curfew and looking all over Sulejow and about Kasia following me and the man chasing us. I showed her the sketch of the man, then of the one with the red door and Cecylia and the man. I watched her face for clues. Did she believe me? She looked shocked when I showed her the last sketch of Cecylia and the man with scary eyes. I folded the sketches carefully, shoved them in my backpack and Cecylia came from out of nowhere, grabbed a chair and gingerly placed her shopping bags down before gracefully lowering herself into the seat.

"What are you guys doing here?" she asked, showing her pearly white teeth. It wasn't a smile. It was more like a showing of teeth. I could count them.

"I could ask you the same thing," Sabilia said. She knew the deflection trick too, and she was good at it.

"Waiting for the last bus. I got permission from the director to do a little shopping." She pulled her bags up for proof.

"Shopping?" I challenged. We could all play this game. Ask questions. Lie. Ask more questions. Lie some more. Add in some attitude and we had a recipe for getting nothing, nowhere. Just chasing our tails. Or gobbling each other up. Or both at the same time.

And with that, the bus pulled up. We all stood at once.

Cecylia swung her bags in the air in an arc and walked quickly toward the bus. "I got some great stuff," she winked at me. "Come on, ladies, we don't want to miss it!" She called over her shoulder. We were right behind her. Once again, she took the front seat.

Sabilia pushed me and whispered, "Let's sit in the middle."

No argument from me. I slid my stuff into a seat and followed it. She did the same. I could see Cecylia laughing with the driver. He seemed to be enjoying the attention. She seemed oblivious to the fact that I had seen her with the man in the sketch. Good.

"What if Daria was in that house?" I blurted out.

I hadn't heard Sabilia's reaction to my information yet, but I couldn't wait. The bus was going to pull out any minute and I needed to know where she stood. I couldn't leave Daria. Why should she willingly go to that man's house? "Stay away from that man. He likes little girls like you,"Panie Piotr had said.

"We have to do this the right way, Adelina," Sabilia said. "We don't have any concrete evidence. Let's get some and move from there. Trust me."

"Not my strong suit."

"Is there anything else you haven't told me?"

"She's pretty rich for a college kid. She dresses a lot like you. Expensive clothes. It probably doesn't mean anything." I put my hand over my mouth. "I shouldn't have said that about you, huh?"

No filter. I had no filter. Daria told me that often. The professor had said he didn't mind a little honesty in this world of hypocrites, but other people did. I didn't know how to control it. Words just tumbled out before I could think about it.

"Wealthy parents," Sabilia said, tucking her hair behind her ear, "and let's just say they aren't pleased with my choice of profession. But Cecylia. That's a puzzle we need to solve."

She kept saying we. We. So she was going to help me. Maybe with the two of us, we could find Daria and I would still have a home at the orphanage. I looked out the window at the dark. Lights flickered from small cottages, tucked behind wrought iron fences. I imagined families sharing a laugh in the kitchen, the tea kettle boiling on the stove. A home. I didn't want to go there. I didn't want to think about that.

"Hey, I can smooth things over with your PPS... tell them you were ill or something."

It was as if she had read my mind. I decided I really could trust her. Fancy clothes and all. I smiled at her.

She continued,"You cannot challenge Cecylia. You must pretend as if you like her, for now, so we can gather intel. Can you do that?" This was going to be tough. Not say what I felt? I would try my best.

"Yes, I can pretend. Gather intel? Who are you?"

"That is not relevant right now. What is important is that you didn't think your friend ran away, right? And the baker, Panie Piotr? He saw her with that man?" She pointed to my backpack where the sketch was.

"Yes, I don't think she ran away. She wouldn't have left this." I pulled out the charm bracelet with one small charm, a small house. "This was her hope. A home." She looked at it curiously.

"It's just a bracelet," she said evenly.

"Trust *me*," I said. "She wouldn't leave this behind."

"When we return to the orphanage, I want you to become friends with Cecylia. Can you do that?"

"Yes, like I said, I can pretend."

"Good. Here, take this," she slipped me a cell phone and then took it back and plugged her number in it. "Don't let anyone know you have it, okay?"

I unzipped my backpack and placed the phone in a pocket.

"And come to my townhouse after dinner tomorrow."

"But residents must not go over there," I stated. Everyone knew that. I couldn't break rules out in the open. We would both be in trouble.

"I'll tell the director I asked you for art lessons."

"Will that work?"

"It will work. Trust me, right?"

"I'll bring my art supplies. The new kit Jim bought me."

"Good thinking. And here. Take this." She handed me a camera. "Take photos. Your sketches are awesome, but we need evidential proof of something, I'm not sure what at this point, but proof, nonetheless."

"Pictures of what?" I felt like I was failing whatever quick course she was giving me. "Couldn't I use the phone for pics?"

"The phone can't be seen. The camera will look like a gift from your PPs. Take pics of everything she does." She nodded her head toward the front of the bus.

Just then, the bus lurched to a stop. We gathered our things. My head was spinning. Make friends. Take photos. Stalk new friend. Art lessons. Fake art lessons. Lie about camera. Hide cell phone.

"You said you saw some files in the director's office that didn't look right," she whispered as we squeezed down the aisle.

"Yes."

"If you see something like that again, take a photo of it."

We stepped off the bus and I headed toward the trail in the woods to the orphanage.

"Where are you going?" Sabilia yelled.

"Home," I yelled back.

"You can't walk that trail at night. Come back. I'll get us a cab. We three can ride together." I turned back and jogged toward them. Cecylia and Sabilia.

Minutes later, we were all three squished together in the back seat. The countryside flew by and I tried to think of something friend-like to say to Cecylia.

"Hey, can I ask you something?" I tried. My brain raced through options. Think like Cecylia, or what you know of her, anyway.

"Sure."

"You said I shouldn't wear pink because of my red hair?"

"Yes," she almost squealed it.

"Do you think you could help me pick out some clothes for my next meeting with my PPs?"

"Yes! Yes, this is going to be fun!" She leaned down and rifled through her bags and pulled out a blue sweater.

Sabilia smiled at me.

CHAPTER
FIVE

THE NEXT MORNING I was awakened by pudgy little hands shaking my shoulder.

"Adelina, we need you," said one of the littles. I shook my head, trying to clear it and remember the mission.

"Yeah. I'm coming."

I spent the next twenty minutes dressing the littles, playing my daily round of *How doth the Little Crocodile* and answering questions.

"Hey, I brought the blue sweater. You're going to look great!" Cecylia waltzed into the room with shopping bags. "When are your PPs coming?"

"Right after breakfast."

She certainly had a knack for clothes. I did look smart in the blue sweater, skinny jeans and ankle boots that she had fished out of the bag. Some parts of the pretending weren't going to be difficult. I didn't have to pretend to like the clothes or her style. I had never owned a pair of jeans or worn anything slightly in style. Not ever. We orphans always stuck out at the local village school, wearing whatever came in the mission boxes, outdated clothes or T-shirts, advertising movies we had never seen.

"I love it!" I told her.

"Thank you," she gushed.

"Your PPs are here," Sabilia said, sticking her head in the door. "You need to get going." The littles, who were climbing all over my bed, were hungry and getting bored, which meant they would be getting into my personal stuff at any second.

"Let's go to breakfast, guys!"

Marge and Jim were waiting in the foyer. I waved to them while I herded the littles into the cafeteria and handed them over to someone else.

"Why don't you invite your friend?" Marge asked as I rejoined her. Cecylia stood on the stairs, beaming.

"Uh, yeah, sure."

"Do you like her outfit?" Cecylia asked, "I picked it out. And I would be happy to join you. I need to ask permission."

She ran up the stairs and we stood there, the three of us, feeling awkward, staring at each other until Jim broke the ice.

"What shall we do today? How about a field trip?"

"That sounds great, Jim."

"How about the church of the Black Madonna? You could do some sketches there, Adelina."

I nodded. It seemed strange. I actually liked these people and every moment I spent with them seemed more natural, more. I don't know the word for it. Comfortable. That was it.

Comfortable-being in a state of physical or mental comfort; contented and undisturbed; at ease

I slung my backpack over my shoulder with all of my supplies and Cecylia joined us, beaming. "Sabilia says it's fine!"

We made small talk in the car and laughed a lot. I didn't expect that. Laughing. I always imagined parents as distant creatures, just pictures on a page of what I wanted in my book of life. They would be like the old photos I had found in books in the library, standing in the background, arms around each other, smiling but distant, and I would live out my dreams because of them, not with them. I didn't expect to like them.

The church of the Black Madonna was amazing. I sketched the statue of the virgin Mary who was said to have wept blood. Cecylia acted as our tour guide. She knew a great deal about the place.

"I've been here several times," she said nonchalantly. The monks were said to have held the Muslims off. Even though they weren't soldiers or trained in battle tactics, they had fought for their lives and for the preservation of the church. The similarities between our situations wasn't lost on me. I wasn't trained as a spy, but here I was, spying and fighting in my own way to preserve my friend and for the only life I had ever known.

Later, we went to the Castle for dinner. Tourists called it that. It was really the Cistercian Abbey, founded in 1176 by the duke Kazimierz II the Just. The village had grown up around it. The church, Saint Thomas Becket of Canterbury, still stood. A remnant of the destruction of the Luftwaffe during World War II still stood, the very wall I had seen Daria beside. Why hadn't I asked them to stop the car?

The professor would have said it was shock. The war did that to people, he had told me. Friends stood by and watched the Jews be herded into trucks in the dark of night, because their minds couldn't comprehend. Their intellect would not accept the truth. And that shock turned into acceptance mixed with fear. What if they were next? So friends kept their mouths shut while countless people, not just Jews, went into the darkness.

When the truth about where they were going came to light, many lived in denial. A few sprang to action and helped, risking life and limb. Jan and Piotrna Żabiński, the zookeepers in Warsaw, had helped save over three hundred people, including the professor. He had told me the stories over and over. Sometimes, a look of fear would transform his face and I almost thought he was that child once again.

Then he would snap out of it and say, "Don't ever forget the past. It holds your future. Back to your lessons!"

The restaurant was dim, with dark hardwoods and old swords and shields hung on the walls. It looked more like a museum than a restaurant.

Cecylia was laughing again, stealing the show. Marge and Jim laughed with her. I smiled.

"I'm going outside for a minute."

Marge followed me.

"You didn't really want her to come, did you?"

"No. Not really."

"Why did you bring her then?"

"Trying to keep an eye on her."

"Does this have anything to do with your missing friend?"

"I shouldn't say."

"You don't have to. I know. You're doing some investigating of your own."

"How did you know?"

"Dear, two things. I'm a writer. I notice details. I saw you slip by the common room yesterday. You looked worried, not sick. And two, I recognize a strong family bond when I see it."

"Yes, family," I said, and I felt a hot tear slide down my cheek. "You guys are great. I mean that. I want to be part of your family. I do, but Daria is my family right now. I have to find her."

Two well-assorted travellers use
> *The highway, Eros and the Muse.*
> *From the twins is nothing hidden,*
> *To the pair is naught forbidden;*
> *Hand in hand the comrades go*
> *Every nook of nature through:*

Each for other they were born,
Each can other best adorn;
They know one only mortal grief
Past all balsam or relief,
When, by false companions crossed,
The pilgrims have each other lost

Marge took my hand. One red curl fell over her eye. She brushed it back and with the same hand brushed my hair out of my eyes. How could we have the same hair, the same thoughts? It didn't make sense to me. "I understand. Family first, right?"

If only I could have Daria and this family, I would have the best family ever. I wanted to tell Marge that. Instead, I said, "I'm not a nice person."

"I know what you're doing and it's not going to work."

"What?"

"You're pushing me away. It's called survival mode."

"You sound like the psychologists."

"We are precisely what you need. Don't you understand? You need people. The most basic of human needs is attachment. Could I ask you a question?"

The air was chilly. I wrapped my sweater around me more tightly. I leaned up against the stone wall that had been built in the eleventh century. How could it just stand here? People came and were gone. Empires rose and fell. The Polish people endured war after war. Invasions. Being fought over and abandoned like an orphan child.

I sounded like the professor.

"Have you ever heard the history of Esther?"

"From the Bible?"

"Yes."

"Father talked about her last week. She was an orphan."

"Right, for such a time as this, remember that phrase. Maybe we aren't here just for the sake of the adoption.

Maybe you and I are here for such a time as this. To help find Daria."

"Would you? Could you?"

"Yes, I can keep my eyes open and I can play along with Cecylia." She winked.

Should I tell her about Sabilia? Should I paint the whole picture? No. I can't. I couldn't reveal everything.

"Hey, what are two doing out here? Let's get some dessert and coffee," Jim said.

"Yeah, and come and take a photo of us with your fancy camera. Where did you get that anyway?"

"From me, " Marge said. "I know it's an extravagant gift, but don't be shy, Adelina. Take some pictures."

"Yeah, of me," Cecylia grinned, and we all laughed.

———

Back at the orphanage, Kasia was waiting by the door. "Adelina, I missed you."

"What's up, kiddo?" And in that moment, it hit me how much Daria's disappearance had affected Kasia. She had lost her and me, both of us, at the same time. I was busy looking for my best friend, spending time with Cecylia and my PPs. Kasia had been abandoned again. I stopped and put down my backpack and pulled out my camera.

"Wow!" yelled Kasia. "Can I hold it?"

"Sure, I thought we could do a scavenger hunt later."

"See you later!" Marge and Jim were waving goodbye.

"Thank you," I mouthed to Marge and pointed at the camera.

"You're welcome," she mouthed back. "See you tomorrow!" she said aloud, and they pushed through the front door and were gone.

"Didn't we have fun today, Adelina? I think your PPs like

me. Don't you? I hope they don't back out like Daria's did. Man, that would stink."

I loathed her all over again. Just when I thought I liked her. I could feel the red flush creeping up my neck. How could I pretend to be friends with her? I'm doing it for Daria's sake, I told myself.

Loathe-to feel disgust or intense aversion for; abhor.

"Everyone likes me best!" she yelled as she ran up the stairs.

"Why later?" Kasia asked, hanging on my arm, "I need your help."

"Turns out, I need your help this time."

"Really?" She twirled around. "For what?"

"A scavenger hunt, but first I have a meeting with Sabilia."

"What for? Can I come?'

"An art lesson and not this time." I snapped a photo of her and shoved my camera back in my backpack. Remember to get art supplies, I reminded myself. You have to make this look real. Kasia followed me all the way to Sabilia's townhouse.

"You can't come in," I said.

"Why? We always do everything together. Art lessons are safe, right? Not like the other night."

We were suddenly interrupted by Cecylia's voice saying, "Art lessons are safe, huh? What does that mean?" How did Cecylia seem to always pop up at the wrong time? And why did she always hear the wrong things? "I'm going for a walk into Sulejow. Want to come, Kasia?"

"Yeah!"

"No! She's coming to my art lesson." I pulled Kasia towards me. Sabilia opened the door.

"Right on time for my art lesson. Come in."

Kasia wandered around the room while I stared in awe. The decor was amazing. A white leather sectional. Bright

Polish pottery with intricately painted flowers in yellows, reds and blues. A teapot and three tea cups sat waiting on the coffee table. I wanted to sketch that pottery. Sabilia watched my 360 degree gaze.

"Wealthy parents," she said using her stock phrase, as if it explained it all away, "and I love Fixer Upper, an American show."

"Were you expecting Kasia?" I motioned toward the three tea cups.

"No, Cecylia's been here, lurking around for the past ten minutes. I wanted to keep your cover in case you needed to bring her in."

"She's going to the village."

"She is? You should go. Follow her. I'll entertain Kasia."

I ran out the door and down the wooded path for thirty seconds before I realized I had left my phone and camera, both in my backpack. I turned back and sprinted to the townhouse. Sabilia was standing at the door with the director. I slowed my pace and hid behind a bristly pine tree, sticky with sap.

"Do you think she knows what is going on?" the director said. "I've been trying to play dumb. I'm not very good at it."

"I don't think she suspects a thing. I have her right where I want her."

"What about her?" the director said, pointing to the townhouse.

"Kasia? She's fine. She doesn't have a clue. I'll keep her busy. I'm introducing her to Fixer Upper."

"What?"

"Never mind. Did you talk to Marge and Jim?"

"Yep. They've agreed to play along. Good people. Let's keep her in the dark about all of this, okay?"

"Of course. I'm a professional."

What is going on? What are they keeping me in the dark about? Marge and Jim are in on it? Playing dumb? I turned to run and slipped on a pile of wet, mushy leaves. I had to get away. I needed to think. Was this just like the professor had said? People were turning a blind eye because they were afraid? Had they ingested the poison?

Poison-1. a substance with an inherent property that tends to destroy life or impair health.

2. something harmful or pernicious, as to happiness or well-being.

Were they under the spell of Cecylia so much that they would keep me in the dark and move forward under her leadership? Wait. What leadership? What was Cecylia up to and what did it have to do with Daria, if anything? Were we all just running around gobbling up lies and following poison trails?

> *I was angry with my friend:*
> *I told my wrath, my wrath did end.*
> *I was angry with my foe:*
> *I told it not, my wrath did grow.*
> *And I watered it in fears,*
> *Night and morning with my tears;*
> *And I sunned it with smiles,*
> *And with soft deceitful wiles.*
> *And it grew both day and night,*
> *Till it bore an apple bright.*
> *And my foe beheld it shine.*
> *And he knew that it was mine,*
> *And into my garden stole*
> *When the night had veiled the pole;*
> *In the morning glad I see*
> *My foe outstretched beneath the tree.*

It wouldn't go that far, would it? I was angry, but could I murder my foe? I rolled the verses over in my head again. Who was my foe? And I watered it with fear. Fear needed to work for me. Not against me. But, how? The professor had spent so much time teaching me about life and half the time I didn't know what he was talking about. We had read this poem together many times. I recited it now because I wanted my foe dead. That was in my imagination. This was real life. I didn't want to kill anyone. I just wanted to find Daria. The rest of these people could go to eat from the poison tree without me. I would do this alone.

"Adelina," Sabilia yelled, "you forgot your backpack!"

I stumbled toward her, shocked and confused. I tried to act out of breath.

"Here," she said, handing me my backpack, "you can catch up with her." She smiled and went back inside.

I ran and tripped over a root, caught myself and kept going. Tears dripped hot and salty into my mouth. Who could I trust? Who was on my side? Was Sabilia really on my side? What sort of professional was she?

From childhood's hour I have not been
As others were; I have not seen
As others saw; I could not bring
My passions from a common spring.
From the same source I have not taken
My sorrow; I could not awaken
My heart to joy at the same tone;
And all I loved, I loved alone.

I recited. Alone. Alone. I could depend on no one. Poe had it right. My joy never got past monotone. And here I was again. Alone.

I saw a pink sweater through the trees. I stopped and leaned up against a tree to catch my breath. I could find Daria on my own. I could follow Cecylia and keep an eye on her. She knew the Scary Man. I had to stop calling him that. I was a teen. Mature. I could formulate. I thought of the professor.

Hiding in the animal cages at the zoo in Warsaw. Waiting for someone to rescue him. I had no one. It wasn't dark yet; that was a plus. Would she go to the bus station? I had to stay back, so she didn't see me. I stood in front of the bakery and tried to act casual. I straightened my hair and pulled down my sweater. I had lost her. No pink sweater.

"Hello!" I heard behind me. "Your American parents came in again today. Wonderful people." It was the baker.

I smiled and nodded my head in agreement while scanning the street.

"Ahhh, you are looking for your friend, no? The blonde with the pink sweater."

"Yes. Did you see her?"

"Ah, yes, just a minute ago. She headed that way with that man. Tell your friends that man is bad news, yes? Have a roll." He shoved a roll in my hand and I ran down the street in the direction he had pointed.

"Tell your American parents to visit me again, yes?" he yelled after me.

I threw a hand up in the air to wave and kept going. The street lights blinked on. It would be dark soon. Then I saw them headed towards a back alley. I needed to see her face. Was she distressed or did she go willingly? She wasn't being dragged. She had gone to his house just two days before. What was going on here? Was the director in on it? Sabilia? My PPs were playing along. My camera. I pulled it out and took some rapid-fire pictures of them talking. They headed down the alley and I crept along the stone wall behind them. They stopped in front of an old weatherbeaten gray door. I moved close enough to hear, hiding in the shadows.

"I've done everything you asked," Cecylia said.

"Did you get the others on board with the plan?"

"Yes, everyone's on board."

"Good girl."

"Can I go home now?"

"No. Go back to the orphanage. You'll have to disrupt another adoption."

Just then, the gray door opened, and a girl stumbled out and fell flat on her face. Her hair was a tangled, matted mess. Scary Man grabbed her by the hair and hoisted her to her feet. Her eyes were glazed. She reached a hand towards me.

"Someone get this girl," he yelled.

Daria! I bit my tongue so I wouldn't yell. Muscular arms reached out the door, grabbed her by the shoulders, and yanked her back in.

CHAPTER
SIX

THE CAMERA HIT the ground with a crackling, glass shattering echo. In one quick motion, I jerked the camera up and pushed myself back against the wall. Scary Man and Cecylia both pivoted their heads toward the dark corner where I hid and I tried not to breathe.

"What was that?!" Scary Man said.

"Probably a cat," Cecylia replied.

He grabbed her around the neck and shook her like a rag doll. Her face turned ghostly green in the dim light that shone above the door. Her perfectly placed hair flew about like a windmill. My perception of Cecylia's part in this whole confusing world tilted on its axis.

Perception-a way of regarding, understanding, or interpreting something; a mental impression.

What part did she play? Did she want to play a part? Had she been force-fed from the poison tree?

"Did someone follow you?"

She tried to shake her head. He let her go, and she gasped for air. Her hands cradled her throat.

"No. You know how careful I am. You know I am." She continued to massage her throat. Her voice was croaky.

"Let's get out of here. By that I mean, you get out of here. I have things to take care of. Fix your hair and get rid of that ugly sweater. Didn't I just give you money for clothes? Get rid of that orphanage garbage."

Cecylia straightened her hair and then her back. "I'm trying to fit in," she spat and walked down the alley toward the street.

"Who is next on the adoption list?"

Did I imagine it, or did her shoulders slump when he asked that?

"Another teen?" he said gruffly. "She had better be a pretty one."

"Adelina," she said softly.

"What? Forget it. Her name doesn't matter. Just do your job. We are shipping this group out to Bulgaria next week. You don't have much time."

"I know what to do. I have it under control. Her adoption will fail." With the last word still hanging in the air, she took off running, and I was left alone in the alley with Scary Man. I pushed myself hard against the wall and wished it would absorb me. He turned and did a series of knocks on the door, and it opened. I memorized the pattern, practicing it over and over in my mind. I was alone and still afraid to move. I sat down and weighed my options. Knock on the door? No, I would be captured. Go back to Sabilia and tell her everything? Could I trust her?

"Everyone's on board," isn't that what Sabilia and Cecylia had both said?

I decided to go it alone. Alone seemed to work best for me.

Alone-separated from others.
   All I loved, I loved alone.

I was pushing myself off the wall when the door opened. I

reeled back and froze. It was Scary Man. He walked down the alley, towards the street, and didn't even glance my way. He marched like a stormtrooper from the Star Wars movie the orphanage owned. We teens had watched the VHS version at least one hundred times before the tape broke. His eyes were forward, a slight lean of the torso forward and quick staccato steps. I waited until he exited the alley and then followed, keeping a safe distance and hiding in the long since closed shop doorways. He walked straight to the bus station and climbed on the last bus to Piotrków Trybunalski. It wasn't any use following him now. I knew where Daria was and that was all the information I needed.

I walked to the church and tried the door. It was open. I slipped in and sat down on a pew. I pulled out the sketch of Scary Man, the broken camera, the house charm, and the blue sweater Cecylia had loaned me this morning. Was it just this morning? It seemed decades ago. I had been full of hope. I was going to be the master spy: take photos, pump Cecylia for information and find Daria, all before dinner. Plus securing the adoption and art school on the horizon. Too bad everyone was on Cecylia's side. Now I wasn't sure whose side she was on. The one positive of the day? Daria is alive! I knew where she was! I just didn't know what to do next. Maybe the priest could help.

"She's right here! I found her!" I opened my eyes. Had I fallen asleep? A blurry face peered down at me.

"Kasia?"

"Sabilia, she's right here," she said, ignoring me. I sat up and rubbed the sleep out of my eyes. Like the disciples in the Garden of Gethsemane, I had failed. Fallen asleep when my friend needed me the most.

"Father Raphael called the orphanage. I was so worried. I shouldn't have sent you. Why didn't you come home?" Sabilia said, her words tumbling over one another and echoing, bouncing off the ceiling and walls.

"I didn't want to."

Sabilia ignored my remark. What time was it? It was still dark. A few candles burned dimly in the front of the church.

"I know where Daria is and I know everyone is on board!"

"What? Where? Tell me so I can get someone there right away! You can't sit on info like this, Adelina." She was angry. We were both angry. The air was full of a tense cloud, ready to burst.

tense-in a state of mental or nervous strain; high-strung; taut.

The priest entered through the side door and genuflected. He walked back toward me, grabbed his robe, and wrapped it more tightly around himself as he sat down beside me. He was tall, lean and handsome. I wondered why he became a priest. Who could devote their whole life to a God who rarely showed up? A scar dominated the left hemisphere of his face from eyebrow to chin. I stared at it and he instinctively touched it.

"Oh, that," he said, as if he had forgotten it existed. "Long story."

"Adelina, where? Focus!" Sabilia interrupted.

I gave her directions. "Wait, there's a secret knock." I showed her and repeated it, and she trotted down the aisle.

"Keep on eye on her, Raphael, I mean Father," she yelled over her shoulder.

"You said I could go to the bakery when it opened!" yelled Kasia.

"It doesn't open for another hour. Stay here!" The huge oak door swung closed behind her.

"Wow," Father Raphael said. "This looks done for." He was holding the broken camera. I didn't know what to say. I was sitting here waiting to see if Daria would be rescued and I didn't know if I could make small talk. Kasia sighed loudly. I glanced at her and she was sleeping peacefully on the pew.

"Adelina, this is some drawing," he picked up the sketch of Scary Man. "Where did you learn to do this?"

I didn't know he knew my name. I went to Mass on Sundays, but I never talked to him.

"I taught myself. There are a few art books in the library at the orphanage. I wanted to go to art school." I said it as if I had dreamed it in a part of life that no longer existed.

"And so you should."

"I really don't want to talk about it."

"I see," he said, putting the sketch down. "Is there something else you'd like to talk about? 'Cause I'm a good listener and I'm not leaving."

I looked toward the altar with Jesus hanging above it stripped down to a loin cloth, almost naked and alone. That's how I felt. *My God, My God why hast thou forsaken me?* I had read that in the Bible in the office. God left his own son hanging on the cross.

Forsaken-abandoned or deserted.

"I don't really believe in God the way you do and if he really does exist, I don't trust him."

"Neither of those are a requirement for talking to a priest."

"Well,......my friend is missing."

"Ahhh, yes, the friend, Daria who was kidnapped."

"You know?"

"I catch on quickly, plus Sabilia filled me in."

"I really blew it. I followed someone last night."

"Cecylia," he said matter-of-factly.

"You know that too?"

"Yeah, we are all on board. Go on." I studied him for a moment. Why was everyone saying that?

"I didn't get a photo of Daria last night. I was so close to her. She reached out for me."

"It seems as if you didn't need it. Sabilia believed you."

"Yeah. Yeah." I played with my backpack strap.

The side door swung open and Sabilia ran in, breathless.

"The girls are gone!" she gasped as she put an arm on the pew to balance herself.

"It's all my fault!" I stood and banged my fists on the hard pew in front of me. "I spooked them!"

"You don't know that, Adelina. Sometimes it's just protocol."

"Is the bakery open yet?" Kasia said as she sat up and rubbed the sleep from her eyes.

"Who cares?" I yelled and ran to the back of the church. I was pretty sure my behavior was sacrilegious, but I couldn't stop myself. I pulled my hair with both hands and held it up in the air. I looked like a freak. *Think. Think. Think.*

Think- to employ one's mind rationally and objectively in evaluating or dealing with a given situation.

"I'm next!" I yelled. "I'm next!"

"What?!" said Father and Sabilia in unison.

"Scary Man said he needed one more girl and Cecylia said it is me. Adelina. Oh, she said something about Bulgaria." I was running faster now in a giant rectangle. Suddenly, I was sailing through the air. My chest hit the ground and with a giant whoosh, my breath escaped. I slid in Superman form, the rug eating the skin off my hands. The burning sensation opened some darkened portal of my mind that stress had hidden away.

"They're not leaving until next week and Cecylia isn't an intern, if that is even her real name!" I had another idea brewing. I rose to my knees and lifted my hands in the air like a prayer. I would be the bait.

"Great work. Do you think you could sit down?" Sabilia said. "We need to figure out their new location."

"I'm sorry, Kasia. I shouldn't have yelled at you. I messed everything up. If I would have come and told Sabilia right away, we might have Daria right now."

"It's okay. I understand. You lost *your mind*. I lose things all the time," Kasia said seriously.

"Why didn't you?" Father said.

"Why didn't I what?"

"Go back and tell Sabilia?"

"Because, 'everyone is on board'. That's what Sabilia and Cecylia both said."

"You're basing your lack of faith on a commonly used phrase?"

I turned on Sabilia, "I heard you talking to the director, 'Do you think she knows what is going on? She doesn't suspect a thing. Marge and Jim. They've agreed to play along. Let's keep her in the dark about all of this.'" I felt myself spit as I said the last sentence. I was on tiptoes and my neck and face were on fire.

Sabilia stared at me. Confusion was written all over her face. "Yes, all true."

"You're helping Cecylia! She said it too!" I screamed it. It echoed from every crack, corner, and crevice.

"No, Adelina. We are on board with you. Marge, Jim, the director. We are on Daria's side." She was calm and firm, which only made me angrier.

"She doesn't suspect a thing!" I glared at Jesus while I yelled it.

"Cecylia. Cecylia doesn't suspect a thing. We are letting her think she has us wrapped around her little finger. Do you think we didn't know Daria's records were doctored?"

"You let her get kidnapped?" I dropped to my knees. I felt sick. I was going to throw up right in front of Jesus.

"Of course not. We had no idea that would happen. We just knew Cecylia was responsible for playing with records. We weren't sure if she was involved yet. I gave her free rein and I feel guilty about that. I'm the one who failed. Not you."

"We both missed it," Father said. He moved forward and put his arm around Sabilia.

"What? You're in on it too? Who are you people?"

"I'm not just a priest. I..."

"You've been our parish priest for a year!"

"I'm not really a social worker," Sabilia confessed.

"*Well, duh!*" Kasia said, finally chiming in.

"What?" we all said in unison, looking at her.

"Well, she knows nothing about orphans. She doesn't act social worky at all. Daria left her charm bracelet. That's important. Even I know that."

We laughed. She smiled. Suddenly, it got quiet. I got to my feet and sat on a pew and looked at Sabilia, waiting for an explanation.

"We're part of a task force, the Internal Task Force For Safe Children (ITFSC) to uncover sex trafficking rings. We've been after this one for years."

"Wait, what? Task force? Sex Trafficking?"

I sat down. This was too much information.

information-knowledge communicated or received concerning a particular fact or circumstance; news.

I sat down and put my head between my hands and rocked back and forth.

My mind flashed back to Daria in her drugged stupor. It made sense now. How could I have left her?

Some say the world will end in fire,
>   *Some say in ice.*
>   *From what I've tasted of desire*
>   *I hold with those who favor fire.*
>   *But if it had to perish twice,*
>   *I think I know enough of hate*
>   *To say that for destruction ice*
>   *Is also great*
>   *And would suffice*

"Yes, " orphans all over Poland," Father Raphael said, taking over. The runaway is a common excuse or cover-up for kidnapping. They get shipped to Bulgaria."

I looked up when Father said this. "Wait. Go back. What's a sex trafficking ring?"

Visions of the world ending in fire and ice were flitting across a screen in my brain. Girls in a fire. Bound. They couldn't escape.

"Sex trafficking is a crime when women, men and/or children are forcefully involved in commercial sex acts," Sabilia said. "False promises are ways in which traffickers bait and enslave their victims. We believe Daria was promised something. She was either kidnapped or went willingly."

"She didn't go willingly!" I jumped up. "She wouldn't. She isn't stupid."

"Adelina, calm down. It isn't a matter of intelligence. It's a matter of vulnerability. She may have believed false promises."

"What do they do with these girls? Like Daria?" I was pacing now. I could see Daria falling out of the doorway over and over, like a video stuck on repeat.

"They sell them," Father Raphael said quietly.

"You can't sell people," Kasia said, "can you?"

Sabilia kneeled down and took Kasia's hands in hers. "I wish you couldn't. I wish you lived in a world that was right. Nothing ever lost. No one ever leaving."

"Don't give me any more details. Not now. Not in front of Kasia. She has heard enough. Just tell me what we need to know." I sat down next to Kasia and put my arm around her protectively. She leaned into me.

sell-to transfer (goods) to or render (services) for another in exchange for money; dispose of to a purchaser for a price.

"Poland is a common hub. A grand central station, if you will, for teen slaves. They are imported here and exported after a few orphans are added to the pot. We've broken up some rings in larger cities and they seem to be relocating to smaller villages." With the last sentence, he touched the scar again.

"Is that how you got that?" Kasia said, pointing to the scar.

"Yes, I did, in a raid, trying to save a little girl. The man in the sketch did this. Ryszard."

"Really?"

"Yes, you don't know how much you've helped us, Adelina. We have been trying to track him down for months," Sabilia added.

"Why don't you just arrest him? I know where he lives!" I jumped up and threw my fist up in the air as if I had the answer.

"It's not that simple. We don't just want him. He is the low man on the totem pole. We want to bring the whole organization down," Father said.

"If we just arrest him, all the girls will be shipped to Bulgaria and disappear forever. And if Cecylia gets a whiff of this and tells him, the same will happen."

"Do you think the bakery is open? I am *really* hungry!" Kasia whined.

Father looked at his watch, "Yes, look at the time. I need to get ready for early mass."

"So, do you believe all this stuff about God or are you just pretending?" I spat.

"I believe it, Adelina. It's about trust. Something you need to learn." At that, he stood and sauntered up the aisle, genuflected and walked out the side door. Funny, that's what the professor had said. I needed to learn how to trust. How could I, with all that went wrong in the world? Yet, the professor did and with all that he went through, he said, "I had a good life, Adelina, and you were part of the good."

"Run ahead to the bakery. We'll be there in a second," Sabilia said. Kasia threw the back doors open so fast she left them swinging.

"I need more information," I said. "Later." My head was spinning. I felt as if it were going to lift off and fly around the church. Sex Trafficking Rings. All I could picture was the ring that one of the teens had. From Lord of the Rings.

One ring to rule them all, one ring to find them, One ring to bring them all and in the darkness bind them.

Was Daria bound in the darkness? Was she being forced to do things against her will? It had gone from kidnapping to slavery in one day. From bad to the unimaginable.

We needed to get back to the orphanage before Cecylia noticed we were missing. I packed up my stuff, and we headed to the bakery. When we rounded the corner, I could see Kasia's head bobbing up and down in front of a glass case. She turned her head and spoke to someone. Not the baker. Who was it?

Scary Man.

"Ryszard," Sabilia whispered.

I hung back. Sabilia did too. "Wait," she said.

Kasia laughed. The baker came to the case and handed her a white paper bag. She took it, opened it, smelled it and closed it back up. The front door opened, the bell jingled and Ryszard stayed inside.

Kasia ran to me, "Look what Panie Piotr gave me for free! I saw that Scary Man and the baker said if I smiled and didn't act scared, he would give me sweeties."

"Look," she said, holding the bag open.

"You girls get a cab back to the orphanage. Have him drop you at the end of the lane." She shoved money into my hands. "I'm going to follow Ryszard." We had moved to the side of the building, out of his line of sight.

"What about Cecylia today? My PPs? My broken camera?"

"Improvise." She tossed me a key. "I have an identical camera in the kitchen. Get it. He's coming. Go!"

We slipped into the nearest alley and waited. After five

minutes, we ran towards the taxi driver's house and I prayed he would be awake. A large doberman barked and lunged at the gate. The front door opened, and the PJ clad taxi driver stuck his torso out.

"You girls need a ride, yes?"

"Yes," I held up the money.

"Come in. Come in." He shushed the dog, and it sat down obediently and whimpered. I opened the gate, and we followed him inside.

"Agnieszka, come make these girls *kawa z mlekiem* while I get dressed," he yelled in a singsong voice. Such a joyful cadence, in contrast to the fear and anxiety of the last few days, calmed me.

"I brought breakfast," Kasia offered. Minutes later, we were sipping hot coffee and eating sweet rolls. The taxi driver waddled down the stairs and grabbed his hat off a hook. Kasia and I stood.

"No, you girls finish," he laughed as if he had made a joke.

"We need to get back. School." I said, as if that one word explained it all. In the last fifteen minutes, I had prayed to a God I didn't trust, trusted two people to find my friend, and then lied. God that I don't trust, forgive me and keep me safe, I prayed.

"Of course. Of course. You must do your lessons so you can be successful like me and my little Agnieszka. Yes?" He squeezed her waist and laughed again. The dog barked and the taxi driver waddled to the window. Kasia followed. I chugged some coffee that all came back up in a choked cough when I saw Kasia's terrified expression.

"You are choking, little girl!" the taxi driver rushed to my side.

I grabbed a napkin and wiped the coffee from my face and throat. "I'm fine. I'm fine. Who is out there?" I said even though I knew in the pit of my gut it was Ryszard.

"A man I do not like to transport." He frowned and a giant crease appeared across his enormous forehead. The crease frowned with him. "I will tell him to come back later. I have important customers." He smiled as if he had solved a great problem. "You girls stay away from the window, yes, and I will tell him I have important diplomats. Yes?" He chuckled and patted Kasia on the head.

He went out the front door. We moved back to the table and his wife shut the curtains.

"That man is bad, girls. You stay away from him. My husband only drives him because he is powerful and can make life difficult for us."

Taxi driver opened the front door and smiled, "It is good. Let us go through the garage, yes? He will come back at nine."

THE TAXI DROPPED Kasia and me at the end of the lane. We ran towards the orphanage, our breath rising like puffs of vapor and the gravel crunching beneath our feet. The lights were on and people were stirring. We sneaked through a back entrance near the infirmary and stored our coats in a closet in case we ran into anyone. Kasia ran to check on the littles and I went straight to the director's office. He's on our side, I told myself. I can tell him anything.

Anything- anything whatever; something, no matter what.

The door was ajar, and I heard a one-sided conversation. He must be on the phone.

"I'll let you know when she gets here...yes, I understand…...we are all concerned. Thank you. Goodbye." Click. I poked my head in.

"Director Josef?"

"Adelina, I have been waiting for you. Come in and shut the door. Panie Piotr just called. He is worried about you and Kasia."

He handed me a mug of coffee and pointed to a chair.

"I think I'm up to speed except for the last hour. Fill me in. What happened at the taxi station?"

I filled in him on Sabilia's plan to follow Ryszard.

"Good. Good. I'm glad you are safe. I'm glad you know everything. We are all on board. I hated deceiving you. We didn't know if Cecylia was involved or not. We had to wait and see. I'm so sorry about Daria. We are going to do everything we can to find her."

"Thanks," I said. I sipped the coffee. Suddenly I felt guilty for ever doubting him.

"No time for that now," he said, sensing my mood. "You've got some serious acting ahead of you today. All the world's a stage. Are you ready?"

And all the men and women merely players;
They have their exits and their entrances;
And one man in his time plays many parts,
I was ready to play mine.

"What's on the agenda?" I said, sitting up straighter.

"Marge and Jim are coming at ten to take you and Cecylia out. You need to play it up. Her ego is her weakness. Let her steal the show and see what you find out."

A light knock sounded, and the door opened about five inches.

"Did I hear my name?" Cecylia stuck her golden head in the doorway.

"Yes, Cecylia, come in. Marge and Jim asked to take you girls out for some fun today. Adelina thought you might want to choose something."

"Shopping! In Piotrkow! Oh," she paused, "Kasia says she needs help with the littles."

"Sure," I said, anxious to get out of there. How was I going to do all this today? I stood up and set my mug down. "See you in a bit," and I was out the door, running.

"I'll pick out your clothes," she yelled after me.

Ten o'clock found me in Cecylia's clothes and make-up, waiting in the lobby. It was worth the price of being dolled up to hear Cecylia prattle on. Keep talking, girl. That's when she would slip. When I got too angry with her, I just imagined her being shaken like a rag doll when Scary Man choked her.

Full of strange oaths, and bearded like the pard,
*   Jealous in honour, sudden and quick in quarrel,*
*   Seeking the bubble reputation*

I tried to hone in on her obsession, clothes, "Where do you get all that money for clothes?" I asked.

"It's a secret, but I kind of work for a guy, a job, you know." Not new info, but if she told me that, she might be willing to share more as the day wore on. I was, like Director Josef said, on the stage. I didn't know the lines or how the play was going to turn out, but I would keep acting.

Marge and Jim came in the front door. Marge winked at me, and Jim gave me a hearty pat on the back. If only they could be my parents.

"What shall we do today, girls?"

"Shop. Adelina wears all the wrong colors for her complexion," Cecylia giggled.

Complexion- 1.the natural color, texture, and appearance of a person's skin, especially of the face. 2. the general aspect or character of something.

What was Cecylia's complexion? Deception? Mockery? Was she in too deep herself to get out? I was confused.

"Let's go. I rented a car." We piled in and sped down the road, making small talk. Cecylia did most of the talking with Marge, doing some strategic questioning. She was good, but so was Cecylia. So shallow. So fake. I bided my time for some real intelligence. It was going to be a long day.

In Piotrkow, we shopped until we dropped, and Jim put his foot down. "I need real food. Let's get some lunch."

We went to Pierogarnia Na Pierogi for some pierogies.

I walked in the door and ran right into Sabilia. She grabbed my arm and whirled me around.

"Ryszard is here," she whispered.

"Should we leave?"

"No, let's see how it plays out. I'll join you."

Sabilia joined us at the table with the excuse that she was shopping on her day off. It was Cecylia's turn to be tense. I hoped that I wasn't that easy to read. I took a deep breath, smiled, pulled out my camera, and pretended to take photos of Marge and Jim. Instead, I was focusing on Scary Man, two tables behind them. He was texting someone. I tried to zoom in on the number. Got it.

Cecylia knocked her water over, soaking her blouse. She jumped up and so did Marge, grabbing some napkins. She sopped up most of the water mess. A waiter rushed over and put in his two cents.

"I so sorry. You don't leave. Please stay. I clean up," he did a bunch of gestures as if he were mopping, yet did nothing to aid us. "My English is good, no?" He stopped and leaned on a chair and grinned, waiting for feedback.

Ryszard looked up. His eyes locked on Cecylia. He stood too quickly and knocked his cup of coffee on the floor. Or did he do that on purpose?

"Maybe you should help your other customers," Jim said firmly. "They seem to be leaving."

He stood and gestured toward the coffee mess.

"But my English, it is good, no?"

"Yes," Marge said. "Good."

"I'll go change," Cecylia said, grabbing a bag of recent purchases. The waiter bowed and went to sop up the coffee.

Sop- Noun.1. a thing given or done as a concession of no great value to appease someone whose main concerns or

demands are not being met . Verb. 2. soak up liquid using an absorbent substance.

Cecylia followed Ryszard as a sop, but didn't always have what he desired. Or did she? I followed Cecylia while pulling up the voice recorder on my phone. If this was a ploy to meet Ryszard to make new plans, I wasn't going to miss it. I walked quickly toward the back where he had exited. No one in the alley. I went back into the lady's room. The attendant pointed to a stall. Cecylia's shoes were visible. A soggy blouse leaked a puddle on the floor and a quiet, gulping sob came from within.

"Cecylia, are you okay?"

"Adelina, is that you? You…*gulp*….came to check on me?"

"Yeah," I lied. Well, I sort of lied.

"I ruined everything. I am just evil. Pure evil."

"What are you talking about?"

"You wouldn't understand. You are pure. Innocent. You have talent. Real talent. I'm just pretty. That is all. You don't know what I have done." She squeaked the last four words and then sobbed.

Was she going to spill the beans? Tell me everything? It got quiet. I looked to the attendant. She shook her head and pointed to the stall again, as if I could pull out a magic bean and fix everything.

"Come out, Cecylia. You can tell me." A click and the stall door swung open. She was wearing the pink sweater from the communal closet. She handed the frilly blouse and some money to the attendant.

"Keep it," she said, then she turned to me and said, "I am going to fix my face and then we are going out there to enjoy the rest of the day. Forget what I said." The act resumed.

She reapplied her makeup along with the fake facade. We went back to the table. Sabilia was gone. I knew she was following Ryszard, and I said yet another prayer to a God I did not trust that she would find some info that would lead us to Daria. Cecylia was slowly cracking like a hard-boiled egg and I planned on playing the act out until she did.

Crack-to break without complete separation of parts; become fissured.

"Everything okay?" Marge asked.

"Fine," Cecylia said, pouring on the charm.

We sat down and ordered. After lunch, Jim opted to stay in a cafe, sip coffee and read while we finished our shopping. Marge and I shopped and waited for opportunities, but Cecylia locked up tight. I was becoming an expert at hiding my phone and texting. Marge didn't have to hide her phone, only the fact that she was texting me.

Marge:

> pink sweater?

Me:

> I know.

Marge:

> What happened in the bathroom?

Me:

> Total breakdown

Marge:

> She is afraid.

Cecylia had three outfits for me to try on and she was her sugary, pseudo self. I tried them on and modeled them. It was actually fun. I felt pretty in them. Cecylia knew clothes. Marge bought me all three. Jim showed up.

"Let's go, girls. I have the car up front."

We drove back to the orphanage in silence. Everyone was too tired to talk, I guess. I pulled out my camera and shot some photos. I was secretly taking shots of every old building the girls could be in. Long shot.

We pulled up in front of the orphanage and Marge reminded us, "Psychologist evaluation tomorrow."

"Yes, last hoop before our final court date," Jim added.

Cecylia followed me in the front door, "I'm going to go take a nap, friend," and she bounded up the stairs.

No rest for the weary. I had a meeting at Sabilia's town-house. She had texted me on the way home: *Strategy meeting. New intel.*

I walked up to my room to grab my art supplies and continue the charade.

"Hey," Kasia met me at the door.

"Hey, Kasia, what did you lose?"

"This time, I found something."

"Really, what did you find?"

"A note. In Cecylia's room."

"Did you take it?"

"No. I copied it."

"How did you copy it?"

"With pen and paper, silly. I put back everything exactly where I got it. I know that kind of stuff is important."

"I've got an art lesson." I took the note and grabbed my gear and headed down the stairs.

"Aren't you going to read it?"

"I will. With Sabilia."

"I'm coming."

I was too exhausted to argue. So many false hopes today. False leads. Stops and starts. I hoped Sabilia had found something substantial. Time was running out.

No speed of wind or water rushing by
>*But you have speed far greater. You can climb*
>*Back up a stream of radiance to the sky,*
>*And back through history up the stream of time.*
>*And you were given this swiftness, not for haste*
>*Nor chiefly that you may go where you will,*
>*But in the rush of everything to waste,*
>*That you may have the power of standing still-*
>*Off any still or moving thing you say.*
>*Two such as you with such a master speed*
>*Cannot be parted nor be swept away*
>*From one another once you are agreed*
>*That life is only life forevermore*
>*Together wing to wing and oar to oar*

The townhouse was crowded and subdued. Father Raphael, the baker, Jim, Marge and Director Josef. It had been transformed into some sort of high tech looking base with screens, maps and faces tacked on a board.

"Adelina, good news. Jim was able to lift the contact list from Ryszard's phone," Sabilia said it as if I were used to this kind of technology and this stuff was normal to me. "We have email addresses. Names."

I was overwhelmed. It was bright and flashy. Kasia looked unfazed, enamored even. She went to the screens and watched the flashing lights on the map.

"So, do you have a where? A location of the girls right now?" I asked. My photos seemed archaic now, so I didn't mention them.

Archaic-very old or old-fashioned.

The baker stood. "I have a list of the abandoned buildings in the area."

"We have a team working through the list," Father Raphael said.

"Plain clothes guys. They will blend in."

"Don't you see, Adelina? This is bigger than just this group of girls. We can bring down the whole ring," Sabilia said excitedly. "There are some big names on this list. *Jackpot, Jim!*" She high fived him.

This wasn't bigger to me. All I wanted was Daria home. That is what my goal was, and that was what was promised. Now, here was a team of sorts, with all the technology at their fingertips, and they couldn't find one girl. Just one. I stood in the middle of the room. It swam in a blinking haze. Everyone was talking.

"We have a hit," Sabilia yelled, "possible location. Waiting for verification." She had put on a headset and was speaking into it rapidly. "No go. That's a no. False alarm. She threw down the headset and went to the board and crossed off a location.

location-a place or situation occupied:

"I know how to find them," I said. No one paid attention. They just kept talking. "I *know* to find *them!*"

Silence. All eyes were on me.

"Use me as bait."

"Too dangerous," Father said.

"We are running out of time, " I reminded. "Put a tracker on me. Surely you can keep track of one teenager with all of this."

"I'm listening," Sabilia said.

"You can't be considering this," Father said. He was pacing now. Agitated.

I ignored him.

"Here's the plan. Marge and Jim, you pull out of the adoption, or at least pretend to go home. Let Cecylia think she succeeded. I am sure she will tell me what to do next." I pulled out the note Kasia had copied that Daria had written and read it:

Cecylia is helping me. She introduced me to a

guy who will help me find work. I'll come back and get my things after I am settled. Don't worry about me. Love, Daria.

"Father, Cecylia is ready to crack. Do whatever it is that you do. She may confess something."

"Which I cannot share if she does."

"What sort of task force is this? You will protect our girl, right?" Jim said, suddenly rising to his full height. "We are trying to save innocent girls here. God will understand."

"The church won't."

"Come on, guys. We are all on board, remember?" I tried.

"To hell with the church," Sabilia joined the argument. "Remember what happened last time?" She pointed to the scar.

"Sabilia, I can't. You know…."

They continued to argue. Man, no wonder they can't crack this case. Sabilia's in love with the priest. The priest is in love with the church. The baker cowered in the corner mumbling about catching the 'bad man'.

"Sit down everyone!" Marge said. "Adelina is right about everything. We need to do it her way. I don't like the thought of it either. But, you have all this technology. Father Raphael, God loves the orphan. He would be proud if you could help just one. You joined the task force to save these little ones, right? You haven't heard our story. Jim?"

Jim's face turned red. He stood up straighter. His frame seemed to take up the whole room.

"Yes, there's a reason we want to help. Besides our Adelina. Our niece was almost abducted."

Marge went to his side. Tears dripped down her cheeks. "Yes, at a truck stop. She believed some guy who told her he could jump start her music career. She agreed to meet him there and they were to ride to Florida with his 'uncle'."

"I don't want to put Adelina out there," Jim said. "I don't. But, we want this hogwash to stop. So does she. She wants her friend home."

Everyone calmed down, and we worked on plans for the next hour. I listened carefully, mindful of what the professor had told me about protocol in the Warsaw Zoo during WWII. When he and his sister stayed there, they had code names, Possum and Rabbit, so Piotra didn't have to use their Jewish names. When Piotra played "Go, Go to Crete" on the piano, that meant danger was close. Everyone hid. His sister Rachel was named Possum because Piotra said she could freeze and play dead like one. Professor Wroblewski was Rabbit because of his swift hops to safety. "Protocol saved our lives," he had told me.

Everyone had a job, down to the baker. I asked lots of questions to make sure I knew the answer in every scenario. Sabilia pulled out a pamphlet that advised girls on how to steer clear of human/sex trafficking rings. Printed on the top was ITFSC. **"What to Avoid"** was on the inside cover. A bullet list followed:

• If someone, whether stranger or acquaintance, promises something that seems too good in return for sex or free work, wait. Listen to the intuitive voice inside your head. Check with family and friends for advice. Do Internet searches or background checks on the person wanting you to go with them. Say no and see how they react. Look for signs of abusive or possessive behaviors. Is the person trying to isolate or turn you against family and friends? If so, avoid that person.

• Do not make decisions under the influence of substances and do not be in the company of people you do not fully know and trust while intoxicated. Traffickers, looking to put someone into prostitution, will take advantage of unconscious people or someone who cannot fight being transported elsewhere. Traffickers will also attempt to take advantage of those with addictions or attempt to create drug dependency.

• If coming from a life of poverty, the lure of a better income or education is hard to resist. Check and double check if the agency or recruiters are reputable. Human traffickers will typically avoid those who are asking too many questions; they want easy targets. Someone looking for a legitimate employee or student will honor the questions, knowing that you would be a valuable employee or student.

There was a loud knock on the door. A hush fell over the room. I hid the pamphlet behind my back. I don't know why. With this whole task force and technology filling the room, the pamphlet was the least conspicuous object in the room.

Conspicuous- adjective

1. standing out so as to be clearly visible.

2. attracting notice or attention.

Sabilia threw a robe over her clothes and cracked the door open and stuck her head out. "I want to help." It was the taxi driver. She pulled him in the room and slammed the door.

"How did you?" she began.

He patted his belly and laughed. "I like the bakery, yes?"

"That is a bad man," the Panie Piotr added while pointing to the photo of Ryszard, as if that one sentence summed it up.

I DRESSED the next morning in one of my new outfits, the lime green blouse and the skinny jeans with the green suede loafers. I slid on the off-white cardigan to complete the look. Cecylia peeked in my room. "Now, the makeup," she said with a giggle. Right on cue, I thought.

"Not too much. Today is my evaluation and I don't want to look fake."

"Well, you will look completely ridiculous if we don't do something about that frizzy hair." She was on my hair, like a lion on its prey. She had brought a giant gold bag of makeup and hair products. I was oiled and straightened, my eyes lined and lips glossed. After she finished, she handed me a mirror with a flourish. I looked amazing. My hair was sleek and shiny. My make-up, understated. My eyes looked bluer.

"Thanks, Cecylia. I mean it. Thanks."

It seemed so surreal. Two teens doing hair and make-up. So normal. So natural. Too bad one of us was aiding a man running a human sex trafficking ring and the other one of us was about to get herself kidnapped to take her down. In the corner of the mirror, I could see the notes I had taken the night before sticking out of my backpack. They seemed to glow and scream at the same time, "Look at me!" Had she seen them?

Villains!" I shrieked, "dissemble no more! I admit the deed! --tear up the planks! here, here! --It is the beating of his hideous heart!

I felt like Poe. The evidence. The charade. Everything screamed guilty while I smiled.

Guilty- adjective 1.culpable of or responsible for a speci-fied wrongdoing.

I wasn't doing anything wrong. Calm down. I was doing something right. If anyone was guilty, it was her. Or was she? Was she a pawn? Was it all Ryszard? It didn't matter at this point. I just needed to follow through with the plan. Daria needed me.

"Great. I'm good, right?" I said while twirling.

"You look amazing!"

I grabbed my backpack and stuffed my papers in.

"What is all that?" she asked.

"Just some art stuff. I printed some stuff at Sabilia's."

I couldn't tell if she had really seen anything or not. We were both great at lying. I needed to pull myself together for a real evaluation before my fake failure. Kasia stuck her head in the door. "Time to go! Good luck. Put your best foot forward!" She stuck a foot forward, pointed her toe and laughed.

"Alright, Kasia. Got it." I tousled her hair and then gave her a side hug.

"Hey, don't be too disappointed if this whole adoption thing doesn't work out," Cecylia said, grabbing my elbow at the same time. She looked sad. Was that sad? Or was it all an act? I couldn't tell.

"Why wouldn't it?" All the while, my brain was sending out warnings. Calm down. Play the part. Play along. Don't give her any reason to suspect you know something.

The psychologist's office was a long, narrow room. One end had two leather couches, a bright area rug, end tables and lamps. The other side of the room had two heavy walnut desks occupied by two women I guessed to be in their forties. They were both dressed smartly and had an air of importance about them. Just watching them made me sit up straighter. Marge and Jim had arrived before me and were already seated on a couch. I had the opposite couch.

"How was your morning?" Marge asked.

"Fine. Yours?"

"You're wearing one of your new outfits."

"Yes. I love it. Thank you." A few months ago, this outfit would have been the focus of all my thoughts. I had never in my life owned clothes like these. I had owned very few clothes at all. Now that I did, they seemed unimportant compared to what was at stake. I would give a million new outfits to have my friend home safely.

Another lady entered the room and took a seat. She was wearing a tweed brown suit with sensible English looking shoes and stockings. She began translating our conversation.

Suddenly, I understood the setup. This was a pseudo living room and these ladies were observing me to see if I knew how to be in a home, that is, if I knew how to be part of a family.

Pseudo- adjective. Not genuine, sham.

I didn't. I thought being kidnapped on purpose was the toughest thing on my to-do list. This little evaluation was beasting it. I didn't have a clue how to act. I was pretty sure I was failing. How do you take a test if you never studied the material in the first place?

"I couldn't sleep last night, so I did some sketches. Want to see them?"

I hoped I was on the right track.

"Sure. Yes. We would love to," Jim said. He looked uncomfortable. Maybe he was having second thoughts.

I had drawn a sketch of Marge and Jim. Marge with her bright blue eyes and copper hair, Jim with his light blue eyes, hair graying at the temples.

"This is great, honey. Where did you learn to do this?" he asked.

"I taught myself from the books in the professor's library."

"It's incredible," Marge added.

"Quiet down. We are going to get started," a firm voice spoke from the opposite end of the room. For the next hour and a half, these women told my story. Every bit of it. My abandonment. Tuberculosis. Attachment issues. Lying. Stealing. I was shocked, embarrassed, and emotionally raw.

Embarrass- cause (someone) to feel awkward, self-conscious, or ashamed.

I looked at Marge and Jim a few times. They looked uncomfortable. Was that shock or disgust? I slumped forward in my chair until finally it was over. Surely, Marge and Jim wouldn't want me now.

A voice said, Look me in the stars
And tell me truly, men of earth,
If all the soul-and-body scars
Were not too much to pay for birth.

My soul-and-body scars weighed too much right now. It was too much. I shouldn't have been born. I never would be adopted regardless of whether we found Daria or not.

What about the part of my story when I met Daria? When she became my conscience and best friend?

Conscience-the inner sense of what is right or wrong in one's conduct or motives, impelling one toward right action.

Sabilia entered and said, "It's time to go." Marge and Jim were whisked away in the other direction. It was over. My fake failure had become real. Cecylia wouldn't have to lift a finger.

Back at the orphanage, I slammed my backpack on the bed. The late afternoon sun streamed through the window. I shut the curtain and fell on the bed myself.

"How did it go?" Cecylia asked. How long had she been standing there? I wanted to punch her, so I punched my pillow instead.

"Not well," I said. "I'd like to be alone."

"I'll come back later,"she said cheerfully.

The stage was set, and I was too weak to be a player anymore. I awoke two hours later to my phone buzzing. I had drool dripping out of the side of my mouth and I was pretty sure I had a zipper crease across my cheek. Kasia sat on the floor watching me.

"You snore."

"Really?"

"Yeah. And you kind of talk and make weird noises. Cool."

"Let me guess. You lost something."

"Bingo. Plus the littles want you to read them a story. They miss you."

I reached into my pocket and pulled out my phone. A text from Sabilia:

> Adoption is on. Act like it failed. Start
> phase one.

Suddenly, the sky seemed bluer. I whipped open the curtains. It was dark. I smiled. Adoption is on! I had a family. All I had to do was get Daria. Bring her home. I had already acted the part. My phone buzzed. It was Marge:

> Goodbye. Love you. Be back in six weeks.
> Stay safe.

Kasia tapped her foot impatiently.

I turned to her. "What did you lose?"

"My favorite stuffed giraffe. I think I left it in the office upstairs." I followed her with a spring in my step and then remembered to act sad, dejected, and depressed. The office door was open an inch or so. I pushed it a bit farther and signaled Kasia to be silent, with a finger to my lips. Cecylia was at Director Josef's computer. She must be following through, despite what I told her.

"Go get my camera, Kasia, quickly." I wasn't sure if this was important anymore, but it was part of my original assignment, so I too would follow through. Kasia was quick. She handed me my camera, and I snapped a bunch of photos. I zoomed in on the computer. My files were up. The screen glowed. Cecylia's face reflected in it. I tried to read her expression. It was blank. She edited my file with no expression. How was she able to do that? This girl was smarter than she looked.

She closed my file and typed in a website. Pics of teenage girls flicked across the screen. Lots of pretty girls with hair and makeup done. Daria! Now I had proof that Cecylia was a vital and active part of this operation. Like a spider, she got these girls in her trap, wrapped them up, and handed them over to Ryszard. A photo of me! I tripped over the door jamb and righted myself. She was too busy to notice. Where did that photo come from? This morning!

I stepped back and snapped more photos. I got the web address. No locations. Just girls and prices. That's when I realized Cecylia was building the website. She was just loading me in. Kasia fell on the door and then on the floor. I jerked my camera behind my back. "Hey, Cecylia. We're looking for Kasia's giraffe" She jerked some ear buds out of her ears and the screen went black.

"Oh, what? Come in, guys." The fake sweet smile was back. She showed her teeth. The giraffe was sitting on the desk. Cecylia grabbed it and handed it to Kasia. "There you go, kiddo!" She stood and exited the office. I stared at the screen and wished I knew how to operate it. Like Professor Wroblewski said, I was old school. I preferred books to technology. Even at school, when I had an opportunity to use a laptop, the only laptop in the classroom, I chose not to. I gave Daria my turn. I looked around for a button.

"Do you know how to work this?"

Kasia pushed a button, and the screen glowed. The tower hummed. "It's on. Director Josef has a few games on here. Want to play one?"

"No. I want to see what Cecylia was doing."

"Oh, that's easy. Go to history." She clicked, and the website came up. "For a smart girl, Cecylia's pretty dumb. The other teens erase their history. Hey, look, it's you."

There I was. Makeup on and smooth sleek red hair. I had a price. I was for sale. Like the washer and dryer in the shop window downtown. Everyone stopped to admire them. They would talk about having them. I wasn't anything more than an appliance in a window. I clicked some more and found the other girls. Including Daria. She smiled at the camera. Her Doris Day bow in place. The photo was taken *before* she was kidnapped. Cecylia was the scout and groomer all in one pretty, evil package. The website made me angry all over again. My body shook. I took a deep breath. We have a plan. What is it that Daria always says? Make a plan. Work the plan.

scout-a person sent out to obtain information.

———

The next morning, Marge and Jim came to say goodbye, and I cried.

My PPs leaving me was harder than I thought it would be. If I called them PPs in my mind, it seemed less personal. Who was I kidding? It was more personal than I had ever known. In a few short weeks, Marge and Jim were just as important to me as Daria.

"Everything is going according to plan," Jim whispered. "See you soon. Those agents better keep you safe."

"Are you sure you want to go through with this?" Marge asked. Her blue eyes were full of tears. I wasn't sure whether she was referring to the adoption or the kidnapping, so I just said, "Yeah."

And they were gone. Back to Warsaw and then to the hills of WV.

"Sabilia says it's time," Kasia said, taking my hand.

I went to my room to pout and be depressed. I didn't need to act. Right on cue, Cecylia appeared. My level of hatred for her had grown in the last twenty-four hours. I tried to channel that anger to my advantage. I liked to control the environment. I had gotten good at it the last ten years. That's what Daria said, anyway. I summoned all my issues and put them to work. Lying. Check. Stealing. If needed. Detachment. Check. Manipulation. Full on. Bring it!

"Sorry about the failed adoption. That stinks."

"You heard? My life is over," I said while hugging my pillow. "Done."

"Maybe not. How would you like to move out of the orphanage? Start life on your own? Have nice things?" She whipped her scarf around her neck for emphasis.

"How?" I said, mustering up some tears.

"I know a guy. He can get you a job. A good one. Do you want to meet him?" She sat down on the bed beside me. I could smell her lavender perfume. It made me want to puke.

"Why not? I'm never going to be adopted." I tried to remain cool. Calm. Collected. Inside, all my emotions were raging. Is this what you did to Daria? Anger. It produced more tears for me. I wanted to choke her like Ryszard had. But I didn't.

Instead, I said, "Thanks, Cecylia. You're a good friend." I meant fiend.

Fiend- (archaic)the Devil. a wicked or cruel person.

I liked the archaic definition the best.

"Great. I can set up a meet. Tonight?"

"The sooner the better."

"Seven o'clock at the Abbey."

"Good. You coming?"

"No. He prefers his interviews to be private."

"Gotcha. I am going to grab a nap before I go."

"Sure. I'll see you." She left. I immediately texted Sabilia: *It's a go for 7 pm at the Abbey.*

I pulled out the notes she had given me and read a few articles.

I had my phone with GPS and the small tracker Father had put in my shoe. Turns out, he wasn't just a priest. Sabilia would alert everyone on the team. I stashed all my stuff in the backpack to drop off at the church for Father. Then I took off.

I AWOKE to the sound of moaning and a strong musty smell. I moved my arm to stretch and something clanked and restrained me. I jerked it. More moaning. Was it me or someone beside me? I sat up and shook the cobwebs from my brain. Where was I? Both of my arms were chained to an old gray metal cot. A surge of panic welled up in my stomach. Bile rose in my throat. The room was dim. I shivered and pulled desperately on my chains. The walls were stone and no help to discover my location. The heavy wooden door was closed.

What happened last night? I tried to sort it all out and swallow my panic. So groggy and sleepy. Had I been drugged? Kidnapped. That was the plan. That's right. It was all part of the plan. The team would be coming for me and for Daria. It was all coming back to me now. I had met Ryszard, and he took me for hot chocolate and we talked. We walked down the street past the bakery. The baker had looked out the window; the taxi driver had done the same when we walked by.

Everyone was in position. Watching me. Tracking me. He had taken me to the restaurant in the Abbey(Castle).

We sipped hot chocolate by a roaring fire. He talked. I listened. He promised me money to go to art school. He must research every girl, promising them exactly what each wanted. He asked to see some of my work. I pulled out a sketch of Kasia and one of the NYC skyline out of my backpack, the fake one I had prepared as Sabilia had instructed. A typical teen girl, one with chocolate and girl stuff. Out of the corner of my eye, I saw Father Raphael. He was on task, too. He sat alone, studying and sipping coffee. Everything seemed to be going according to plan.

The whole team is in place. What could go wrong? Did something go wrong or was this part of the plan? I turned on my side and looked at the girl on my left. The moaning girl. Her blonde hair stuck to her face. Her muscles were wasted, her frame shrunken. She twitched and her hair fell away from her face.

"Daria!"

She opened her eyes and mumbled, "Adelina, I knew you would come."

"Daria, I'm here. I came to…" She turned toward the wall and fell silent.

The girl on my right fidgeted and pulled her chains.

"What? Where am I?" she screamed.

"Shush!" I commanded, turning my attention to her.

"What?" she yelled.

"Be quiet. I'm pretty sure that whoever kidnapped us will come in and do something horrible. Like drug us again." I turned to check on Daria. She had curled up in the fetal position.

"Drug us again?"

"Yeah, drug us again. How exactly did you get here? What's the last thing you remember?"

"I was having a drink with this guy, Ryszard. He was sweet. He's going to help me find a job."

"Really?" Was this girl dense? Didn't she know what was going on?

"Yes, he said he knew some people in fashion and would help me find a modeling job."

"What's your name?" I asked. She was yanking on her chains and I could see panic rising in her. "Look, let's try to be calm. I think the only reason no one has come in is because they think we are still out cold."

"Okay," she whispered. She had long, straight, raven black hair and hazel eyes. A striking combination. Her tall, lean frame fit with the model criteria. Last night's makeup was smeared, but she still looked beautiful.

"I'm Joanna. I'm seventeen." She filled me in briefly. Similar situation. Only difference? She had a family. She didn't know anyone named Cecylia, so maybe Ryszard had other minions or she used a different name.

"Who are you?" she asked.

"Adelina. I'm here to rescue her." I pointed at Daria.

"Doesn't look like you're doing a great job. Do you have a plan?"

"Yes, I have a whole task force behind me." I didn't tell her that one was a baker, the others a taxi driver, and a priest. It was the quiet pre-dawn hour. No one seemed to be stirring. Daria was sleeping. I felt confident that my team would bust down the door at any moment, so I filled Joanna in on everything from the beginning. Daria's failed adoption. Cecylia, the new girl. My PPs. Sabilia.

"So, you're like a spy?"

"Kind of," I agreed.

Joanna relaxed at my surety of rescue. She filled me in on some of her modeling aspirations, as if she would be pursuing them within the hour. I was sure she would. I heard a rustling outside the door. The sun had made an appearance and was streaming through the window.

I put a finger to my lips and then mouthed, "Act asleep."

We both put our heads down. I closed my eyes and prayed. God, where are they?

The door creaked open. Heavy booted footsteps. They stopped next to me. A large, heavy hand grasped my shoulder and shook it.

"This one is still out. Ryszard must have really dosed her." He chuckled. I squeezed my eyes tighter.

"This one too. What is he giving these girls?" he yelled to whomever was standing in the doorway. He moved over to Daria's bed. I opened my eyes to check on Joanna. She was faking well. He was shaking Daria. The metal frame of her bed creaked a sad, sickening squeak.

"This one's dead. Get her out of here."

My eyes widened, and I tensed to leap, chains and all, out of bed.

Joanna's eyes opened wide. "*No!*" she mouthed.

I froze. I wasn't sure if it was grief or fear. This one's dead. This one's dead kept repeating itself in my head.

Dead-adjective no longer alive.

Two men came in and took her. I heard the locks click on both sides of her bed and they carried her away, wrapped in a sheet. She was gone. She had died while I was talking. Boasting about the rescue team and how I was a spy. All the planning meant nothing now. Maybe those men would come back in and drug me enough to forget about everything. Maybe I would die. I wanted to. My face burned red with anger. She couldn't be dead. Hot tears trickled down my cheeks. I heard a guttural sob. It was coming from Joanna.

"We're not getting out of here, are we? I mean we are going to die or be prostitutes or something. Your team failed."

All the war stories the professor had told me came rushing back. Stories of people dying in the ghetto right beside him. They weren't shackled or drugged. Rather, they had another sort of shackle. Ignorance. Hate. Anti-Semitism that drove humans to atrocious acts such as starving and gassing men, women, and children. Professor Wroblewski lost his mother in the ghetto. Her mind went first. She couldn't come to terms with the fact that she couldn't feed her own family. She shut down. "Her despair became her shackles," Professor Wroblewski had told me. I hadn't understood at the time. Now, I did. Despair wrapped around my mind like a noose, tightening and squeezing out every hope. Hope was naked now, stripped of her feathers. Without those light and fluffy feathers, she was ugly.

The door flew open and Cecylia ran in. She didn't look her chipper self. She had a large blue bruise on her right cheek and small bruises that looked like thumbprints on her neck.

"Shush, girl. I can hear you out there," Cecylia ordered. Joanna gulped and put her head under her pillow.

Cecylia extracted a key from her skinny jeans and opened my shackles. I fell out of bed and rubbed my wrists.

"Get out of here," she whispered harshly. "Enough is enough."

She said the last phrase as if it explained everything. She rolled me out of bed and opened the window.

"Go," she whispered as a tear trickled down her cheek.

"Daria is dead," I mumbled. "I don't care what happens to me."

"Well, I do. You're my friend. Do you think I want to do this to you?"

The door opened again, and I watched the brown work boots advance toward me from my position under the bed.

"What's going on?"

"This one had to go to the bathroom. She fell out of bed after I released her. She is still too drugged to know what is going on." Large, burly hairy hands lifted me up like a rag doll and plopped me back in bed.

"I know. I checked these two. Lock her back up and give me the key."

I pushed my face into the moldy mattress and tried to disappear.

"Get your own key. Ryszard told me to check on these two." The old Cecylia had re-emerged. She locked me up and marched from the room.

What now? I waited for work boots guy to leave before I opened my eyes. The next time he came in, I would be awake, maybe scream and be violent so he would jab me with a needle full of mind-numbing, sleep-inducing drugs. Joanna cried quietly until she fell asleep.

Ping. Ping. Ping. I looked around. Joanna was asleep. The door was closed. I looked at the window. A small pebble hit the window, and a face pressed against the glass. The small nose smashed flat. The blue eyes were wide and straining. Kasia! How had she gotten here? How long had she been here?

I sat up.

She saw me and smiled.

"Go away!" I mouthed.

She just stood there grinning. The door opened, and I turned my attention there. It was brown boots. I prayed he hadn't seen her. I turned my head in a quick swivel to take in the window. Her face had vanished.

"Awake now? Good. Best you don't scream. No one to hear you." He smiled, revealing a broken front tooth. The breakfast tray he held looked ridiculously dainty in his muscular arms. He set it on a table beside my bed. Strange. I didn't know kidnap victims were fed a hearty breakfast.

"You are different from the other girls, no? You don't fight or scream. Too many drugs. I tell Ryszard often. Too many drugs."

I went out on a limb. "Is that what the girl died of?"

He looked at Daria's bed. "Her? I don't know. None of your concern. She was fighter, that girl."

How could brown boots talk about her as if he cared? As if it mattered what she died of?

"Why do you do this?"

"What?"

"Kidnap girls."

His facial expression changed from polite to scary. The veins in his neck pulsed.

"Okay. *Eat.*" he said and left. So I ate. The eggs and oatmeal. I drank the juice. I felt woozy. Everything was fuzzy. A pink fuzzy sweater floated in. A voice called to me from far away, as if I were in a tunnel.

"Don't eat the food, Adelina...."

CHAPTER
TEN

SOMEONE WAS SHAKING ME, or I was dreaming.

"Wake up!" It was Joanna. She wasn't shaking me. She was kicking my back.

"What? Leave me alone." Everything came back to me. Kidnapped. Not rescued. Daria is dead. Want to die. The professor had told me of that first night he and his sister spent in the cage at the Warsaw Zoo. Strange. Fuzzy memories about that story flitted across my mind now. When he had told me about feeling scared, cold and alone, as if his world had ended, I hadn't understood. I just wanted him to get onto the next poem. That's not the way the professor worked. I liked the poems because they had a wonderful cadence. That was the word he used. I loved memorizing them because it kept my mind off other things. He loved teaching me because each poem had a connection to some event in his life. I suppose he taught me well, because in the haze of my darkest hour, I thought of a poem.

> *Take this kiss upon the brow!*
> *And, in parting from you now,*
> *Thus much let me avow-*

You are not wrong, who deem
That my days have been a dream;
Yet if hope has flown away
In a night, or in a day,
In a vision, or in none,
Is it therefore the less gone?
All that we see or seem
Is but a dream within a dream.
I stand amid the roar
Of a surf-tormented shore,
And I hold within my hand
Grains of the golden sand-
How few! yet how they creep
Through my fingers to the deep,
While I weep- while I weep!
O God! can I not grasp
Them with a tighter clasp?
O God! can I not save
One from the pitiless wave?
Is all that we see or seem
But a dream within a dream?

"Your friend was here again. She said to keep you awake and alert," Joanna told me.

"I don't want to be awake and alert. And she is not my friend."

"Hey," she said, kicking me in the back again, " I saw that big guy with the brown boots drag some little girl away from the window."

I sat up. Alert now. Awake now. "Kasia!"

"You know her?"

"Yes, I think she followed me here. But, how?"

The door opened and brown boots came in with a cafeteria tray.

"You are both awake, huh? Those super drugs finally wore off. Two days!"

"Two days?" I said weakly. He laughed. He put our trays down on the rusty metal table between our cots. He exited and said to someone, "Those two make my job easy."

The food smelled enticing, but with this new info, I didn't want to be drugged again. I had to rescue Kasia. The girl who always lost things had found me. Was there anyone left to find her?

I really had to pee.

"How do we get a bathroom break around here?" I asked. Joanna jerked her chain and dropped it on the metal cot.

Brown boots stuck his head in the door. "You girls going to make trouble for Ivan now?"

"No," Joanna said quickly, "she has to pee."

"No funny business," he said as he unlocked my chains. "Come this way."

He led me out a door and down a dank, musty hallway. It had a single light bulb hanging precariously from a frayed wire. I took it all in. My desire to end my miserable life had been put on hold. Until I rescue Kasia, I told myself. I needed to study my surroundings. Find a way of escape. I needed a plan. We passed a room with the door slightly ajar. I peeked in to see half a dozen girls chained to beds, all asleep. Drugged. In the corner was a small form curled up in the fetal position. Kasia.

Drug-a habit-forming medicinal or illicit substance, especially a narcotic.

The bathroom, though small, had a single toilet with a rusty ring on the inside where the water line no longer reached. The sink had similar rust marks where the water had dripped. Both were white porcelain from an era gone by. What really caught my eye was the small rectangular window above the toilet. It was about eight inches high and two feet wide. I could fit through it. Not now, though. Not only did I need a plan, I needed an ally or two.

I flushed, then washed my hands while brown booted Ivan stood on the other side of the door. Another problem to deal with. Ivan. How many more of them were there? I thought about passing out to see if he would call for help, then I remembered how easily I had been picked up the last time. Hmmm. Should I become a problem for Ivan, the kind he didn't know the answer to?

"Hey, Ivan," I called, "Ummm, I started my period. I need some feminine products."

Silence.

"I get someone," he said finally. "You stay here." I heard his heavy footfall down the hallway. I opened the door and peeked out, careful not to make too much noise. There was a door directly across the hall. It was closed. I tried the knob. It wasn't locked. I pushed it slowly, opening it just enough that I could peer in with one eye. I held my breath. Ryszard was sitting at a card table with his back toward me. He was on the phone.

"We're shipping the girls out tomorrow. Things are getting too hot here. I saw that priest. You know the one. Father Raphael. Yeah, I messed up his face...... I don't know what he is doing here.......It might be personal........Right, it was his little sister.......Okay.......Bulgaria. Usual place....Yeah, renting a truck. We have nine girls. One is pretty young, but I am sure you will find a use for her."

I heard brown boots shut a door, and I slipped back into the bathroom. A matronly woman with a hair net over her dark, graying hair poked her head in the bathroom and handed me a brown paper parcel with a few feminine prod-ucts inside.

"Thank you."

She nodded her head and left. Was that guilt or fear on her face? Nevertheless, I had a better picture of the operation. She must be the cook. There were a few guards, including brown boots, Ryszard, Cecylia and a chemist, somewhere, maybe not onsite.

When I got back to the room, I looked for my backpack. If I got lucky, I could draw everything I remembered. Then Joanna and I could come up with some sort of escape plan.

"What are you looking for?"

"My backpack."

"Under your bed."

I fished it out and pulled out my sketchpad and pencils. My shoes were gone, thus the tracking device. My phone too.

"Hey, are your shoes here?"

"No, they probably take them so we can't run."

Well, at least maybe they didn't know about the tracking device. The operation seemed to be pretty low technology, except for the website.

"You can eat, you know. The food is safe. Your friend with the pink sweater said."

"Cecylia?"

"Yeah. She bribed the cook."

No wonder the cook looked like she had a boiled egg caught in her throat. She was just as guilty as Cecylia and caught in the middle of all of it. Sex trafficking rings. Kidnapping teens and children. Drugging them. Transporting them out of the country. And we were next. My team hadn't shown up, and it was after the birds, as we Polish said. (Too late, nothing could be done.)

The door swung open and Cecylia sashayed into the room in a pink blur. She plopped on my bed. "We need a plan."

"We?"

"Yeah, I didn't sign up for this. I'm done."

"So, how did you get involved?"

"No time for that now. Ryszard is away arranging for a truck."

"Can't you just text Sabilia?"

"No. Ryszard won't let me do anything that doesn't go through him first. I set the system up myself, but he tweaked it."

Joanna had been pretty silent to this point. We had drawn maps, worked out complicated scenarios and plots.

"The bathroom window," Joanna said.

"What?!" We both looked at her.

"It's pretty easy to get to the bathroom here. Adelina, you just had Ivan search for feminine products, right?"

"Yes, I did." Still not getting it.

"Only one of us needs to escape."

"Right. Out the bathroom window and go get help, right?"

"Adelina, it has to be you."

"No, I can't leave Kasia."

"You have to in order to save her. Can't you see?"

Sacrifice-   an act of offering to a deity something precious; especially : the killing of a victim on an altar

destruction or surrender of something for the sake of something else.

Who else would be sacrificed? And where was the team?

"Yeah, we can't all go. All you have to do is get to your team and we are all saved," Joanna pleaded.

"We're only about 10 km away from Sulejow. That's it. You can run," Cecylia added. "I need to stay here and maintain my cover to protect the girls."

Cecylia explained to me how to get back into town. It was confusing, but I could do it. It wasn't a straight shot and there were no real roads.

I had to do it. I had to leave Kasia. What were my other options? Stay and wait for rescue? What if they were close right this minute? Then again, what if Ryszard went for Father Raphael? If he found the priest, he might find the baker or the taxi driver. Neither of them could stand up to

Ryszard. They might be injured, or worse, killed. I had to warn them.

"Okay, here's the plan. We'll keep it simple like Joanna says. I ask to go to the bathroom. Ivan comes and gets me. Joanna, you are going to have to do some acting," I said.

The plan had to begin now before Ryszard returned from his errand. Right now, we were supposed to be drugged, so everything seemed quiet. Joanna would strip to her under-things and scream, yell and have a meltdown. She would probably have to endure being drugged. Everyone would run to her and I would run to the village. The church or the taxi driver, I couldn't decide. Ryszard might be there confronting Father Raphael. Another person I had to sacrifice. The taxi driver. No one would suspect him and he could drive me anywhere. I could use his phone. It had to work.

I shook my chains and banged them against the metal frame. Brown booted Ivan appeared.

"I have to go," I stated simply, clutching the brown paper bag of feminine products for effect.

CHAPTER
ELEVEN

IVAN KEPT his eyes to the ground while he shuffled over and unlocked my chains. I glanced at Joanna. She feigned a drugged stupor. Her face relaxed and a drop of saliva sat at the corner of her mouth. Great!

I closed the bathroom door and crinkled the brown paper bag loudly. The screaming began shrill and loud. Chains banged up against the cot, sharp and metallic. Brown boots sounded down the hall. I didn't wait. I jumped on the toilet and pushed open the window. I slithered out and flipped to the ground just like I had done from the upper bunk in the orphanage. The rain had stopped and an autumn sunset sank on the horizon. That helped me get my bearings. Head west. My feet sank deep into the mud. I pulled them out one at a time with a loud suctioning pop. It sounded loud. Too loud. I focused on the run ahead, looked at the old stone building, and memorized the details. I took a deep breath and blew out, my breath rising in a vapor, and I ran. I hit something hard. I stumbled.

"What are you doing out here?" I fought to maintain my balance and looked up into the face of Ryszard.

"I ….uh…," He pushed me to the ground, his face twisted and red.

"Get back inside, now!" He gave me another hard shove. My back sank in the mud, coating me. I put my hand down to push myself up on my side. He smacked it out from under me like it was a kickstand on a bike. My shoulder hit a rock, and I froze. I was numb. Everything moved in slow motion. This couldn't be real. We had a plan. A simple plan. A good plan.

Plan-1.a scheme or method of acting, doing, proceeding, making, etc.,developed in advance.

"We're finished! I'm not standing by anymore." A flash of pink flew by me. I guess Cecylia wasn't maintaining her cover.

"No one leaves until I say so and then only in a truck or a body bag. Got it? Back inside," he laughed as if he had just told a joke. I crab walked backwards. He came towards me with a knife. The silver blade shone, taunting me. Then I saw her out of the corner of my eye. Kasia. I shook my head. NO!! I didn't want him to turn around and see her. How did she get out?

He thrust the knife at me and missed as I dodged it. He bent down, and we both grabbed for the knife. His hand got there first. I pulled mine back from his like I had touched a hot iron. When he righted himself, I lunged toward him with all of my weight pushing on his chest with both hands. A sharp pain. I dropped to my knees. Red, thick blood oozed out of my left forearm. The knife stood at attention. I gritted my teeth and looked up at my attacker. He grinned, leaned over me and exhaled a putrid puff of breath as he laughed.

I leaned against the building.

Cecylia rushed at him, screaming, "Not again. You're not hurting another girl!"

She jumped on his back, scratching his face with both hands. I watched as small lines of blood ran down his face, making him look even more evil with his grin intact. He whirled around, flung her off, and knocked her in the head with his balled fist. She crumpled and went down.

Kasia took over. She grabbed him around the waist. He laughed. I looked down at my arm and vomited on the ground. *I need help, God, please help me.*

Kasia had backed off.

Vomit-1.to eject the contents of the stomach through the mouth; regurgitate; throw up.

"You're not getting away. Just give it up, girls," he said as he turned his back on me. He tripped on a brick and I saw my chance. Sweep the leg. I swung my leg and made contact with his as he tried to regain his balance. Kasia rushed up and pushed him at the same time. He went down hard, bouncing his head off a brick. He groaned and pushed himself up on one arm. He was close enough that I could touch him.

I looked at my arm with the knife still protruding from it and then at his face. His gaze was squarely on the knife, too. I could sense his next move.

Cecylia lay on the ground, still dazed. Kasia stood over Ryszard, awaiting my instruction. Then he turned his attention to Kasia. I had to do it. I jerked the knife out and blood spurted upward. In a surge of adrenaline, I plunged the knife into his back. It was an awkward thrust. He twisted his head and looked at me. His eyes looked shocked and startled. He wasn't laughing anymore. With a sickening thud, he fell backwards, driving the knife deeper. Someone had pushed him. Who? Panie Atoni and the taxi driver's faces floated over me in a haze. Was I dreaming?

"That is a bad man!" Kasia was in Sabilia's arms.

Father Raphael reached down and picked me up. Where had he come from? Had Father Raphael pushed Ryszard? I heard a loud whirring sound. Was that a helicopter?

Then the darkness closed in on me.

CHAPTER
TWELVE

MY MOUTH FELT COTTONY DRY. I raised my right arm to my mouth and a plastic IV tube swung with it. I looked down. I was tucked under white crisp sheets. I sat up quickly and a wave of nausea swept over me.

"Careful, sweetie. You need to take it easy. We stitched up your arm and we are administering morphine for the pain." A white uniform floated in front of me with bright purple hair.

"Where am I?" I asked, gingerly placing my head back on the pillow.

"The hospital."

"What happened to Kasia? Cecylia? Joanna?"

"Calm down. I don't know. I'm just the nurse. Maybe your friends can tell you."

Director Josef appeared in the doorway with Kasia peeking out from behind him.

"May I come in?"

"Yes."

He talked as he walked toward a chair. "Ryszard is in custody. Wounded but stable. All the girls are here at the hospital."

"I helped. I found you!" Kasia added.

"Wait. Where's Cecylia?"

"She wasn't sure you would want to see her. She had a mild concussion. They let her go home. Her mother hired a nurse."

"I didn't kill Ryszard?"

"No. You missed his heart. You did puncture a lung. They will get him to talk. You rescued all of those girls, Adelina. You broke the case wide open." He leaned forward and patted my leg. "The whole team was there. Waiting for backup before they made their move. I guess you got tired of waiting. You moved the timeline up."

"Except Daria. I didn't move the timeline up enough for her." I closed my eyes and hot tears dripped down my cheeks.

"Hey, she would want you to have this," Kasia said. She put the house charm bracelet on my wrist. "Don't lose this. It is important. Daria will want it later."

The purple-haired nurse stuck her head in the door. "You need to let her rest."

"Wait. What do you mean 'Daria will want it later?'" I tried to sit up and pain shot through my arm. I fell back, panting.

"Well, I don't know why they didn't tell you," purple-haired nurse said. "Daria isn't dead. She had been overdosed. I remember her name because you kept saying it when we stitched you up."

Kasia and Director Josef smiled. "We didn't want to tell you," the director added. "They weren't sure if she would make it through the night."

"We found her," Kasia said and slumped against the director. He leaned over and picked her up. She put her head on his shoulder and slept. He smiled and patted her on the back. "See you soon. Get some rest."

Then I was alone with my thoughts, hope and a charm bracelet. Alone didn't feel the same this time. It felt hopeful.

"Hope" is the thing with feathers -
That perches in the soul

Hope-a feeling of expectation and desire for a certain thing to happen.

Hope had perched in my soul. It sat like a bird full of brightly colored feathers waiting for the morning.

What had the professor said that had gotten him through those dark nights in the zoo cage? Hope for the future. Going to America to be with his father.

I have stood still and stopped the sound of feet
When far away an interrupted cry
Came over houses from another street,
But not to call me back or say good-bye;
And further still at an unearthly height,
One luminary clock against the sky
Proclaimed the time was neither wrong nor right.
I have been one acquainted with the night

What was my hope? What would come from this dark night?

"Hey, I know it's late, but can I come in?" Joanna said as she peeked her head in the doorway.

It was hours after everyone had gone home. There was one dim fluorescent light above my bed that blinked intermittently. I had dozed on and off, but I could use some company. Everything seemed so surreal. It was over. Daria was alive. I had stabbed Ryszard. Cecylia had tried to save me. I had been dreaming of toucans with lime green beaks and feathered bibs.

"Come in, " I said.

She grabbed a chair and scooted it next to my bed.

"You saved my life." Tears dripped down her cheeks. She wrung her slim hands and her long legs searched for a place to go. She twisted them together and slid her feet under the bed.

"We saved each other's lives," I said.

"Yeah, but I was stupid. Believing I should chase my dream like that."

"No. Chasing your dream isn't stupid. It is the way you chased it. Our dreams are important, but the journey is just as important." I looked around for my backpack. She instinctively knew what I was looking for and handed it to me. I pulled out a sketch. "I always dreamed of going to art school in NYC and living in a city. I thought if I got adopted then I could make that dream come true. I was wrong."

"But you just said..."

"Just listen. My dream is to go to art school, but how I get there may be different than I expected. Expecting people to make our dreams come true as if they are magic is wrong. Relationships matter." I knew I was all over the place. I couldn't seem to find the way to put into words the journey I had gone on with Daria. I tried again, "All Daria ever wanted was a family. To belong. A home. All I ever wanted was a family so I could do what I wanted. You see? You can't put your dreams on a pedestal and pursue them by stepping on other people. You need people. You need to belong." I still wasn't sure if she got it. I wasn't sure that I had gotten it. I just knew that Marge and Jim were important. I belonged with them. It didn't matter whether I lived in NYC or the hills of WV. I could do my art. I did it here.

"Where are your parents?" I asked.

"They went home. They are coming back tomorrow. I get to go home in the morning."

"Good. Good." I played with my sheets with my good arm. Home is how this all got started. "Make sure you don't take them for granted. Tell them your dream. They'll help you achieve it, the right way. No more meeting strangers for hot chocolate. Hey, have you seen Cecylia? I really wanted to see her."

"Yeah, she said you wouldn't want to see her, because of Daria and all."

"How did she get involved in all of this?"

Then she was there in the doorway wearing that fuzzy pink sweater - or a replica of the orphanage one.

"I had to come back and tell you how sorry I am."

She hovered in the doorway, rocking back and forth on her feet.

"Come in, we were just talking about you."

She hesitated, searching my face. I offered my best grimace smile.

"Ryszard is my step-father."

"What?!"

"Yeah, weird. Scary. I know. You see, I am from an old aristocratic and wealthy family. My mom, well she lived a pretty charmed life. Waited on. Spoiled. Sheltered. My dad and the staff managed everything for her. Before that, my grandfather did. My grandfather died five years ago. My dad died suddenly six months ago."

"I'm sorry."

"So sorry," Joanna echoed.

"So my mom married the first guy who came along. Ryszard was sweet. He knew what to say and when to say it."

"Yeah. So true," Joanna added.

Cecylia paced back and forth at the foot of the bed.

"It happened so fast, you know. Mom wouldn't listen to me. To anybody. They got married. He fired the staff and hired his own people. He changed, but mom remained in her bubble."

"He didn't change," I cut in. "He just fooled everyone."

"Yeah." She hung her head, watching her feet as she paced," He told me he had a job for me and if I didn't do it, he was going to kill my mom. Just like that. Cool as ice."

"Move into the orphanage and recruit girls for his sex trafficking ring?" I asked.

"He didn't say it like that. He said that he would get these girls jobs, like they wanted this sort of thing. I didn't know how bad it was going to get. I'm sorry. I really thought if some orphan wants to be a prostitute, I wasn't really doing anything too terrible. I was wrong. Really wrong."

"All that shopping and the diva complex?"

"I had to sell all of this. I had to be ditzy so no one would suspect I was doing anything. My mom thought I was at computer school, so I would take the money Ryszard gave me and show up with shopping bags and smile. Adelina, you were my friend. I couldn't…" She began to weep uncontrollably. Her body collapsed in a heap. Joanna jumped up and knelt beside her. She stroked her back.

"I almost …..killed…..that…..girl…."

Purple-haired nurse rushed in. "Why hasn't this girl been treated?" she demanded.

"I uh…I don't know."

The nurse supported Cecylia and led her to a room across the hall. She peeked her purple head in ten minutes later, "I gave her something to help her sleep. I suggest you girls get some rest."

I can't really blame Cecylia. I can't be angry with her anymore. I had used so much energy hating her and she was only trying to preserve the only family she had, her mother. How many nights had I lain awake in the orphanage late into the night, giggling with Daria and imagining the day when I had a family, when we both had families. Daria had a much better idea of what that meant. She knew it meant sacrifice. I thought it meant self-service, such a wide gap, like the Grand Canyon I had read about in the United States.

Canyon-a deep gorge, typically one with a river flowing through it.

A voice said, Look me in the stars
*   And tell me truly, men of earth,*
*   If all the soul-and-body scars*
*   Were not too much to pay for birth.*

Cecylia had a family and in a weird way, she had shown me what it meant to choose family. It meant denying yourself. She was suffering the soul-and-body scars of her birth. There really wasn't a canyon between our stories. They both ran deep with the river of shame. A shame neither of us could explain. Shame of being an orphan for me. Shame of doing what she thought she must to save her mother.

I thought back to the first day I had met Marge and Jim. What an idiot I had been. I had so many rotten thoughts that day. They focused on me. What did the psychologist say? Survival mode. I needed people. I needed to attach. I knew that now. That's what Marge said. I didn't really know exactly what that meant, but I wanted to try. I didn't need art school. I wanted it. Just like I liked the idea of getting on the subway in NYC and flitting around the city. That was an empty dream, not because I didn't want to learn more about art, but because things without connection, without family, without people who love you aren't fulfilling. They are meaningless.

My arm throbbed. I pushed the call button. Purple-haired nurse came in.

"Can I have something for the pain?"

She checked the I.V. and adjusted it. "There you go. Get some sleep."

Sleep wouldn't come. It taunted me as I thought of the weight of what I had gone through. I pulled at the white sheets, trying to cover the cold chill in my soul. Those girls, taken from homes. Those girls, taken in by a promise, a lie that all their dreams would come true. They left the thing most valuable. The fluorescent light blinked above my bed and went out. I looked toward the window where the moon shone brightly. The harvest moon. A quote the professor had repeated often when he spoke of WW II camped out in my mind.

Many that live deserve death. And some that die deserve life. Can you give it to them? Then do not be too eager to deal out death in judgement. For even the very wise cannot see all ends.

I couldn't see all ends. The professor had spoke of those who were silent or those who herded Jews into cattle cars in the dark night only to protect their own families. "How difficult it was to sort out who should die after the war. Who should be punished for all those who did die?" he had said. Those words were like a foreign language to me when he first spoke them. Now, they were starting to make sense.

The next day was a hazy blur. The pain increased or the adrenaline wore off. I'm not sure which. Cecylia slept most of the day. I saw her mother, tall, slim, blonde and wearing a pink tweed suit with black heels and accompanied by an entourage of staff. Her purse hung on her forearm like an accessory, and she walked like she was headed down a runway instead of into a cold, sterile hospital room. I could see the resemblance.

Joanna came in and said her goodbyes and introduced me to her parents who thanked me repeatedly and gave me a gift. A set of paint brushes. Joanna cried. I cried, finally able to release some of the tension that had built up in my body since this whole ordeal began. Some of the anxiety slipped away with the tears. Just a tiny bit. She promised to stay in touch and then she was gone, back home with her family.

It was kind of a letdown. No Sabilia. No Father Raphael. Not even the taxi driver or the baker. Being alone no longer appealed to me. I longed for the connection that these people had given me. I wanted to talk to Father and tell him that I believed. That God had come to my aid when I needed Him.

I decided to try my hand at prayer again. I prayed for each of the girls. They were all being treated for the drugs in their system. As the day wore on, I drifted in and out of sleep and more people, probably family members, drifted in and out of the hospital.

One day the purple-haired nurse brought a wheelchair into my room, "Hop in," she said. I wasn't exactly hopping, I kind of shuffled across the floor and slid in gingerly.

"Where are we going?"

"Someone wants to see you!"

Purple-haired nurse, or Sasha, as her name tag said, wheeled me down the hall and through another set of glass doors into another patient's room.

"I knew you would come!" Daria! She floated like a translucent ghost on the fluffy pillow. "Thanks for rescuing me."

I stood, my knees weak from excitement and shaking from the pain of exertion. We hugged delicately, each of us too fragile to squeeze too hard.

"I thought you were dead," my face flamed red and hot tears dripped down my cheeks. "I thought I failed."

"Of course you didn't," Sasha said, "You are a hero! I'll be back in fifteen minutes girls, talk fast. You both need to rest."

"I refused to eat the food," Daria said quietly.

"What?!"

"I figured out after the first night. My hot chocolate was dosed. I got away. I ran. I hid. Ryszard found me the next day," she looked sad and defeated.

"So what happened next?"

"I guess I had become a problem. Some huge guy with brown boots on started putting the drugs in me whatever way he could. I fought hard. Not hard enough." A tear dripped down her cheek and ran into her mouth.

"Hey!" I said, scooting closer, "I'm here. We made it. We

are alive. It's not your fault. I fought too and look what that got me." I pointed to my arm and put on my best smile.

"Yeah," she said, rallying a bit. "You fought for me. For all those girls. I'm proud of you. Adelina." Then she turned her head away, towards the window. "I'm tired. So tired."

I called for purple-haired nurse and went back to my room. I thought victory would taste sweeter. The after-effects were sometimes bitter. Trauma wounds. Daria was wounded differently than me. She was wounded inside. My arm would heal. Would her heart?

wound-an injury, usually involving division of tissue or rupture of the integument or mucous membrane, due to external violence or some mechanical agency rather than disease.

an injury or hurt to feelings, sensibilities, reputation, etc.

A week later, the director came to collect me. I was heading home in the orphanage van. It felt comfortable and familiar, like a warm pair of fuzzy socks.

Kasia waited at the glass door in the entryway. She leaned her face against the glass and squashed up her nose, just like she had in the abandoned building when I was kidnapped.

"I'm glad you're back. The littles missed you. You wouldn't believe how many things I've lost this week."

I followed her up the stairs to my room. My empty room. My artwork didn't look appealing to me anymore. I reached up to grab the sketch of NYC and ripped it down with my good arm.

"And they want to see you in the cafeteria right now."

"Who?"

"The kitchen staff. They said they want to see 'our little hero'. I think that's what they said." She pulled my good arm and led me towards the steps. I followed her down the stairs, through the empty foyer and into the darkened cafeteria.

"Are you sure?"

"Surprise!" The lights came on and brightly colored confetti flew at my face. I tried to take it all in. Jim and Marge rushed forward and enveloped me in an embrace. "We're so glad you're okay, honey." Marge said, tears dripped down her pink cheeks.

"And we're darn proud of you," Jim added with a catch in his throat.

surprise-to strike or occur to with a sudden feeling of wonder or astonishment,as through unexpectedness.

Sabilia hovered beside them, "You did a great job. A real spy." I was going to sit her down and get the whole story when this party simmered down. No time now.

Father Raphael stepped in front of me. Marge and Jim stood like guard dogs, not leaving my side. "God answered my prayer and kept you safe," he said.

Panie Piotr shoved a plate towards me, "I bought cookies for you, yes, eat. Eat. "

The taxi driver. Laughing. Congratulations. Pink balloons. Confetti. This had Cecylia written all over it. She stood in front of the window to the kitchen where we returned our trays. The counter was covered with a pink satin cloth, white lilies in a vase and silver trays of cookies. She linked arms with a more mature, stately version of herself. Above her head was a room spanning banner that read, "Welcome home, Adelina!"

I gazed out the window of the the Lot airliner and watched the cottony clouds go by. I was going home for the first time. A real home with a real family.

So much had happened in a short week of being home from the hospital. Marge and Jim had finalized the paperwork for my adoption. There was a flurry of activity after that. A week in Warsaw. A check up. The Embassy. Jim had stomped around there to show them who was boss. Everyone seemed to stand a little straighter when he walked by. I was learning so much about parents that I hadn't expected.

Yesterday, at the hotel, I had turned on the TV. Marge had taken the remote and quickly snapped it off. "You can't watch that show." Her face was red. Was she angry? Embarrassed? I couldn't tell.

"Why?"

"It's inappropriate."

"We watched it all the time at the orphanage," I explained.

She sighed heavily, "Adelina, I don't want you to watch that anymore."

I had slumped in my chair and crossed my arms. I hadn't thought about this part of family. In the orphanage, the staff gave us some rules like when to go to bed or meal time. The rest of what we did was pretty much up to us as long as we stayed on the premises.

A little later, I heard Marge talking to Jim in the other room.

"Jim, did you see the garbage Adelina was watching? Kasia, too. The people on the show were naked. And the language...."

"Calm down, Marge. We will have time to parent her when we get home. We aren't responsible for the choices someone else has made for her so far."

Parent her. What did Jim mean?

Parent-noun

1.a father or mother.

Verb

1. be or act as a mother or father to (someone).

I thought I was on their good side, the whole rescuing the girls stuff. What did it matter what I watched? Were they going to tell me what to do every minute of every day?

Marge had come back in Kasia's and my room and found a children's show for Kasia. Kasia was satisfied. Actually, she was super excited to have the attention. I taught Marge how to play Black Peter before we went to dinner and the rest of the day went smoothly. I tucked the information away. Kasia did whatever was asked of her. This made me feel a bit better about the situation. I had told Jim and Marge I couldn't leave her behind. I had begged. Cried. Cajoled.

Cajole- persuade someone to do something by sustained coaxing or flattery.

Marge's response to my plea was to find a host family near our home for a month. Jim was on the phone and furiously filling out paperwork. He made multiple trips to the post office to overnight and fax documents. What happened after the month of December was up to the family, Kasia and God. Kasia's English was great, thanks to hanging out with me all the time. When she lapsed into Polish, I shouted, "English only!" She had already managed to lose something on the plane and had the flight attendants scurrying to find it. Thankfully, Kasia was wearing her heart T-shirt and Marge had managed to find three more of them at an underground shop in Warsaw. Kasia's joy had overflowed when Marge plunked down the money for them. Marge had them wrapped in pink tissue paper and put in a white box.

"I'll carry them," Kasia had offered.

"Oh, no you won't," Jim had said while playfully mussing her hair. "I will. We don't want them to get lost now, do we?"

Kasia giggled. "I'm always losing things."

Marge, Jim and I had looked at her, laughed and said in unison, "We know!"

Those moments of family togetherness I loved. I loved how Marge and Jim had accepted Kasia and all her quirks. They didn't make fun of her like kids in the orphanage did. I hadn't sorted all of these family things out. Some of it was so foreign. Welcome, but foreign. Moments of assurance and acceptance on Marge and Jim's part often made me bristle. I was glad they kept trying. I wasn't going to tell them that.

Daria. There were no words. Purple-haired nurse had wheeled her into the party. She had awakened, but she wasn't the same. She was broken. Sad. It made me angry all over again. We only had a few minutes here and there before I left for good.

"I can't leave you, Daria," I had said.

I had overheard the nurse telling Director Josef about Daria's night terrors. "Physically, she's ready to leave the hospital. Mentally, she isn't. She wakes in the night, crying and screaming. Fighting."

"I see," he had answered, "I'm not sure what to do."

"There is a couple who visit her regularly. They tell me they had been in the process of adopting her. Any way that could move forward? And some counseling?"

At that point, Kasia had come for my help and I didn't hear the rest of the conversation.

"You have to leave me, Adelina," Daria had said. "You have a family."

We cried together for joy and sorrow.

"It was the best of times, it was the worst of times, it was the age of wisdom, it was the age of foolishness, it was the epoch of belief, it was the epoch of incredulity, it was the season of light, it was the season of darkness, it was the spring of hope, it was the winter of despair."

I quoted this section to her in our last visit. I understood what it meant. It was the season of darkness. It was the spring of hope. Two seasons at once. I left her, a string from my heart to hers, stretching across the Atlantic.

I pulled out my phone to look at the photos from the party. Daria, pale and skeletal in the wheelchair. Sabilia and Father Raphael had told me their story. They were siblings! Who knew? The comments at her townhouse about, 'remember last time' were a tiny piece of the puzzle. Their younger sister, Aneta had fallen prey to Ryszard. She just wanted to go out and have a good time. Although Father wouldn't admit it, she had probably confessed to him that she was seeing someone older, the same storyline as Daria.

The confusing part for the priest and Sabilia was that Aneta wanted for nothing. Her family were aristocrats who had actually held onto their status and money. Their estate was one of the 20,000 that had been damaged and/or occupied during World War II. Because of their grandfather's wise moves pre-war and a lengthy reconstruction project in the early nineties, all three siblings grew up in the manor. Their father had bought a few more estates and had been restoring them and opening them up as hotels and retreat centers. Only two thousand of the twenty thousand were repairable.

Aneta, even though she was a teen, was totally into the process. She did research for her dad and helped with modernizing ideas while keeping the old world charm intact. Sabilia had already joined the task force when her sister disappeared. She never suspected human trafficking would affect her own family.

"I followed Ryszard one night after Aneta disappeared," Father Raphael said. "I wasn't sure he was the man who had kidnapped Aneta. I was just following my gut, following the bread trails, and acting on her confession. He went to an old abandoned building on the outskirts of Warsaw. I followed him into the building. He didn't hear me until I saw the girls chained to beds. I must have gasped."

That's when Ryszard had attacked the priest, slashing his face with the knife. Father Raphael was knocked unconscious and when he awoke, he was alone in the building. They never saw or heard from Aneta again. The case in our little village opened up a whole new nest of info and capturing Ryszard could give some valuable information.

Kasia tapped me on the shoulder, "Look!" I looked up to see a pink blur with a blonde bob marching down the aisle towards me.

"Second class is so cramped! How do you survive back here?"

"Cecylia, what are you doing here?"

She grinned and glanced around. "Come join me in first class. We're moving to the States. Mom just wants to put all this behind her."

Kasia stood. "I want to see the first class." Marge nodded and we three headed up to the more spacious part of the plane. Cecylia showed Kasia the great features while I looked out the window. Kasia tired quickly and was ready to head back to our seats.

We landed in Chicago. Jim gathered our things, slinging three bright floral Vera Bradley bags over his shoulder and grabbing his brown leather satchel. Kasia clung to me as Jim charged down the aisle and Marge took the rear, holding us together like front and rear guards.

The Chicago O'Hare airport was the antithesis of Warsaw's terminal. Warsaw was grey. Stark. Cold. Chicago bustled. It breathed life. Marge suggested we get some food before our next flight. I drank in the sights and sketched them in my mind.

"Hey, I'll order," Jim yelled above the noise. "They speak English."

Marge, Kasia and I stood off to the side of the fast food line and waited. A blur of pink surrounded by suits caught my eye . Then Cecylia was beside me. Smiling. She gestured to the men in suits.

"Bodyguards. Mom insisted. She might be going overboard."

"I think it's a good idea," Marge said.

Cecylia flipped her hair, "I just wanted to say goodbye. We're staying with Mother's cousins in Chicago while we decide where to settle. Here's my new number. Text me." She wiped a tear from her eye and sniffed.

"Come visit," Marge said.

"Yes, please," I added. I wasn't sure how to say goodbye and I'll miss you. So, I didn't say it.

"Really?" she said, looking me in the eye.

I looked at my shoes.

"Yes, we can go to the outlets," Marge said.

"Yes, Adelina needs a new wardrobe."

At that she turned on her heel, flanked by her body guards, and disappeared from the crowd. I sniffed and wiped a tear from my cheek.

"She probably won't come," I said to Marge. Strange. I felt a huge loss at Cecylia's parting. How could a relationship go from hate to love? Cecylia hadn't learned to distrust until Ryszard came into her life. I distrusted everyone. Then I trusted her. She had never been pushed around or threatened. I was every day. Sure, she was bossy. What was the word? Spoiled. Now she was tough. I could see it. Man, I was going to miss her and it didn't make sense.

I took off running in her direction, "Cecylia, wait!"

She and her bodyguards turned in one seemingly choreographed movement. Like a jerky dance move.

"Hey," I said, catching my breath with my hands on my knees. This was stupid. What was I doing? This wasn't like me. I didn't want to to do whatever I was doing. "I'm really going to miss you." That was lame. Why did I say that? She was probably going to make a snotty remark and walk away.

"I'm going to miss you, too, Adelina. We're friends, right?"

So, I was wrong. Where did I go from here? What would the professor say?

"Yes, of course. Do come visit. Don't just say it." It sounded stupid coming from my mouth. *Do come visit. Really?*

"I will." She touched my shoulder like she was going to give me a hug. Instead, she just shook my hand. "I will. It's a deal. Who else are you going to get to do your hair?"

We both laughed. Her mother stepped towards me and the bodyguards moved with her. They looked like an Oreo with pink filling. She said, "You have heard the news that Ryszard has escaped? I am concerned for you girls. Please be careful." I nodded and gave her hand a quick shake and she and her entourage slipped into the crowd.

The rest of the trip was a tired blur. How could Ryszard have escaped? Where was he? I suddenly felt exposed. Maybe those bodyguards were a good idea. After another flight to Pittsburgh International Airport, we disembarked to find a welcoming committee. Friends of Marge and Jim's hugged me and snapped photos. So much crying. My new siblings joked with me about scheduling bathroom time, bedrooms and stuff I didn't understand.

"Welcome, Adelina," Rob said. "I'm your older wiser brother."

Faces. Brightly colored sweaters. Dark pressed jeans. Clean new boots. A stark contrast to the faded wardrobes I was used to. My new eldest sister, Laura, draped a lemon colored pea coat around my shoulders. I felt dizzy. I sat down on a bench. Jim put an arm around me and pulled me up. "Party's over, people. Dinner at our house Sunday. We'll tell you the whole story then."

Hours later, I shifted in my seat and opened my eyes. The SUV pulled in a driveway. The house from the photos glowed in front of me. The white columns glittered with tiny lights. The balcony lights shone and a front door beckoned. I pulled out the sketch I had made of the house with the word home written on the bottom.

Home-the place where one lives permanently, especially as a member of a family or household.

———

Read the next in the series-The Girl Who Was Targeted

BONUS

Want to read the first chapter of the next in the series?
Turn the page!

SNEAK PEEK

THE GIRL Who Was Targeted Chapter 1

The text read. It was from Cecylia.

I texted back. I had been 'home' with Marge and Jim for seven months. I called them Mom and Dad now, most of the time. I had been wishing Cecylia would visit. Now, she was coming.

"MOM! Cecylia's coming!" I opened the library window and yelled out. Marge was weeding her flower garden in the front and Jim had gone to get some mulch.

"Come out and tell me about it," she said, still pulling weeds.

I walked out the front door and plopped down on a wicker loveseat. I was reading the texts to her when a large black SUV pulled up in front of the house.

"This is strange," Marge said. She stood and pulled her garden gloves off.

Marge loved her privacy. I had learned she was an introvert. Marge and Jim had bought this place, the home and property at the end of a neighborhood because Marge needed it. The home on seven and a half acres was so well hidden that most people had a hard time finding it, including the UPS man. Marge used Amazon Prime a lot. You would think the UPS man would get it right. Amazon saved her the trouble of going out, she would say. One click is all it took. Still, we were five to ten minutes away from restaurants, shopping, church and the homeschool co-op. Sometimes the house seemed like a giant revolving door with older sister Laura coming with her littles (which made me miss mine). Robert loved to have bonfires with his friends. The music was loud and the S'mores sweet. He usually let me hang out with his friends until about ten p.m., which is when Jim came out looking for me. That was enough time for me anyway. An hour.

I think I was finding out so much about myself by watching Marge. I needed time alone to sort things out. I relished time alone. When the dust settled after the bustle of activity, Mom went to her office to write and I settled in the library. A real library with a round dark walnut table that sat on a large pedestal with ornately carved lions at the bottom. It had lived in a monastery at one time. Fitting, I thought, to remind me of the one in Sulejow. It sat in someone's basement for thirty years before Mom bought it and refinished it. The best thing about the library? It had books. Whole books. No one tore out pages and made cigarettes to smoke. No one smoked period, which was weird. Everyone in Poland smoked. I spent hours pouring over books I had wanted to finish at the orphanage. Of course, I was interrupted here too, mostly by siblings. Robert always said, "Adelina, you don't have to read all the books in the library your first year here."

Jim always defended me. Marge, too. "She's catching up," she'd say and then she'd smile

The SUV rolled to a stop and the driver's side window opened.

"Adelina?" a square-faced, suited man asked. Before Mom or I could say a word, the rear passenger side door opened and Kasia popped out.

"Hey!" she yelled, running toward me across the green lawn. "You're never going to guess what happened!"

Before she could tell us, another door had opened and Sabilia stepped down. Her blonde hair, silky smooth, grazed her shoulders and she wore a form-fitting mint green sleeveless dress and heels.

"Adelina!" Despite the heels, she ran to the porch and bounded up the stairs. She wrapped her arms around me and gave me a tight squeeze.

"Marge, hi. Sorry to stop by unannounced."

Marge laughed. "It's great to see you, Sabilia. Stopped in unannounced is a bit of an understatement, isn't it?"

"Yes," she laughed, "I guess you're right." She squeezed me once more and then let me go.

Kasia had joined us on the porch. She scanned the yard. "Where's the pool? Can we swim?"

I grabbed her hand and pulled her toward me into a giant bear hug, "I've missed you!"

"First things first," Sabilia said.

"Let me make some coffee," Mom said, "then we can talk. I made some muffins. Give me a minute."

"I'll help." Sabilia followed her into the house.

"You know where the pool is, remember? You can tell me what's going on!"

"I know. I've just never seen it uncovered. It was winter last time I was here.......WOW!" she said as she rounded the corner. She stopped. "It's huge. It's so blue. Can I get in?"

"Focus, Kasia, why are you here?"

In December Kasia had spent a month with a host family close to us. It hadn't quite worked out the way we planned. She hadn't been permitted to visit, although Marge made a point to take me to see her once a week. During those visits, the host Mom and Marge drank coffee in the kitchen and the host Mom had poured out her woes.

"She's a little too high needs for our family," I had overheard. I had quickly guided Kasia into the basement family room. Kasia didn't need to hear her faults listed in front of her. Instead, we played Wii bowling.

On Christmas Eve, Marge, Jim, Robert, Anne and I had taken Kasia some gifts. Laura had stayed at the house with Lucy and Ivan, my niece and nephew. They were busy making Christmas cookies. Kasia had been elated to see us. "I don't like it here," she cried on my shoulder while I held her on my lap. "They don't like me."

She had opened her gifts and cheered up. Marge had bought her a hoodie with a giant heart. Jim had picked out a charm bracelet with a heart. He was such a softy sometimes. I had heard Robert say that. I wasn't sure what it meant until

Jim stopped at the jewelry store in the mall during our Christmas shopping trip.

"Jim, she's eight years old. What are you going to buy her?" Marge had asked.

"Every little girl needs jewelry," he had winked at me and bought the charm bracelet. He also bought Mom a ring and asked my opinion about it before he shoved me out of the store. The stone looked orange like a pumpkin. It matched Mom's hair, so I said, "Yes, that one." I knew nothing about jewelry.

Mom, Anne and I had bought the hoodie, some jeans and tennis shoes. I also had to buy her a book, *The Secret Garden.* Anne had suggested I read it and I loved it. I thought Kasia would too. I planned to read it to her.

It was on Christmas Eve that the host Mom had told us that Kasia was going back to the orphanage for good.

"We're having my family over tomorrow. All of my siblings and their children. We will have a full house." She looked at me as if I understood what she was saying. Her mouth turned down in a frown. I had thought her beautiful in the beginning. Long dark hair the color of chestnuts and amber colored eyes. She reminded me of a character in a fairytale. I had first thought her a princess. Now, I thought her a witch.

Robert had pulled Dad aside in the entryway. I had followed. "Dad, do something. Are you going to let this witch get away with it? With hurting Kasia?" Robert had said. His face was red and fists clenched. "I'm going to the car!"

This had made me feel better. I wasn't the only one who saw her that way. From the foyer, I heard Mom say, "Why doesn't Kasia spend the day with us then?" Robert stopped, his hand on the door knob. He looked at Dad.

"Oh, could she?" Host Mom replied.

"Of course," Jim had said loudly and in two steps he was back in the kitchen. Robert right beside in matching his steps. Dad cleared his throat, "Let's pack her up now. She can spend the night."

So Kasia had spent the last few days of her visit with us. We played games, sang songs, ate tons of cookies and Kasia played with Lucy and Ivan. Laura's husband Daniel joined us for Christmas day before he had to get on a plane and fly away for another business trip. Laura and the kids stayed with us for days after, making the house lively and fun. The whole Hunter family had taken her to the airport and seen her off. A bubbly flight attendant had taken charge of her at the gate. We all shed tears. Kasia had clung to me.

"I can't lose you!" she sobbed.

In January, Mom and Dad had begun the paperwork to adopt her, only to be told someone else had already begun the process and been approved. We hadn't heard anything since.

Kasia was peeling her sandals off and dipping her foot in the pool.

"It feels great!"

I ran down the bank. "Did Sabilia adopt you?"

"Yep!" she said, stepping down another step until the water covered her knees, "That's what I was trying to tell you!"

"Girls, come up here!" It was Marge. She and Sabilia were on the deck, muffins and coffee in hand.

"I want to swim!" Kasia said, stepping out of the pool.

"After we talk and you get settled," Marge answered.

"You're staying? They're staying?" Kasia was too busy stomping up the stairs to answer me.

"Yes, for a few days," Sabilia said and she handed me a coffee.

Just like old times, I thought. Those days in the orphanage seemed like a lifetime ago. I loved the way Sabilia treated me. Like a human. My new family treated me the same. My coping mechanism (Marge's name for it) had died down quite a bit. I still memorized poetry and sometimes it popped in my head when it applied to a situation, but I didn't have to recite it as often to calm myself. Same with my dictionary habits. The first day of homeschool co-op was horrific. All I did was define words and recite poetry. In the middle of class once, I answered with a verse. Talk about mortified.

Mortify-to subject to severe and vexing embarrassment : shame.

Just thinking about it sent me into my old habits. This situation with Sabilia wasn't helping. Why was she here? What was going on?

I sat down gripping my coffee with both hands so as not to spill it.

"We need your help, Adelina. We followed all the leads we had from Ryszard and the organization. The last lead led us here."

"What?" I stood up and my coffee cup hit the deck. Coffee spread out on the deck while the fiestaware cup bounced in slow motion.

"To WV?" Marge said as she stood and put her arm around my shoulders. I just watched the coffee spread.

spill-to cause or allow to run or fall from a container, especially accidentally or wastefully.

"Yes, we've taken down some other rings in other countries. Some of these girls end up back on the street. I'll get into that later. One of our contacts here in the States said she had seen Ryszard."

Marge and I sat down at the same time. Robert opened the back door and stuck his head out. "What's going on, Mom? Adelina, are you okay?" He disappeared and reappeared with a pitcher of water which he poured on the coffee puddle. It streamed through cracks on the deck to the patio below. He picked up the coffee mug and sat down beside me. He stuck his hand out to Sabilia, "I'm Robert." Kasia flung herself on his lap. "I want to go swimming, Robert!"

Just then we heard the sound of the truck being driven into the front yard. Jim was back with the mulch.

"I'll go fill Jim in," Marge said as she stood. "Adelina, will you be okay?"

"I'm here, Mom. I've got this. Go talk to Dad," Robert said. "Kasia, go put your suit on." Kasia bounded in the house, slamming the door behind her.

"If Ryszard is here, why do you need my help?" I was finally able to formulate a sentence.

"He may have set up a ring in this area and he may be looking for you. We're not sure. If he is looking for you, we need to protect you."

"But, you said you need my help. So, you mean use me as bait again."

"Oh no you don't," Robert said, raising to his full height. "That didn't work out so well the last time."

Kasia was back, swinging her towel around. "I'm ready!"

"Adelina, why don't you take Kasia down to the pool while we finish this discussion?"

Robert looked so much like Jim right then. He shooed me down the stairs to the pool. Kasia was right behind me. As soon as we were on the pool patio, Kasia threw her towel down and jumped in. She bobbed back up squealing. "It's perfect!" she yelled. I sat down in a chair to watch her. I glanced up at the deck where Jim, Marge, Robert and Sabilia were now talking. I couldn't make out exactly what they were saying. The pool filter and air conditioner were too loud.

"It won't be the same," Sabilia said. Jim answered. I couldn't hear the words. I recognized the posture. He wasn't going to budge. No, I wasn't going to be helping this time. I turned my attention to Kasia.

"Where do you live, Kasia?"

"What? We're moving here for awhile. Father Raphael, Sabilia and I are looking at some houses tomorrow."

Hmmm. Cecylia was coming. Moving here. Sabilia moving here. Sounds like someone already had a plan in place. Anne joined us at the pool. "Robert said for me to keep an eye on you." She pushed my shoulder with her hand. "You okay?"

"I'm fine," I lied. She had her suit on. The orange suit matched her red hair. We could be sisters. Oh wait, we were sisters.

"Go get your suit on. I'll watch her for a few minutes."

"Anne eeeeee, get in!" Kasia yelled. Anne ran to the side and did a cannonball, splashing me, and Kasia squealed again.

I ran up the stairs and went to get my suit on. Anne, Kasia and I spent the next hour playing in the pool. It felt good to play and get my mind off the reason Sabilia was here. Anne didn't mention it. We dove for the rings and played tag. Anne was good at distracting me. At cheering me up. It wasn't until right before lunch, when we went in to change that it hit me.

I was in my room sliding back into my shorts and I saw his face. His evil grin. I looked at the purple scar on my arm where I had been stabbed and the fear washed over me. I stood up. Poetry sped through my mind like Flash. My mind couldn't settle on a poem. The words were getting mixed up. Anne poked her head in the door, "Lunch is ready." I tottered. The world was spinning. "Adelina, sit down!"

She rushed over and took my arm. "Tell me about it."

"I just keep seeing his face."

"Ryszard's?"

"Yeah."

"Are you doing that poetry thing again? Maybe if you recite something it will help."

"I can't. It's all a jumble."

"Adelina, you are the reason he was captured the first time. You took him down. You can't let this fear overtake you."

I took a few deep breaths. "I know you're right. My body just doesn't want to cooperate."

"Then, do it afraid. I'm here. I can help. Robert's here. Laura. Daniel. Mom. Dad."

"I'm here," Kasia stuck her head in the door, "and it's time to eat. Marge said."

We went down the steps together. Everyone was in the kitchen. Robert and Dad were making sandwiches while Mom served fruit salad.

"I want to help, Sabilia. I want to take Ryszard down for good," I announced.

"Great!" Sabilia said. "We have a task force here in WV. We'll take you to our headquarters and get you settled in."

"No!" I said a little too quickly. "I'm not going to a head-quarters or whatever you have set up. "I looked around the kitchen at my family."This is my headquarters. This is my task force."

"Yeah," Robert said, flinging his sandwich onto his plate. "We're her task force. Mom? Dad?"

"Yep!" they both said in unison.

"She's not going into the lion's den alone this time," Jim said.

"Cecylia too!" I said, remembering the text. "She's coming tomorrow!"

We settled into lunch, everyone talking at once. It was like old times.

"This is the most unorthodox task force ever," Sabilia said loudly and slumped back in her chair.

I smiled. It was the best task force ever.

Her phone buzzed. "A text from my brother," she said in explanation. She stood, waving her phone around in the air like a flag. "Aneta is alive! Someone saw her here in the States!"

I dedicate this book to those teens I met in the orphanage, all those years ago in Sulejów, Poland. You captured my heart. You were gorgeous girls with the sparkle of life still in your eyes. I don't know where you are today and that makes me feel guilty. As if I didn't do enough. I wrote this book for you and all those who are like you, who don't know how to define home, who don't have a family or an advocate to speak for you. I speak for you. I write for you. If one of you is saved because of what I do, I count that as success.

Special thanks to my revision teams and all those coffee meetings where we discussed and rewrote. Thanks, Carly Jones, Lori Shaffer, Alec Coen and Rebekah Schoonover for being part of the revision team. You guys rock!

Thanks to hubby, Jerry for listening to all of my ideas, and reading the finished work!

Special thanks to Theresa Ingles, copy editor, and proofreader!

INDEX

RESOURCES

Zoe International at <u>http://gozoe.org</u>

International Justice Mission at <u>https://www.ijm.org</u>

In the US - Home Land Security at <u>https://www.dhs.gov/blue-campaign/what-human-trafficking</u>

National Human Trafficking Resource Center: <u>1-888-373-7888</u> for help or to report suspected trafficking.

NOTES

The places in Defining Home are real.

- Piotrków Trybunalski and Sulejów are both places the Guires frequented when we adopted our children.
- Dom Dziecka or the Children's Home, where 3 of our 4 children lived, 2km outside of Sulejów, has since been closed.
- The wooded path from the orphanage is real. The Guires used the path Adelina used to walk to Sulejów.
- The Guire family used the taxi service described in *Defining Home.*The doberman was our greeter too!
- The Guire family visited the bakery and were asked to pay a million dollars for a dozen rolls.
- We stayed in the castle. The Cistercians Abbey, founded in 1176, now houses a hotel.
- The bus line is how we got around. I rode the bus from Sulejów to Piotrków Trybunalski every day.
- Most small shops advertised the LEGO logo. There were no LEGOs in the orphanage.

- The orphanages in Poland use the communal closet system.
- The cleaning ladies did open all the windows when they were cleaning!

What about the story?

The story is fiction, although many facts are weaved in. The professor's story is actually three histories intertwined. The facts about Poland and World War II are real. Sulejów was destroyed by German bombs. Piotrków Trybunalski was the site of the first Polish Jewish ghetto.

Here are a few of the sources I used:

Hiding to Survive by Maxine B. Rosenberg

The Zookeeper's Wife by by Diane Ackerman

———

Stories like Daria's and Adelina's happen every day. I wrote this book to save teens like them and like YOU. Make sure you read over the suggestions Adelina read in the pamphlet:

- If someone, whether stranger or acquaintance, promises something that seems too good in return for sex or free work, wait. Listen to the intuitive voice inside your head. Check with family and friends for advice. Do Internet searches or background checks on the person wanting you to go with them. Say no and see how they react. Look for signs of abusive or possessive behaviors. Is the person trying to isolate or turn you against family and friends? If so, avoid that person.
- Do not make decisions under the influence of substances and do not be in the company of people you do not fully know and trust while intoxicated. Traffickers, looking to put someone into

prostitution, will take advantage of unconscious people or someone who cannot fight being transported elsewhere. Traffickers will also attempt to take advantage of those with addictions or attempt to create drug dependency.

- If coming from a life of poverty, the lure of a better income or education is hard to resist. Check and double check if the agency or recruiters are reputable. Do they have references from people living where they want to send you? Make sure all contracts signed are in your native language so that you will understand all the details. Ask lots of questions. Find out, from another source, what a reasonable travel and recruiting expense would be. Ask for pictures of housing and names of people, companies, or schools that can be contacted. Human traffickers will typically avoid those who are asking too many questions; they want easy targets. Someone looking for a legitimate employee or student will honor the questions, knowing that you would be a valuable employee or student.

STAY IN TOUCH

Hi! Building a relationship with my readers is super important to me. If I could, I'd sit down and have a cup of coffee with you. Since I can't do that, I'd love to keep you in the loop.

Hop on over to kathleenguireauthor.com to sign up to follow me by email. I'll keep you updated on new releases.

You can also email me - Kathleenguire@gmail.com

Last but not least -

Please leave a review. I count on readers like you!

COVER DESIGN CREDIT

Get Covers

ABOUT THE AUTHOR

Kathleen Guire is the mother of seven, four through adoption, former National Parent of the Year, author, teacher, and speaker. She loves connecting with readers through her website (Kathleenguireauthor.com).

For more information,
about Kathleen, check out her website and follow her on social
media!
www.kathleenguireauthor.com
kathleenguire@gmail.com

ALSO BY KATHLEEN GUIRE

What to read next?

The Girl Who Was Targeted

Cathy Divine

De la nuit

vers

ma lumière

———————————

CreateSpace 2018

De la nuit vers ma lumière

Copyright © 2018 Cathy Divine

ISBN **198587007X**
ISBN-13: **978-1985870079**

Préface

Il existe des personnes qui ne laissent pas les autres indifférents. Elles portent sur elles et en elles, quelque chose de plus, quelque chose qui brille, vibre. Ces gens-là rayonnent de l'extérieur comme de l'intérieur. Comment cela est-il possible ?

Cela nous fait dire qu'il doit bien exister autre chose de plus puissant, et que nous ne maîtrisons pas forcément, dans notre vie matérialiste. Pourtant, lorsque nous étions enfants, nous connaissions ce phénomène, au fond de nous. C'est lui qui nous aidait déjà à grandir. En devenant adulte, nous avons occulté cette valeur première, qui, pourtant, devrait nous porter chaque jour un peu plus, sur notre chemin de vie.

Cela, certains l'ont compris. Ils inondent d'amour leur cœur, et, par rayonnement, irradient de joie leur entourage. Il existe des personnes qui sont là pour ne pas laisser les autres dans l'indifférence.

Le cheminement n'est jamais facile, pour accéder à l'excellence de la lumière. Le monde nous montre toujours ses deux facettes : Le Yin et le Yang, le jaune et le noir, le jour et la nuit. Cela a toujours été et sera, jusqu'à la fin des temps. Néanmoins, nous pouvons choisir la face du miroir dans lequel nous désirons nous regarder. Quelle véritable image désirons-nous voir renvoyer ? De quel côté de la fenêtre voyons-nous la lumière ?

Lorsque je suis à l'intérieur de ma demeure, il y fait plus sombre qu'à l'extérieur. Je regarde par la vitre et j'y aperçois la lumière du jour. Lorsque je suis à l'extérieur, je suis baigné par les rayons de l'astre du jour, et cela me réchauffe. Pourtant, si je regarde par la fenêtre de ma maison, je n'y vois presque rien, c'est trop sombre. C'est pourtant la même fenêtre, et j'en connais parfaitement les deux faces. Sans ombre, la lumière n'est rien. Sans lumière, la nuit ne peut exister.

N'oublions jamais que c'est toujours dans le noir que nous pouvons le mieux apercevoir un rayon de lumière, et, ainsi, mieux nous diriger vers elle.

Il est donc important d'accepter, à chaque instant, ce que nous vivons, ou avons vécu par le passé. Ce n'est que de cette manière que l'on pourra apprendre à s'aimer soi-même. Nous pourrons alors commencer à faire rayonner cet amour en nous et le faire déborder autour de nous. Ainsi la lumière pourra éclairer les coins les plus sombres, et les noirceurs faire ressortir, dans son contraste, la beauté de la clarté.

Cette alchimie secrète, que l'âme doit apprivoiser, Cathy Divine en a cherché la formule. Elle a trouvé certaines réponses qui lui ont permis d'avancer sur le chemin qu'elle s'est choisie. Dans ce livre, elle nous ouvre son Cœur, sans crainte, en esquissant son parcours de vie. Elle nous montre également que la lumière existe réellement. Elle nous explique pourtant que rien n'était gagné, que ce fut difficile. Elle met enfin à notre disposition, tout un ensemble d'outils, qui pourra nous servir à nous élever vers l'excellence du Cœur et de l'Amour.

Il ne tient qu'à nous de savoir ce que l'on désire réellement. Si on pense que l'on n'a pas la force de se sortir de notre torpeur, de notre mal-être, c'est que, inconsciemment, on ne désire pas réellement changer les choses.

Il est un fait certain et incontestable : Plus je reste dans le noir, et plus il m'est difficile de regarder la lumière. Ce qui me fait dire que rien n'est acquis d'avance, rien n'est facile. Plus vite vous règlerez les problèmes qui vous rongent, vous hantent, plus vous apprécierez la douceur de ce rayon d'Amour qui brille tout au fond de vous. Plus vous vous estimerez, et plus vous ferez grandir cette flamme intérieure. Plus elle s'amplifiera en vous, plus vous éclabousserez votre entourage de votre beauté intérieure.

C'est l'orientation que Cathy Divine a décidé de donner à sa propre vie. Elle a pu tester diverses solutions thérapeutiques. C'est ainsi que son parcours lui a permis de rencontrer différentes personnes qui l'ont aidée dans son évolution. Elle est rapidement passée du sujet de patiente à celui de praticienne, notamment dans les domaines qui touchent aux énergies. Elle a su tirer parti de tous les enseignements octroyés par les soins qui lui avaient été prodigués, ce qui lui a permis d'évoluer rapidement dans ses différents domaines de prédilection. Elle vous livre ici tous ses secrets, tous ses enseignements, qui ont pu l'amener là où elle en est aujourd'hui, avec un amour infini et toujours grandissant.

Certains de ces supports thérapeutiques, j'ai également pu les approcher de près, voire les utiliser, à des fins d'études sur « les mondes invisibles » qui nous entoure. Je dis très souvent que tout est lié. Il n'y a pas de mauvaise méthode lorsque celle-ci est travaillée avec son Cœur. Ce principe appliqué peut se décliner sous toutes ses formes et en toutes occasions. Il est d'ailleurs de plus en plus utilisé dans les hôpitaux ou cliniques, dans les soins conventionnels comme dans le palliatif.

Cathy nous démontre ici que tout est possible, lorsque l'on s'aime d'abord et que l'on aime les autres. C'est dans un style spontané et plein de douceurs envers nous tous qu'elle nous conte à la fois son histoire et ses problèmes maintenant estompés, avant de nous délivrer ses enseignements guérisseurs.

Edmond Girou

Chercheur – Auteur - Conférencier

Avant-propos

"Aujourd'hui et pour tous les jours à venir, ce sera toujours aujourd'hui.

Aujourd'hui, je me libère de mes chaînes.

Aujourd'hui, je prends conscience de mon plein potentiel.

Aujourd'hui, je sais qui je suis, où je vais et qui je veux avoir près de moi.

C'est maintenant que je tourne mon regard vers le bonheur, l'amour, la paix, la lumière, l'harmonie, car nous y avons tous droit. "

On a tous un but précis, un objectif à

atteindre, une mission à réaliser. Nous ne sommes pas ici pour rien. Nous sommes ici pour grandir, évoluer, apporter du bonheur et de la joie dans ce monde qui ne marche plus droit.

Ceux qui s'éveillent, s'écoutent et œuvrent pour un monde meilleur, grandiront et s'élèveront pour essayer d'atteindre une forme de vie angélique.

Il est difficile de sortir du schéma que l'on nous a tracés. Mais à ceux et celles qui ont la patience, la volonté et la lucidité d'avoir recours à leur soi réel, pourront briser les chaines, et briller de mille rêves.

Nous avons tous une mission, un objectif, un but, pour arranger les choses, quel que soit son impact.

"Un jour, dit la légende, il y eut un immense incendie de forêt. Tous les animaux terrifiés et atterrés observaient impuissants, le désastre. Seul le petit colibri s'activa, allant chercher quelques gouttes d'eau dans son bec pour les jeter sur le feu. Au bout d'un moment, le tatou, agacé par ces agissements dérisoires, lui dit : « Colibri ! N'es-tu pas fou ? Tu crois que c'est avec ces gouttes d'eau que tu vas éteindre le feu ? » « Je le sais !», répond le colibri, « mais je fais ma part. »".

Moi aujourd'hui, j'ai choisi de n'être que Paix, Amour, Lumière et Harmonie, et c'est ensemble, que, demain, nous bâtirons un monde meilleur, un monde juste, un monde rempli de sérénité, là ou le soleil brille de mille éclats d'un printemps trop longtemps dégradé.

"Je me suis regardé dans un miroir,

puis j'ai souri,

j'en ai pleuré,

puis j'ai fini par en rire,

ainsi mes yeux se sont haussés,

sur ma motivation la plus bafouée,

devenir aussi solide qu'un diamant,

devenir mon propre maître savant."

A tous ceux et celles qui œuvrent pour un Monde Meilleur.

14

Yves Eleutheria

Auteur du livre "Journal d'un Eveillé." Créatespace 2017

La nuit

Comme beaucoup de personnes, ma vie n'a pas toujours été facile.

Mes parents ont divorcé, je venais d'avoir huit ans, mon frère six et mon petit frère quatre. Le juge avait décidé que nous devions vivre avec notre père. Il refit sa vie huit ans plus tard.

Les souvenirs restent en mémoire. J'ai été élevée dans les conflits familiaux, dans les critiques, les jugements, les reproches. J'ai toujours été dévalorisée.

J'ai beaucoup souffert du manque d'amour de mes parents et de ma belle-mère. Mon cœur n'a jamais connu la douceur, la tendresse. Je peux dire aussi que j'ai été manipulée au point d'avoir rompu le lien avec ma mère pendant vingt ans. J'ai toujours agi pour faire plaisir à mon père dans le but de recevoir son Amour, un je t'aime et surtout ne pas le décevoir. J'aurai tellement aimé vivre dans une famille sans histoire, et se sentir aimée, mon cœur était vide et j'ai grandi ainsi.

Lorsque parfois, un rouge gorge venait dans ma chambre, j'avais le sentiment que c'était mon papy qui venait me rendre visite, et ça me redonnait le sourire.

J'avais eu une enfance difficile. L'adolescence était du même acabit.

En grandissant, je m'apercevais qu'il n'y a pas de hasard dans la vie. Tout a sa raison d'être. Lorsqu'un souhait n'est pas exaucé, c'est souvent pour nous diriger vers un meilleur chemin. J'avais foi.

Vers l'âge de vingt-sept ans, j'ai été poussée, sans le vouloir, à acheter un livre sur les lois spirituelles du succès, ce qui m'a permis d'ouvrir les yeux. Je compris que la vie ne devrait pas être dans le jugement, la colère, ou la haine. Il devenait évident pour moi, qu'il fallait accepter les gens tels qu'ils sont, et de les aimer de tout son Cœur.

Plus tard je me mariais et eu trois enfants. Quatorze ans après, je décidais d'ouvrir un cabinet en tant que magnétiseuse-énergéticienne. Mais mon cœur était vide et je ne m'épanouissais pas dans ma vie de couple, alors qu'il en était tout autrement dans mon travail. Je pris alors la décision de quitter mon mari.

Dés lors, je reçus des signes hors du commun. Je venais de comprendre qu'il me fallait écrire mon premier livre.

Aujourd'hui, je reste toujours coupée de toute ma famille, hormis ma mère. Mais maintenant, j'accepte cette séparation. Je la vis comme une renaissance. Il m'a fallu effectuer beaucoup de travail sur soi. Apprendre à s'aimer profondément, à se donner de l'amour sans être dans l'attente d'en recevoir. Apprendre à se faire confiance et à se faire respecter.

La chose la plus importante à mes yeux, que

j'ai su faire, est de pardonner. Ainsi je retrouvais la paix intérieure tout en continuant à les aimer. Je leur dis merci de m'avoir fait évoluer. Ces expériences vécues m'ont permis de me faire grandir et de devenir la femme que je suis actuellement. Pour cela je remercie mes parents et ma famille.

Aujourd'hui, je continue à cheminer sur une route d'Amour et de Lumière.

Premiers rayons de lumière

Je m'appelle Cathy Divine, j'habite dans le Lauragais entre Toulouse et Castelnaudary, j'ai été aide-soignante à partir de 1999 et en 2009, j'ai appris que ma mission sur Terre était de soulager les douleurs des gens par le magnétisme que j'ai dans les mains.

Pour commencer, je vais vous expliquer comment j'ai été incitée à écrire un livre.

Etant ouverte spirituellement, le jour de mon divorce, le 4 mai 2015, j'ai demandé à l'Univers de recevoir un signe. Il me fallait être rassurée sur le fait que quelqu'un, là-haut, devait bien pouvoir m'accompagner sur mon parcours terrestre.

Une fois les papiers signés au tribunal, j'ai repris la route pour rentrer à mon domicile. Arrivée devant mon portail, je trouvais une pièce de 20 centimes de francs par terre. Cela me paraissait très étrange, puisque nous n'utilisions que l'euro depuis plus de quinze ans. J'ai vite compris que c'était un signe du ciel. Je savais que je n'étais pas seule, et j'ai remercié avec amour.

Une fois rentrée chez moi, j'ai allumé mon ordinateur pour lire mes messages. A ma grande surprise, j'ai reçu une publicité m'informant que j'avais la possibilité d'écrire un livre sur le magnétisme et sur mes activités professionnelles.

A partir de là, j'ai fait le rapprochement avec la pièce de 20 centimes de francs et cette proposition à écrire. J'ai compris tout simplement comme une évidence, le message de mon guide, qui souhaitait que j'écrive un livre pour transmettre aux personnes quel chemin j'avais emprunté pour en arriver à exercer mon activité de magnétiseuse guérisseuse, qui consiste à soulager les douleurs physiques et morales des personnes.

Je me sens épanouie dans cette mission que je pratique avec mon Cœur, dans l'Amour inconditionnel.

Découverte d'un don

Il est important de savoir que le magnétisme est un fluide que tout le monde possède. Il est plus ou moins développé selon les personnes.

Le magnétisme transmet l'énergie, rétablit l'harmonie, l'équilibre du corps, de l'âme et de l'esprit. Il peut se révéler à tout âge et s'amplifier par une pratique permanente, c'est une méthode naturelle.

C'est avec grand plaisir que je vais partager avec vous la découverte de mon don puis mes différentes activités qui se sont greffées pour aider mon prochain.

Un jour, les rêves m'ont apportées une

solution qui s'est avérée utile pour mes souhaits : à plusieurs reprises, je me suis vue soulager les douleurs des personnes en utilisant mes mains. Dans mon rêve on m'appelait pour accompagner les personnes en fin de vie. Je me voyais les paumes des mains dirigées vers le ciel, et il en sortait une lumière violette.

A cette époque, je ne comprenais pas pourquoi je faisais ces rêves.

Un jour, une amie m'a conseillée de m'inscrire sur un forum, où une médium donnait des consultations de contacts avec des défunts. Apparemment toutes les personnes étaient satisfaites. La vie continuait-elle après la mort ? Au fond de moi je l'ai toujours su, mais je souhaitais avoir une confirmation de la part de cette personne.

Je finis par rencontrer cette femme, en septembre 2009, à Marseille. Elle m'a, ce jour-là, donnée des messages de ma grand-mère Germaine et de mon oncle Robert. Ce fut une journée inoubliable. Mon cœur a été rempli de joie. J'étais très émue d'avoir reçu des messages aussi précis, dans les moindres détails. J'avais l'impression de revivre tous ces bons moments gravés dans mes cellules. Quel Bonheur !

Mon oncle m'avait délivrée un message d'espoir, ce jour-là. Il m'encourageait à utiliser mes mains. Ma mission sur terre devrait être de soulager les Êtres en souffrance.

Mes larmes ont coulé lorsque la femme exprima ces mots de la part du défunt : « Je serais toujours près de toi, je vais t'accompagner pendant les soins et ton guide sera là pour transmettre l'énergie de guérison aux patients. »

Je lui avais également parlé des rêves que j'avais faits à plusieurs reprises. Elle me répondit via son guide : « j'interviens à travers les rêves pour te transmettre des messages, c'est ma façon de t'éclairer ».

A cet instant, j'ai compris que ma vie allait changer. J'allais m'occuper des personnes pour soulager leurs souffrances.

Je n'ai plus aucun doute, mes anges sont près de moi. J'ai toujours senti leur Amour, comme ils peuvent aussi ressentir que je les aime. Je sais qu'ils veillent sur moi et me guident sur ce beau chemin de Lumière et d'Amour.

Une nouvelle aventure allait commencer !

L'apprentissage

Lorsque j'ai appris que j'avais la capacité de faire du bien autour de moi en utilisant mes mains, je me suis demandé comment j'allais m'y prendre.

Je me suis inscrite sur un forum de magnétiseur où il y a eu des échanges enrichissants. Une personne m'a conseillée de magnétiser un citron, de le prendre dans mes mains plusieurs fois par jour, je devais constater les modifications. En effet, au bout de trois semaines, le citron est devenu marron, tout léger, dur.

Qu'est-ce que cela voulait dire ? On m'expliqua que lorsqu'on arrive à magnétiser un citron, on serait capable de magnétiser les personnes.

J'ai ensuite essayé de poser mes mains sur

mes enfants. Ils n'ont rien ressenti de particulier et moi non plus ! J'ai persévéré dans ma pratique. J'ai tenté de calmer un de mes fils qui pleurait car il avait du mal à faire la sieste. J'ai posé mes mains naturellement sur sa tête, il s'est calmé et il s'est endormi.

Nous le savons tous, il n'y a pas de hasard dans les rencontres mais que des rendez-vous ! J'ai donc débuté le magnétisme à distance sur une autre amie médium qui avait des douleurs. Je lui ai dit naturellement de m'envoyer sa photo puis de s'allonger le temps du soin.

J'ai mis la photo dans mes mains, en demandant de l'aide à l'Univers pour que mon amie reçoive les énergies de guérison, puis j'ai prié avec mes prières et celles du cœur.

J'ai remarqué que lorsque je priais, je baillais beaucoup. A la fin de la séance, elle m'a signalée que ses douleurs avaient diminué. Elle avait ressenti une énergie circuler en elle.

Je vous avoue que j'étais un peu perplexe. J'ai pensé qu'elle me disait cela pour me faire plaisir ! Par la suite, j'ai donc proposé mes services à mes amies proches. J'ai remarqué également que je baillais à chaque fois que je faisais un soin à distance mais pourquoi ? J'ai demandé à mon amie médium si elle pouvait me renseigner afin que je puisse comprendre. Elle m'a répondu : « Mon guide me dit que tu évacues la mauvaise énergie, le mal-être, le stress, les douleurs… par des bâillements ». Cela m'a réconfortée d'avoir une réponse.

J'ai pratiqué gracieusement les séances de magnétisme à distance pendant six à huit mois pour me convaincre que mon travail était efficace, que les personnes étaient bien soulagées.

Ensuite il m'est venue l'idée de faire des séances de magnétisme en direct mais sur qui ? Je me suis dit : « je fais confiance en l'Univers, mon guide mettra une personne sur ma route pour que je la soulage ».

En effet, en sortant de chez moi, j'ai vu ma voisine qui boitait et qui souffrait. J'ai compris qu'il fallait que je lui propose mon aide pour la soulager. Suite à ma proposition, elle a accepté volontiers le soin énergétique. Nous sommes allées dans sa maison, je lui ai demandé de s'allonger sur son lit, j'ai allumé une bougie puis j'ai mis la musique douce pour apaiser son âme.

J'ai fait ma demande à mon guide pour apporter de douces énergies de lumière à ma voisine. Je me suis laissée guider par mes mains. Je les positionnais sur les différentes parties de son corps pour évacuer toutes ces tensions, ces douleurs, par les bâillements. A l'instant où je ne bâillais plus, j'avais compris que le soin était fini. A la fin de la séance, elle pouvait à nouveau marcher normalement et sans aucune douleur !

Étant heureuses toutes les deux du résultat, nous nous sommes pris dans les bras, en pleurant et en souriant, quel moment magique ! Quelle belle expérience gravée dans mon cœur.

Ce jour-là, j'avais pris conscience qu'il fallait que j'aille de l'avant, aller plus loin, afin que je puisse exercer mon activité dans de bonnes conditions. Comme tout thérapeute, j'ai acheté une table de massage, puis créée mes petites cartes de visites pour les déposer dans le but de me faire connaître. J'ai rapidement compris que la meilleure publicité était le « bouche à oreille ».

N'ayant pas de salle de soin, j'ai commencé à recevoir mes patients dans ma salle à manger. Je pratiquais les après-midis ou les week-ends, après mon travail initial d'aide-soignante. Les personnes que j'avais reçues avaient tout type de douleurs : des hernies discales, migraines, sciatiques, entorses, spasmophilie, eczéma, arthrose, stress, cancer, etc. Suite aux soins effectués, ils m'ont tenue au courant, j'ai pu constater que dans les 48h ou même avant, les résultats étaient satisfaisants. Les gens étaient soulagés, et parfois même, avaient vu disparaître leurs douleurs.

J'ai le souvenir d'un cas où une personne avait une hernie discale. Elle avait du mal à se mouvoir. Il était prévu que son docteur l'opère. Après trois séances de magnétisme, il n'était plus question d'opération étant donné que la personne avait retrouvé sa santé et ne souffrait plus.

Un vrai bonheur d'avoir des retours positifs suite aux soins effectués avec Amour. En effet, elles avaient retrouvé la joie de vivre. Elles avaient retrouvé le sommeil. Elles étaient plus détendues. Vu les bienfaits occasionnés, cela m'encourageait à poursuivre dans cette voie.

En tant qu'aide-soignante, j'avais travaillé dans divers services et dans différentes régions. Je garde un bon souvenir de ce beau métier que j'ai exercé avec mon cœur.

J'ai toujours eu de bons contacts avec les patients, souvent ils me faisaient sourire lorsqu'ils m'appelaient : le rayon de soleil ! Parce que j'étais gracieuse, j'ai toujours aimé apporter un peu de chaleur dans le cœur des gens, afin qu'ils retrouvent le goût à la vie, le sourire. J'ai aimé mon travail qui a été fait avec beaucoup d'Amour et de respect envers autrui.

Vous devez vous demander pourquoi j'ai quitté mon travail étant donné que j'aimais ce métier.

Chaque jour, j'avais du mal à me lever pour me rendre sur mon lieu de travail. J'ai commencé à avoir des angoisses, un certain mal-être. Avec l'accord de la directrice, j'ai obtenu un nouveau contrat qui m'a permis de travailler les matinées. L'idée m'est venue de pratiquer le magnétisme les après-midis, puis j'ai pensé qu'en diminuant mon temps de travail, mon état de santé s'améliorerait. Eh bien non, ce n'était pas la grande forme ! A partir de là, j'ai écouté mes ressentis en allant chercher la solution au fond de moi. Je me suis laissée guider par ma petite voix intérieure. Je savais que la solution était en moi, pour retrouver cette sérénité.

Je ne voulais pas me l'avouer, mais je savais très bien ce qu'il allait se passer. Mon idéal de vie était de quitter mon travail. Ainsi, je pourrais faire ce que j'aimais, au plus profond de moi : les soins en magnétisme, pour soulager les personnes en souffrance. Là, je me sentais épanouie.

Par une pratique régulière, je proposais gratuitement mes services à mes ami(es)s proches. Les résultats étaient plus surprenants que mes attentes. J'ai pris confiance en moi, et c'est tout naturellement que j'ai décidé de quitter le milieu médical. Je ne me sentais plus à ma place dans cette société essentiellement omnibulée par le matérialisme. Je retrouvais dès lors ma santé et ma joie intérieure.

Au fil des jours, les résultats allaient plus loin que mes espérances, j'ai décidé de créer ma salle de soin en septembre 2011 afin d'accucillir les patients dans mon bel Univers ! Et à partir de janvier 2012, je me suis lancée officiellement en auto entrepreneur.

L'aventure ne s'arrêterait pas là !

Soins à distance

Aujourd'hui, je n'ai plus besoin de photo pour donner des soins à distance. Juste un nom, un prénom ou une voix me suffit, pour canaliser l'énergie de la personne.

- Le client et moi-même fixons le rendez-vous et me signale de quoi il souhaite être soulagé.

- Une fois l'heure fixée, je demande à ce que la personne s'allonge 10 min avant, dans le but de se détendre, et si elle le souhaite, elle peut allumer une bougie et / ou de l'encens.

- Essayez de faire le vide dans votre esprit.

-Fermez les yeux et relaxez-vous en commençant par des petites respirations...un moment unique et privilégié rien que pour vous !

- Pendant le soin, il se peut que vous ressentiez des gargouillements dans votre ventre, du froid, c'est tout à fait normal. Vous pouvez avoir des bâillements pendant ou après le soin ou vous endormir paisiblement.

- De mon côté, j'évacue l'énergie négative, le mal-être, le stress…, par des souffles forts et bâillements que je ne contrôle pas.

La séance dure 25 min.

Une fois celle-ci terminée, j'effectue un petit suivi. Je demande à la personne, par exemple, de me donner ses ressentis durant le soin, ainsi que l'évolution quant au niveau de la douleur.

J'ai pu constater que les gens étaient apaisés en fin de soin.

Elles retrouvent le moral avec diminution ou disparition de la douleur dans les 48h et même avant.

Je ne promets aucun résultat car je me dis que tout le monde ne peut pas être réceptif aux soins que je pratique dans l'Amour inconditionnel.

Quelques témoignages :

« -Ma petite fille est née à 5 mois et demi de grossesse. Elle faisait 980gr. Elle a fait une hémorragie cérébrale. Ce petit bout ne devait pas vivre car en plus elle avait un problème au cœur. Nous avons passé des moments difficiles.

Lyana a fait des arrêts respiratoires. Cathy a envoyé un mail à ma fille pour avoir des photos. Cathy a envoyé des forces à Lyana, ce dont elle avait besoin pour pouvoir être opérée du cœur et pouvoir surmonter tous ses problèmes de santé.

Aujourd'hui notre pitchoune va bien, les médecins disent que c'est une miraculée. Ils ne comprennent pas ce qui s'est passé. Nous, on sait.

Sans Cathy, Lyana ne serait plus auprès de nous. Je ne la remercierais jamais assez. Ma Cathy, tu es notre sauveur et j'espère un jour pouvoir te rencontrer et te dire de vive voix : MERCI. »

« -Je suis ravie des séances de magnétisme de Cathy. Elles ont eu lieu à distance et les résultats obtenus (je souffre d'eczéma) sont plutôt inespérés : aucune trace depuis 2 mois alors que cet eczéma était présent quotidiennement depuis 7 ans. De plus je tiens à saluer l'omniprésence de Cathy par téléphone ou par mail, toujours attentive aux résultats des séances et à l'évolution de notre bien-être. »

« -Ma petite fille Loeva souffrait de somnambulisme au point de se blesser et de n'avoir aucun souvenir au réveil. La dernière fois elle avait des marques sur le cou et dormait à même le sol.

Avant il y a eu d'autres épisodes où elle s'est réveillée sur la marche de la maison à l'extérieur etc. j'ai demandé à Cathy de venir en aide à ma petite fille. Après une séance à distance, Loeva n'a jamais eu de crise. Ma fille ne lui a pas dit qu'elle allait être magnétisée et curieusement Loeva s'est levée en expliquant qu'elle avait eu comme un mal au ventre et c'est comme si un aimant lui avait retiré cette douleur. Je te remercie Cathy pour ce bien-être. »

Je vous livre ici une prière que j'utilise pendant la séance de magnétisme à distance. Lisez-la avec Amour, avec votre Cœur :

Ce traitement prière est pour X

Elle est détendue et en paix, équilibrée, sereine et calme.

Son entendement, son esprit sont l'entendement l'esprit de Dieu.

L'intelligence curative qui crée son corps transforme à présent chaque cellule, chaque nerf, chaque tissu, chaque muscle et chaque os de son corps selon le prototype de Dieu.

Silencieusement, tranquillement, tous les prototypes mentaux négatifs sont écartés, dissous et la vitalité, l'intégrité et la beauté de l'Esprit se manifestent dans chaque atome de son Être.

Elle est à présent réceptive à cette puissance de guérison qui coule à travers elle comme un fleuve, la rendant à la santé, à l'harmonie et à la paix parfaite.

Toutes les discordes, toutes les images

pensées laides sont à présent balayées par l'océan d'Amour et de Paix coulant à travers elle et il en est ainsi. Amen

(Joseph Murphy [1] – la prière guérit)

---

[1] Joseph Murphy - Expert en sciences divines et écrivain.

Soins collectifs et réseaux sociaux

Je vais vous raconter comment j'en suis arrivée à proposer des soins collectifs avec mes ami(e)s, grâce aux réseaux sociaux, à partir du juin 2017.

je travaillais à l'extérieur de chez moi, ce jour-là, pour subvenir au besoin d'une personne. A un moment donné, j'ai entendu dans ma tête : « soin collectif ». Oui j'ai eu l'information par mon âme qui m'a insufflée de me lancer à soulager plusieurs personnes en même temps. Est-ce possible ? Jusque-là, j'avais toujours fait des soins individuels, mais pourquoi pas ! Tout est possible, nous avons tous des capacités, à nous de vouloir les exploiter ou pas.

Ce qui est sûr, c'est que j'avais compris le

message de l'Univers. Dans tout ce que j'entreprends, j'écoute mon cœur, mes ressentis. Là, je savais qu'il fallait que je pratique les soins collectifs par le biais des nouvelles technologies. Lorsque je me suis lancée, je l'ai fait gratuitement sur quelques mois. Ayant des retours positifs, j'ai proposé des séances à don libre et, de temps en temps, je le faisais gratuitement. Au fond, je suis sûre également que si j'organisais des séances collectives en direct dans une salle, cela fonctionnerait également. Peut-être un jour serais-je amenée à le faire. Je n'ai pas encore tout exploité. Chaque chose en son temps. J'ai confiance en mes ressentis, aux messages universels que je reçois.

Comment se déroulent les séances ? Chaque personne s'inscrit pour faire le soin. Les personnes qui n'ont pas ce type de compte ont la possibilité de voir le planning sur mon site internet. Elles ont alors la possibilité de me contacter pour me dire qu'elles désirent y participer.

Ensuite, le déroulement se fait comme une séance de magnétisme individuelle à distance. Dix minutes avant l'heure indiquée, vous vous allongez pour vous détendre afin d'accueillir l'énergie des Guides et tout l'Amour que je vous enverrai. Vous recevrez les énergies de Guérison, d'apaisement pour que votre âme soit en Paix.

Pour ma part, rien ne change, je peux avoir 1 personne comme 10 ou 50, cela ne me fatigue pas. C'est un travail qui ne me demande pas d'effort car envoyer de l'Amour, des belles énergies, c'est quelque chose de naturel chez moi. Tout le monde en est capable, il suffit d'être dans l'ouverture du cœur dans l'intention de faire du bien à son prochain.

Je suis très heureuse de faire du bien autour de moi, de voir les âmes apaisées.

Depuis peu, il m'arrive d'avoir un message inspiré de ma petite voix pour le groupe collectif, comme pour finaliser le soin dans l'Amour.

Pour terminer, je fais un tirage d'oracle pour chaque personne qui a participé à la séance. Je me connecte à l'Univers et demande à ce que je sois guidée pour donner le message à la personne concernée. Tout se fait naturellement, dans mes ressentis, pour apporter un bien-être à la personne, à son âme.

Voici quelques témoignages des personnes qui ont assisté aux soins collectifs en magnétisme :

- *« Bonjour Cathy, un soin vraiment génial, je t'explique : la chaleur qui monte, une vraie puissance, d'abord les mains, les bras, les pieds, les jambes, les cuisses puis les épaules, le cou ! Je me suis sentie très bien, un bain d'Amour ! Merci beaucoup ».*

- *« Merci Cathy, une douce chaleur pendant tout le soin, comme enveloppée comme un cocon, et j'ai entendu un mot tout au début « chat vert »je n'ai pas d'explication pour l'instant, merci encore pour ce moment magique. Namasté. ».*

- *« Bonjour Cathy, j'étais présente hier soir pour le soin, j'ai ressenti des fourmillements dans les mains, dans les pieds, une forte chaleur, voire même ouverture du plexus solaire et cœur. Une détente du corps et sur la fin beaucoup de frissons en haut du dos.*
Au milieu du soin j'ai eu besoin de chanter la mélodie « il était une fois dans l'ouest » ne me demandez pas pourquoi c'est comme ça, mais j'ai apprécié, donc merci à vous et à vos guides. ».

Vous pourrez retrouver tous les témoignages sur mon site internet. Vous trouverez l'adresse à la fin de ce livre.

Tout le monde n'a pas la capacité de percevoir les énergies qui circulent. Pour certaines personnes, cela peut être frustrant. Mais cela ne veut pas dire que le travail ne se fait pas. En effet, les personnes qui n'ont pas eu de ressentis, ont remarqué qu'elles étaient plus sereines dans leur quotidien.

Je vais vous conter une petite histoire qui m'a assez surprise. Je pense fortement que l'Univers a voulu me tester !

Dans mes soins à distance, j'utilise un certain protocole. Je suis perfectionniste !! J'allume une bougie, de l'encens. Je prends ensuite mon petit livre où se trouvent mes prières préférées pour les soins, et je demande de l'aide avec mes propres phrases qui viennent du cœur.

Nous étions en été 2017. J'étais partie en vacances avec mes enfants. J'ai eu deux appels téléphoniques pour un soin en magnétisme, puis une purification, le tout à distance. J'avais bien signalé que j'étais en vacances, mais apparemment c'était urgent. Ça ne pouvait pas attendre. Alors me vient une pensée :

- « Je suis sûre que vous me testez, et si vous m'envoyez ces personnes-là c'est que je suis capable d'arriver à faire ce travail sans mon rituel ».

Je me suis alors connectée à l'esprit de la personne, juste avec ses nom et prénom. J'ai pratiqué le soin comme je le fais d'habitude, mais sans ma bulle de confort.

Comme je vous l'ai déjà expliqué, dès que je demande de l'aide, je baille et à ce moment-là, je sais que je suis connectée avec mon guide, les anges. Je sais qu'ils sont tout près de moi et qu'ils m'accompagnent pour faire les soins. Ils sont présents tout simplement, quotidiennement dans ma vie. En fin de séance, la personne a été soulagée et durant le soin, elle avait eu des ressentis identiques aux autres individus.

De la même manière, lorsque j'ai fait la purification de la maison à distance, et accompagné les âmes dans la lumière, la personne a tout de suite trouvé un changement radical. Elle ne sentait plus la présence des entités.

Ces deux expériences m'ont permis de comprendre que je n'ai pas besoin de mes rituels pour faire les soins, juste de continuer à être dans l'Amour et peu importe où vous vous trouvez, le résultat est positif. Je me suis même retrouvée, un jour à faire un soin à distance, tout en me promenant sur les berges du canal du Midi ! Tout cela paraît incroyable, magnifique et magique !

Vous vous êtes certainement posé la même question que moi : comment ça peut fonctionner réellement ? Comment cela se passe t-il dans l'invisible ? Je suis curieuse par nature. Je n'ai pas de réponse, mais je sais que j'ai de bons retours. Un jour, je finirai bien par savoir comment ça marche.

Tout finit par arriver au bon moment ! Lors d'une conférence à Escalquens (31), j'ai fait la connaissance d'une médium Malorie. L'Univers nous a rapprochées. C'est une belle personne avec un grand cœur. Nous avons fait des échanges. Je lui ai donné un soin en magnétisme et elle m'a donnée une consultation de médiumnité. J'ai eu l'occasion de lui demander comment un soin à distance ou les soins collectifs pouvaient fonctionner. J'avais hâte d'en savoir plus à ce sujet.

Voici la réponse de son guide : « Lorsque tu demandes de l'aide, lorsque tu pries, tes guides sont là, tout le monde est avec toi. Ils prennent tout l'Amour que tu as dans ton Cœur pour le partager à toutes les personnes à qui tu viens en aide. » Cette réponse m'avait beaucoup émue. Ses paroles avaient touché mon âme bien sensible.

Je n'ai plus à me poser de questions, je ne m'en pose plus d'ailleurs. Je n'ai qu'à continuer à travailler dans l'Amour inconditionnel, dans l'ouverture du Cœur. Je sais que la magie est souvent là et opère, vu les résultats positifs en retour.

Comme me l'a signalée Malorie, je suis aidée par les plans supérieurs, et par mon guide qui se prénomme Georges. Nous ferons un bout de chemin ensemble pour qu'il puisse m'apprendre certains enseignements. Plus tard, il donnera le relais à un autre guide, qui m'aidera à son tour à faire grandir mon âme. En attendant, j'ai confiance en mes capacités, j'ai la foi en l'Univers, je ne suis jamais seule. N'oubliez pas, vous n'êtes jamais seuls. L 'Amour vous accompagne.

De la nuit vers ma lumière

De la nuit vers ma lumière

Soins en magnétisme direct

Je débute toujours les soins par un dialogue avec la personne qui m'explique, si elle le souhaite, la raison de son rendez-vous.

J'essaie de la guider en lui parlant avec mon âme pour éclairer sa situation. Je lui donne quelques conseils pour la rassurer et l'accompagner sur son chemin. Je lui explique ma façon de travailler dans le soin énergétique.

Tout au long de la séance, vous êtes bercés par une musique douce vous permettant de lâcher prise et de vous évader !

Pour commencer, la personne s'installe habillée sur ma table de massage. Je suis simplement guidée par mes mains qui m'indiquent où il y a des blocages, des tensions. Je nettoie les zones sombres pour laisser couler la Lumière.

Durant le soin, vous allez entendre mes bâillements ou des souffles forts importants. J'évacue votre mauvaise énergie, le stress, tout type de douleurs par ces rictus que je ne contrôle pas. En revanche mon guide est présent pour que vous receviez l'énergie de guérison.

Je débute le soin par un nettoyage de votre Aura qui se situe au-dessus de votre corps physique. Vous allez m'entendre bailler. Une fois le nettoyage terminé, je pose mes mains sur votre corps physique. Je mets les mains sur la tête, la gorge, le cœur, la partie abdominale, les bras, les jambes jusqu'à la plante des pieds. Je reste sur chaque zone indiquée tant que je baille. Une fois que je suis arrivée aux pieds, je finalise mon travail en vérifiant s'il y a encore des tensions du corps. Si c'est le cas, vous m'entendrez de nouveau bailler. Sur cette dernière partie du soin, je suis dans l'empathie. Je vais poser mes mains plus longtemps sur les zones du corps et essayer de ressentir, de canaliser une information qui pourrait m'indiquer où je dois déposer l'énergie de guérison.

Un jour, j'ai mis les mains sur les genoux d'une personne et d'un coup j'ai senti sur mon corps physique, une douleur dans le bas du ventre. Naturellement je demande à ma cliente si elle n'a pas de douleurs à cet endroit précis. Sa réponse a été positive, elle m'a répondu qu'elle a un fibrome et que cette région-là est parfois douloureuse. Cette information m'a permis de comprendre qu'il fallait que je pose mes mains sur cette zone indiquée pour que je continue à travailler en profondeur.

Lorsque j'ai fini de vérifier mon travail en libérant vos tensions, je vais vous demander de vous mettre à plat ventre pour faire le même procédé qu'au début du soin.

Une fois la séance terminée, je finalise par un modelage intuitif du dos, de la tête et des pieds pour que l'énergie puisse continuer à bien circuler dans votre corps, à apaiser votre âme et votre esprit.

Vous pouvez retrouver sur mon site, tous les soins de bien-être que je propose pour retrouver la sérénité. Il est bien entendu que je ne promets aucun résultat sur les soins effectués qui, je le rappelle, sont pratiqués dans l'Amour inconditionnel. Même si j'ai de bons retours, je ne me mettrais jamais en avant pour vous dire que je vais réussir à vous soulager. Ne pensez surtout pas que je suis une magicienne, c'est simplement l'Amour qui guérit. Je suis certaine que tout le monde est capable d'aider son prochain, il faut juste vouloir ouvrir son Cœur et vouloir faire du bien à son prochain.

L'essentiel du travail est réalisé par mes guides invisibles qui m'accompagnent tout le long de la séance. En canalisant et en transmettant de l'énergie au consultant, je me laisse traverser, c'est tout ce que j'ai à faire... La Magie est bien là !

Les sept corps subtils

Je vais vous expliquer succinctement pourquoi je mets les mains au-dessus de votre corps physique.

Il est important de savoir que nous sommes

des Êtres constitués d'énergie. Si des blocages énergétiques existent, ils peuvent se manifester dans le corps physique sous la forme de symptômes.

Le but de la guérison par l'énergie du cœur est de libérer ces blocages en intervenant par l'imposition des mains sur les corps subtils qui enveloppent le corps physique. En opérant en douceur sur les différents corps énergétiques, j'effectue une lecture invisible du patient. Je travaille au cœur de l'ensemble des différentes couches invisibles de l'Être. Je mets dans mes mains tout l'amour nécessaire pour soulager ou guérir durablement. Lorsque l'énergie du cœur est imprégnée de l'amour inconditionnel, elle guérit.

Nous avons 7 corps subtils énergétiques qui constituent la totalité de notre Aura.

- Le corps physique

- Le corps éthérique

- Le corps émotionnel

- Le corps mental

- Le corps spirituel ou corps causal

- Le corps bouddhique

- Le corps divin

Je rééquilibre le flux énergétique permettant ainsi à la personne de retrouver l'harmonie et la bonne circulation de l'énergie vitale.

Les chakras

Le mot chakra signifie roue, c'est un centre énergétique qui est localisé sur l'axe du corps au nombre de 7, que nous ne pouvons pas voir, ni toucher.

Lorsque la personne a des douleurs physiques ou morales, elle affaiblit ses chakras. Il est donc important de les rééquilibrer. Cela va permettre à l'énergie de recommencer à circuler harmonieusement dans les corps subtils et dans le corps physique.

Cette énergie va nous aider à évacuer le stress, les émotions refoulées, responsables des dysfonctionnements.

Lorsque je rééquilibre les chakras, la personne retrouve l'énergie et l'harmonie.

1er Chakra :

Le chakra racine de couleur rouge est situé au niveau du périnée. Ce chakra capte l'énergie de la terre pour la transmettre aux corps subtils et aux organes du corps physique pour assurer leur bon fonctionnement. Lorsque ce chakra est rééquilibré, vous avez davantage confiance en vous, une certaine force et du courage.

Lorsque ce chakra est déséquilibré, vous pouvez ressentir de la colère, de la rancune, avoir des problèmes osseux (dents, dos, jambes, etc…)

2ème Chakra :

Le chakra sacré de couleur orange est situé entre l'ombilic et le pubis.

Lorsque ce chakra est équilibré, vous avez une certaine joie de vivre, une relation équilibrée, épanouie.

Quand ce deuxième chakra se referme, vous pouvez ressentir de la mélancolie, avoir des pensées suicidaires, des déséquilibres hormonaux.

3ème Chakra :

Le chakra solaire de couleur jaune est situé au niveau du plexus solaire ou de l'estomac.

Lorsque ce chakra est équilibré, vous ressentez une certaine liberté, sans attente et ni reconnaissance.

C'est le centre des émotions et lorsqu'il est perturbé, vous pouvez ressentir des douleurs abdominales, avoir des nausées, un manque de confiance.

4ème Chakra :

Le chakra du cœur, de couleur verte est situé au centre de la poitrine.

Lorsque ce chakra est équilibré, vous ressentez la paix, le pardon, l'amour inconditionnel, la compassion pour les autres.

Lorsque ce chakra est déséquilibré, vous pouvez avoir des problèmes respiratoires comme l'asthme, des problèmes cardiaques.

<u>5ème Chakra</u> :

Le chakra laryngé de couleur bleu est situé au niveau de la gorge, c'est le chakra de la communication.

Lorsque ce chakra est équilibré, vous arrivez mieux à vous exprimer, vous avez confiance en vous.

Lorsque ce chakra est déséquilibré, vous pouvez avoir des extinctions de voix, des acouphènes, des difficultés à dialoguer.

<u>6ème Chakra</u> :

Le chakra frontal ou 3 œil, de couleur bleu indigo est situé entre les sourcils.

C'est le chakra de l'intuition, de la clairvoyance.

Lorsque ce chakra est équilibré, la personne laisse le mental au repos et fait davantage appel à son intuition qui se développe en pratiquant la méditation. Si vous vous laissez guider par votre intuition, vous trouverez des solutions aux problèmes ou de percevoir l'avenir.

Quand ce chakra est déséquilibré, vous

pouvez souffrir de sinusite, avoir des difficultés à trouver le sommeil, avoir du mal à prendre des décisions.

7ème <u>Chakra</u> :

Le chakra coronal est situé au-dessus de la tête, de couleur violette, son énergie est lié au monde spirituel, il nous connecte à la partie divine, des guides.

Lorsque ce chakra est équilibré, la personne pratique la foi, connaît sa mission sur terre et sait la mettre en pratique.

Lorsque ce chakra est déséquilibré, vous pouvez avoir des troubles de l'équilibre, la nuque bloquée, la fermeture à la vie et aux autres.

Quelques témoignages de mes soins en magnétisme direct

- *« Ce mail est un test pour moi car depuis deux mois je n'arrive pas à me mettre devant mon pc sans douleur aux cervicales. Là je n'ai rien !! Je n'arrive pas à y croire, là où la médecine, le kiné et le reste n'ont rien pu faire pour moi, vous, en une demi-heure, vous avez fait disparaître ma souffrance. Je ne sais comment, mais ce que je peux vous dire c'est que c'est réel !! Alors un grand merci de m'avoir délivré de cet enfer qui depuis deux mois me faisait souffrir. J'ai encore quelques courbatures en bas du dos mais rien de grave, mon corps est en train de faire le ménage !! »*

- *« Je te remercie pour le bien que tu m'as fait lors de ta première séance de magnétisme, cela fait 15 jours que je ne prends plus de médicament pour la douleur. Depuis 9 mois, je souffrais d'une arthrose cervicale, plusieurs traitements à base de cortisone, 2 infiltrations, mais en vain très peu d'amélioration, ça me tarde de te revoir, pour la deuxième séance. Encore une fois merci de faire du bien sans effort et sans traitement. A très bientôt. »*

- *« Je suis allée voir Cathy alors que je souffrais d'une hernie discale L4-L5. Malgré la cortisone, les antalgiques et des séances de Kiné, j'avais toujours des douleurs intenables au bas du dos, des tensions dans la jambe et des fourmillements dans le pied, avant de décider de retourner voir mon médecin pour une éventuelle opération ou des infiltrations, je suis donc allée voir Cathy pour une séance de magnétisme, et on le croit ou pas, mais quelques jours après... plus de fourmillement dans le pied et plus aucune douleur aux lombaires et dans la jambe !!*

- C'est incroyable mais je suis un témoin de plus, des bienfaits que Cathy peut nous apporter !

- Merci Cathy de faire bénéficier de votre don à tous ceux qui ont la chance de vous connaître. »

Voici une petite expérience que j'ai vécue en janvier 2017 :

Ma matinée a été remplie de joie. J'ai décidé de partager mon expérience avec vous. Je suis allée rendre visite à une dame de 91 ans pour lui faire un soin de magnétisme. Une gentille petite dame assise sur son fauteuil m'expliquant qu'elle a des douleurs liées à l'arthrose, ça la handicape pour se déplacer, elle a des difficultés pour se peigner car elle a du mal à lever ses bras. Suite au soin de magnétisme, elle a pu lever ses bras sans aucune difficulté, puis elle a pris son déambulateur pour marcher. Elle a remarqué qu'elle pouvait poser son pied à plat, chose qu'elle avait du mal à faire jusqu'à maintenant, puis elle a remarqué qu'elle se déplaçait plus rapidement. Sa petite fille me l'a confirmé et a vu la différence. Gratitude à mes Guides guérisseurs qui sont toujours là pour m'accompagner pendant le soin.

En rentrant chez cette dame, mon cœur a été rempli de joie, je ne savais pas pourquoi ? cela m'a rappelé certainement lorsque je pratiquais mon travail d'aide-soignante à domicile, le contact avec la personne, un très beau souvenir. Ce matin, j'ai pris conscience qu'il fallait que je fasse des soins à domicile ou ailleurs pour soulager les douleurs des personnes. Je me laisse bercer par les énergies de mon Cœur et de l'Univers qui savent me guider vers la Lumière. Gratitude. Je vous envoie plein d'Amour.

Une personne me contacte pour me dire " j'ai vu sur votre site que vous aidez les personnes qui souhaitent arrêter de fumer, mais moi j'aimerai vous rencontrer pour que vous m'aidiez à ne plus manger des sucreries, des bonbons" qu'elle mange régulièrement dans la journée. Je demande à la personne de m'amener ses bonbons pour les magnétiser puis je lui ai fait un soin. Trois jours après, elle m'a contactée pour me dire qu'elle n'a pas remangé un bonbon et qu'à la vue des bonbons, sa gorge se noue donc impossible d'en manger un, puis 9 jours après, elle a perdu 3 kilos. La cliente est contente du résultat et moi aussi. Gratitude.

Les ressentis des clients pendant un soin en magnétisme

Les ressentis sont différents d'une personne à une autre.

Elles ont souvent le ventre qui gargouille, elles peuvent ressentir du chaud, du froid, des fourmillements, des émotions peuvent apparaître. Certaines personnes m'ont déjà signalé qu'elles avaient eu l'impression que quelque chose partait de leurs pieds, une sensation d'être libérée, de se sentir plus légère.

Quelques douleurs peuvent apparaître et disparaître rapidement. Ce sont les effets secondaires du magnétisme.

Il arrive également que des personnes ne ressentent pas l'énergie circuler cela ne veut pas dire que le soin n'a pas été efficace.

J'ai toujours le même témoignage à la fin d'une séance : les personnes ressentent un bien-être pouvant amener à l'apaisement ou à la disparition de la douleur initiale.

Les effets du magnétisme, durant un soin en direct ou à distance

Il se peut que la personne baille pendant ou après le soin. Une sensation de fatigue, d'être vidé mais apaisé. Lorsque les personnes rentrent à leur domicile, elles m'ont déjà signalée que les après-midis, elles dormaient presque durant deux heures. La première nuit, il se peut qu'elle soit agitée ou bien le contraire. La personne retrouve sa vitalité, le goût à la vie.

Le lendemain de la séance, des douleurs peuvent être plus intenses, pour partir ensuite graduellement. Ce n'est pas une obligation d'avoir des douleurs qui réapparaissent.

Les personnes soucieuses portent un autre regard sur les choses qui avaient beaucoup d'importance. Elles prennent du recul.

Avec une séance de magnétisme, je préconise

de se reposer au lieu d'aller faire une activité intense parce que l'énergie continue à travailler sur votre corps.

Les différents maux

En dialoguant avec les clients dont je me suis occupée, j'ai pu constater que leur mal-être est lié au travail, au rythme de vie, par des soucis personnels et bien d'autres raisons.

Les contrariétés ont une influence sur le corps physique. Elles se manifestent par le mal de dos, les migraines, les sciatiques, les tendinites, des hernies discales, les maladies, un mal-être…

Lors des consultations, je conseille aux clients de prendre soin de leur âme. Je les incite à faire une activité qui leur procure du plaisir, de la joie. Je leur dis de faire ce qu'ils aiment le plus souvent possible, pour que leur corps soit détendu.

Il faut savoir, par exemple, prendre du temps pour écouter en conscience une musique douce afin de pouvoir s'évader un petit peu dans le but de lâcher prise, se promener en plein air, pour faire le plein d'énergie, un massage. Malheureusement pour beaucoup de personnes, c'est très difficile car voici les retours que j'ai pu entendre : « je n'ai pas le temps ».

Dans notre société, nous sommes tous conditionnés à faire les choses avec un rythme rapide, par obligation, faire certaines tâches les unes après les autres sans se poser. C'est à croire que l'Être humain agit comme un robot, je dirai que l'homme ne prend pas le temps de vivre. Ne serait-il pas bien d'apprendre à écouter son corps, à le respecter pour vivre plus sereinement ? Je dis souvent : « Sachez vous apporter de l'Amour chaque jour pour que votre âme puisse rayonner ». Vous verrez bien la différence ! Le plus important, bien sûr, étant de la mettre en pratique pour en ressentir les bienfaits.

« En faisant ce que tu aimes le plus souvent possible, ton âme sera épanouie. Tu rayonneras la Lumière et tu t'élèveras dans les vibrations d'Amour. Gratitude. » Cathy Divine

Le magnétisme – que peut-il soulager ?

Voici la liste des divers maux que j'ai pu soulager, même voire disparition de la douleur.

- les maux de tête, les sinusites

- les douleurs cervicales

- les maux de dos, les hernies discales, les sciatiques

- le mal-être, le stress

- la spasmophilie

- la cruralgie

- les entorses, les tendinites, l'arthrose

- la fatigue, le manque d'énergie

- soucis de sommeil

- les personnes atteintes du cancer

- les personnes ayant la maladie de Crohn

- l'état grippal

- l'arrêt du tabac, la dépendance aux sucreries

- les colites

- l'eczéma, le psoriasis et bien d'autres maux.

Le magnétiseur

Le magnétiseur est canal, il reçoit souvent l'énergie de ses guides qu'il transmet à la personne, et il évacue la mauvaise énergie du corps par des principes qui lui sont propres.

De la nuit vers ma lumière

Vers l'Amour inconditionnel

L'amour inconditionnel est la forme d'amour la plus pure car il donne tout et ne demande rien en retour.

Le plus proche exemple de cet amour est celui que ressent un parent pour son enfant.

Comme je vous l'ai dit, je travaille dans cet amour inconditionnel car mon intention la plus pure est de faire du bien à mon prochain, pour qu'il retrouve la joie de vivre, la paix, la santé morale et physique.

Je pense fortement que pour faire ce travail, il faut aimer les gens et leur vouloir du bien.

« L'énergie du Cœur guérit avec la puissance infinie de l'Amour Inconditionnel »

Cathy Divine

Comment ressentir l'amour inconditionnel ?

Pour ressentir l'Amour inconditionnel, il est conseillé de pardonner aux personnes qui nous ont blessées. C'est un acte qui doit être réalisé par vous-même pour retrouver la sérénité dans tout votre Être.

Lorsque vous pardonnez, vous ne devez en aucun cas ressentir l'envie de vengeance, de la rancune auprès des personnes qui vous ont blessés. Au contraire, l'amour doit prendre place dans votre Cœur.

Il est important d'avoir des pensées lumineuses, de belles intentions pour les personnes qui vous entourent. Lorsque nous pardonnons, les blessures du cœur finissent par se cicatriser et nous retrouvons la liberté d'aimer et la joie de vivre.

Le pardon est la clé qui ouvre la porte de

notre cœur, pour laisser sortir l'Amour inconditionnel.

De la nuit vers ma lumière

De la nuit vers ma lumière

expliquer comment je suis également devenue passeuse d'âmes.

Un jour, un client est venu me voir en consultation, il m'a raconté sa situation assez troublante, en me disant que sa femme était décédée et qu'il ressentait sa présence, avec des manifestations dans la maison. Les membres de sa famille étaient perturbés. J'ai tout de suite compris qu'elle avait été guidée vers moi pour que je lui vienne en aide.

C'est donc tout naturellement que je lui ai proposé mon aide. J'allais faire de mon mieux pour accompagner l'âme de l'autre côté du voile afin qu'elle repose en paix.

La personne accepta. Je lui avais juste demandé le prénom et le nom de sa femme. Le soir, au calme, j'ai allumé une bougie, en priant pour cette âme. J'avais demandé le soutien de mon guide pour l'accompagner à passer cette porte de Lumière. Le lendemain, le veuf me contacta pour me signaler que sa famille et lui-même ne ressentaient plus la présence de la défunte. Ce jour-là, j'ai compris que ma mission était celle de passeuse d'âmes, un acte que je fais avec beaucoup d'Amour, avec mon Cœur.

Vous devez surement vous demander si je vois les âmes ?

Un jour, lors d'une conférence médiumnique, j'ai signalé que je suis passeuse d'âmes et que je ne comprenais pas pourquoi je ne voyais pas les âmes. Voici la réponse qui me fut donnée : « ce n'est pas une obligation de les voir mais tu les verras bientôt ».

Pour le moment je ne les vois pas avec mes yeux mais avec mon cœur.

Je vous livre ici quelques messages reçus :

- « L'Amour est une énergie qui te guide vers la Lumière »

- « Continue à sourire aux Etoiles pour les élever dans la Lumière »

- « Envoie de l'Amour dans le ciel, les étoiles mettront de la couleur dans ton Cœur »

- « La prière devient magique lorsqu'elle est prononcée avec sincérité avec ton âme »

- « Soyez attentifs aux signes que vous recevez de l'au-delà, comme les plumes, les chansons, les papillons, les nombres qui vous indiquent que vos Anges vous aiment, ils sont tout près de vous »

- « Ton Ange aime te voir sourire. Si tu souris à la Vie, il va sourire aussi, ton Ange sera heureux. Si ton Cœur pleure, ton Ange sera triste...Les Anges sont en Paix plus que nous ! Pensez à allumer une bougie juste pour vos Anges c'est une façon de leur envoyer de l'Amour, votre Amour et de les élever dans la Lumière. Faites-le avec votre Cœur et avec le sourire. Continuez à penser à eux dans la joie du Cœur Avec Amour. »
Cathy Divine

Les témoignages

« Bonjour à tous, je viens témoigner. Depuis un certain temps je ressentais une présence qui m'étouffait, je n'étais plus libre, pas facile de parler de cette situation autour de moi. Une nuit je me suis retrouvée face à un problème. Ma couette venait d'être enlevée et j'ai ressenti que l'on me sortait de mon lit.

Un autre soir, j'étais à mon bureau et là je ressens deux bras qui passent par-dessus mes épaules se plaquent le long de mon corps et deux mains qui me compressent la taille et me plaquent contre mon dossier. La nuit suivante les mains toujours présentes, me serraient la taille - là je me dis : il y a qu'une personne à qui en parler. Je contacte Cathy qui m'écoute et me rassure. J'ai eu dernièrement un décès, mon oncle. Cathy me dit que c'est lui qui est présent et n'est pas passé de l'autre côté de la lumière, elle me dit : je m'occupe de lui, je vais faire le nécessaire - effectivement, je confirme je suis mieux, je ne n'ai plus cette présence. Elle lui a permis de rejoindre les personnes qui lui sont proches, qui ne sont plus parmi nous. Je fais une énorme confiance à Cathy Magnétiseuse Passeuse d'âmes, je vous promets, vous pouvez lui faire confiance, le travail qu'elle effectue est une merveille, Cathy tu es un ange. »

- « J'ai " connu " Cathy par hasard sur le réseau social. En bref, j'ai perdu deux êtres chers tragiquement. Pour commencer, un grand frère, décédé à la naissance et né deux ans avant ma propre naissance. J'ai toujours ressenti sa présence, comme celle d'un ange gardien. Mais dernièrement et depuis quelques mois, sa présence me devenait oppressante, j'avais le sentiment qu'il était bien présent dans ma vie et je le sentais *désemparé... Ensuite, il y a une quinzaine d'années, le compagnon de ma mère s'est suicidé... On dit toujours que ce genre de décès tragique empêche l'âme du défunt de trouver la lumière... Et c'est ce que je ressentais également mais j'étais assez sceptique quant aux " dons " des passeurs d'âmes... J'ai donc décidé de contacter Cathy et de lui exposer mon ressenti.*

Aujourd'hui, elle a accompagné mes deux amours vers la lumière, avec la force de son amour et ses prières pour les y aider... Et bien mon ressenti à distance fut presque instantané. J'ai ressenti une énorme fatigue, beaucoup de tristesse, quelque chose d'inexplicable avec de simples mots... Mais je dois avouer que depuis quelques heures, je ressens réellement que ces deux âmes sont allées vers la lumière avec l'aide de Cathy. C'est une évidence, je ne les sens plus tourmentées mais enfin apaisées et moi de même.

Merci Cathy, de tout cœur. »

- « J'ai contacté Cathy tout à fait par hasard. En 1993, vingt ans que ma mère a été assassinée, sa présence à mes côtés était pesante, j'ai vécu 20 ans de mal- être. J'avais pris un appartement au-dessus d'un magasin de fleurs, elle-même était fleuriste, j'ai été secouée un soir

dans mon lit alors que je ne dormais pas c'était très troublant ! Cathy a su trouver les mots, maman est partie dans la lumière il y a deux jours. Merci à Cathy pour sa générosité et sa bonté amour, paix et lumière. Je me sens libérée, apaisée, je ne ressens plus la présence de ma maman. »

- « Bonjour à tous, Je viens témoigner car depuis 8 longues années j'avais un esprit près de moi mais qui n'était pas mauvais pour autant, dû à une séance de spiritisme fait dans le passé, il s'est attaché à moi et réciproquement jusqu'à prendre beaucoup de place dans ma vie.... Mais maintenant il est dans la lumière et je remercie Cathy pour son super travail. »

- « Bonjour Cathy, je voulais vous raconter ma nuit et les choses qui se passent autour de moi.... Après des mois de lourdeurs, de chagrin de plus en plus lourd à porter malgré les mois qui passent. La forte présence de mon frère, l'odeur de cigarette pour sa présence, nos contacts d'échange par la pensée et le fait que je lui parle comme s'il était avec moi tout le temps. Hier soir, vous êtes intervenue pour l'aider à aller dans la lumière. Pour lui et pour moi. Après vos prières, une sensation de vide et d'apaisement pour moi. Ma nuit a été comme elle n'a pas été depuis des mois, les cauchemars ou hurlements hantaient mes nuits.

Cette nuit, un ange est venu me dire au revoir et m'a montré l'avenir.

J'ai été dans une osmose totale, un bien-être extraordinaire. J'ai vu et ressenti une ambiance, une famille, un amour de la part d'un homme, un compagnon. Ce que j'attends depuis toujours. Est-ce un message, le futur ? Je l'espère. Des faits ensuite, ont eu lieu, mes mésanges qui avaient déserté mon jardin, à ma grande désolation sont là ce matin. Une amie d'enfance avec qui je n'avais pas eu de contact depuis 30 ans m'a mis un gentil message sur le réseau social. Étrange non. Je suis à l'écoute du bonheur. Je suis calme, j'ai prié pour lui et pour moi. L'avenir ou les jours qui viennent me diront la suite. Merci à vous Cathy pour cette aide, ce bien-être, vous êtes la lumière. »

Je souhaite partager avec vous une expérience qui m'a permis de comprendre qu'au final, je n'avais pas besoin du nom et du prénom de l'âme pour l'accompagner dans la Lumière.

Suite à un soin de magnétisme à distance que j'ai effectué sur une cliente, celle-ci m'a signalée qu'elle s'est sentie davantage stressée et que son sommeil a été perturbé. Elle m'explique que depuis un moment, elle se sentait observée, qu'elle n'était pas bien dans son corps.

Ne trouvant pas cela normal, j'ai de suite pensé qu'une âme était dans son logement, et se nourrissait de son énergie, ce qui pouvait expliquer son état de mal-être.

Je lui ai proposé mon aide pour accompagner l'âme dans la lumière, ainsi elle pourrait retrouver la paix dans sa demeure.

Je lui ai envoyé une prière, je lui ai conseillé d'allumer une bougie, et à une heureuse précise nous avons lu, chacune chez soi, la prière. Lorsque j'ai fini de prier avec Amour et accompagné l'âme avec l'aide de mon guide de Lumière, j'ai contacté la personne pour avoir ses ressentis. Elle a vécu un instant particulier. Elle avait vu comme des petites étincelles et entendu du bruit. Elle a retrouvé de suite la paix intérieure et ne se sentait plus observée. Le lendemain, elle m'a signalée avec joie, qu'elle avait pu dormir. Le calme était revenu dans sa maison.

Ainsi, j'ai compris que je pouvais aider énormément de personne et qu'il n'était pas nécessaire d'avoir l'identité de l'âme. Suite à cette expérience, des personnes ont été mises sur mon chemin pour que je leur apporte mon aide. Les résultats ne peuvent être satisfaisants que lorsque le travail est fait avec le Cœur, dans la Foi, et dans l'Amour inconditionnel.

« Laisse-toi guider par la Lumière de ton Cœur. »

Cathy Divine

Prière de passeur d'Âme.

Petite âme tu m'attendais, mets ta main dans la mienne. Il est temps pour toi de quitter ce monde

Petite âme, n'aie pas peur, je suis là, je t'amène vers la lumière

Ne te retourne pas, laisse tes soucis, tes parents, tes amis

Suit la petite lumière et ne te retourne pas

N'aie pas peur, Dieu ne punit pas, va sans crainte

Je reste là et j'appelle tes guides afin qu'ils te

montrent le chemin

Ne tremble plus, à présent tu t'en vas, je t'embrasse une dernière fois

Fini les pleurs, les peurs, tu es belle et tu franchis la porte

Tu es belle, tu es heureuse, tu rayonnes d'Amour

Je t'aime petite âme

(Auteur inconnu)

<u>Purification des lieux de vie</u>

En quoi consiste le nettoyage énergétique d'un lieu ?

Cela consiste à libérer les mémoires ancestrales et à nettoyer le lieu énergétiquement et spirituellement, afin qu'il puisse de nouveau rayonner, remonter et vibrer d'amour et de paix.

Les maisons, les terrains, les locaux professionnels, les lieux de soins sont porteurs d'empreintes énergétiques.

Les murs, les objets, les espaces possèdent leurs propres mémoires, aussi bien négatives que positives. Il peut également y avoir des âmes, perturbées ou non, qui laissent planer leurs empreintes vibratoires sur les lieux.

Toutes ces vibrations restent actives dans le temps et provoquent, à la longue, des troubles pour les habitants du lieu : mal-être, fatigue, stress, insomnies, échecs, maladies, une baisse de clientèle pour les lieux professionnels.

Pourquoi faire un nettoyage énergétique ?

Cela permet :

- de faire de votre lieu de vie, un lieu de repos physique et psychique, un lieu de ressourcement ;

- d'instaurer ou réinstaurer des énergies saines dans votre maison ;

- de vendre ou louer plus rapidement une maison, un terrain, une boutique.

<u>Pour les professionnels :</u>

- d'augmenter la fréquentation de votre commerce ;

- de rétablir de bonnes vibrations sur son lieu de travail.

Purifier son lieu de vie, c'est purifier sa vie et se purifier soi-même. Régulièrement je purifie ma maison, ma salle de soin pour vivre et travailler dans de bonnes énergies. C'est tellement agréable de ressentir des vibrations de paix.

Un jour, à la sortie de l'école, un papa me pose des questions par rapport à mes activités professionnelles. Il me fait part de ses petits soucis au niveau du travail, certainement un blocage me dit-il, une certaine fatigue dans la maison.

Je comprends rapidement que l'Univers a guidé cette personne vers moi pour que je fasse une purification de sa grande et très ancienne bâtisse. Selon mes ressentis, il y avait beaucoup d'âmes qui vivaient dans cette maison, ce qui pouvaient expliquer leur mal-être, les petits blocages. Naturellement, je lui ai proposé mon aide gracieusement pour faire une purification en direct. Une fois le rendez-vous fixé, je me suis présentée chez lui avec mon matériel et mes prières. Une fois la purification terminée, je me suis sentie vidée, fatiguée, il me tardait qu'une seule chose, de rentrer chez moi pour prendre une douche de lumière, pour me nettoyer et me ressourcer.

J'ai su par mon amie médium, qu'il y avait dans cette maison des entités du bas astral qui en ont profité pour pomper mon énergie !

A partir de là, je me suis promise que je ne ferai plus de nettoyage énergétique d'un lieu de vie à domicile car cette expérience m'avait refroidie.

L'Univers a mis sur ma route des nouvelles personnes pour purifier leur lieu de vie que je pratique maintenant à distance.

Comment je procède pour effectuer le nettoyage d'une maison à distance ?

Je demande à la cliente de se procurer du charbon et de la résine d'encens tel que le benjoin ou du Saint-Benoît, qui sont très connus pour ses puissantes propriétés purificatrices et protectrices.

La cliente et moi-même fixons le rendez-vous. Durant le nettoyage du lieu, je propose à la personne d'allumer une bougie (peu importe la couleur). Elle devra ensuite enflammer le charbon et le mettre dans une vieille casserole. Une fois le charbon incandescent, y déposer la résine d'encens qui va se consumer.

A partir de là, la personne me contacte pour me signaler qu'elle est prête pour passer les fumées d'encens dans toute sa maison. Ensuite je me mets en condition pour la purification en étant connectée à mon guide. Une fois que la cliente a mis l'encens dans toutes les pièces, je lui demande de sortir pendant une heure pour que le travail se fasse au niveau des énergies. Au bout d'une heure environ, lorsque la personne revient chez elle, je lui conseille d'ouvrir ses fenêtres durant 10 min pour aérer et de dire en visualisant : « je demande que toutes les mauvaises énergies partent de chez moi ». Elle sent alors comme un voile qui a été enlevé, qu'il y a plus de clarté dans la maison. La personne se sent mieux.

En général, je profite également de ce moment de purification pour accompagner les âmes dans la Lumière, avec l'aide mes guides spirituels, mes anges.

Témoignages de purifications de lieux de vie

- « *Cathy a effectué un nettoyage de mon appartement à distance, le résultat est immédiat. Je me sens libérée, je retrouve l'énergie qui circule à nouveau dans mon corps et que je n'avais plus depuis longtemps. Merci Cathy de tout mon cœur pour le travail effectué dans une grande simplicité avec autant d'amour. Avec toute mon amitié.* »

- « *Un grand merci à toi Cathy du superbe travail de purification que tu as fait à 2 reprises, pour mon domicile. Grâce à cela j'ai pu retrouver une sérénité et une énergie plus positive ainsi qu'un apaisement quasi immédiat, merci encore de ce don que tu offres en toute humilité, douceur et simplicité. »*

- « Je tiens à vous témoigner ma reconnaissance suite aux soins que nous avons reçus, ma petite famille et moi. Je n'oublierais jamais le bonheur que j'ai ressenti à mon réveil à l'issue du soin. Moi qui avait tant de mal à dormir à cause des douleurs, j'avais retrouvé un équilibre sur ce plan là. Concernant la maison, il y avait cette énergie, cette lumière qui dure encore. Je pense que vos soins s'imposent de temps en temps. Cathy est une perle, elle est disponible, n'est pas avare de bons conseils. Merci Cathy »

- « J'ai connu Cathy par ma mère, elle m'a fait un soin et un nettoyage de ma maison, car je me sentais triste, et j'avais peur d'aller dans certaines pièces de ma maison. Suite au soin et le nettoyage de la maison, je me sens épanouie, j'ai retrouvé le sourire, je dors mieux. Quand je rentre du travail, je ressens un apaisement dans ma maison et je n'ai plus peur. Je remercie Cathy car elle apporte beaucoup d'énergies, je l'encourage à continuer. »

- « Merci Cathy pour ton aide. Je viens de changer d'habitation et j avais du mal à me sentir

vraiment chez moi ! Cathy m'a proposé de faire une purification à distance du nouvel appartement ! Le résultat ne s'est pas fait attendre, dès mon retour chez moi, tout me semblait plus clair, plus léger, plus calme, la lumière me semblait différente ! Vraiment mille mercis pour cette purification, du très bon travail. »

- *« Suite au décès de ma maman, je ressentais une certaine lourdeur à chaque fois que je devais me rendre dans sa maison. Il me fallait procéder au déménagement de ses affaires car la maison est en transaction de vente.*

Je ressentais le besoin de la purifier, ayant entendu parler de cette méthode, j'ai contacté Cathy qui m'a tout de suite inspiré confiance par sa simplicité et sa bienveillance.

J'avais le souci de libérer l'âme de ma mère de son vécu. J'ai donc procédé à la purification et quand je suis revenue dans la maison une fois fini, je me suis sentie d'abord très fatiguée et pour la première fois je me suis allongée sur le canapé pour un moment de détente. Quelque chose avait changé !

A tel point qu'après, j'ai commencé à trier ses affaires. Avant, je rentrais dans cette maison comme dans un temple sacré avec le cœur serré, n'osant rien toucher. Cela devenait un problème puisqu'il me fallait la vider. Dans la soirée, une vision très intense de ma mère, m'est apparue. Elle venait me voir pour m'embrasser, elle rayonnait de gratitude et semblait tellement heureuse. Je pouvais presque la sentir, c'était vraiment troublant. Puis elle s'est éloignée, j'ai senti qu'elle partait en paix, au loin je pouvais deviner une foule de silhouettes blanches qui l'attendaient, je ressentais l'amour de ces âmes pour ma mère, j'ai compris qu'elle n'était pas seule et qu'elle se réjouissait de rejoindre tous ces êtres chers à son cœur ! J'ai beaucoup pleuré, je me suis sentie tellement émue de cette expérience !

Merci Cathy ! »

Je vous ai déjà signalé que je ne vois pas les âmes puisque mon guide intervient à travers mes rêves pour m'envoyer des messages, à moi de savoir les interpréter !

Un jour, une dame m'a contactée pour une purification de maison ainsi que pour accompagner des âmes dans la Lumière. En effet, sa fille et elle voyaient des entités dans leur maison. Cette situation les perturbait beaucoup. Elles étaient fatiguées et avaient quelques soucis de sommeil. Nous avons fixé un rendez-vous. Deux jours avant l'intervention, elle me contacte pour me dire qu'il y a de plus en plus d'âmes dans sa maison. Je ressentis que des âmes avaient dû se donner rendez-vous.Elles savaient que j'allais les aider à monter sur ce chemin lumineux.

En fin d'après-midi j'ai fait la purification des lieux et j'ai guidé les âmes vers la Lumière. Une fois le travail terminé, la personne m'a contactée pour me dire qu'elle ne voyait plus toutes ces entités, et qu'elle ressentait un vide dans la maison.

Après ce travail prenant, je décidais d'aller me coucher. Au petit matin, j'ai fait un rêve assez particulier :

« J'entends quelqu'un frapper à la porte. J'ouvre, et je découvre un Être lumineux assez grand, cheveux blond, les yeux bleus. Il se présente comme étant Saint-Expédit[2]. Rapidement, j'aperçois beaucoup de personnes dans ma cage

---

[2] Saint Expédit était un commandant romain d'Arménie converti au christianisme

d'escaliers qui montaient les marches, j'ai pris peur et j'ai fermé la porte ».

A mon réveil, je me suis dit que j'avais fait un drôle de rêve. Qu'est –ce qu'il voulait pouvoir dire ? Qu'est-ce qu'on a voulu me faire comprendre ? Comme à chaque soin que je fais, je contacte la personne pour savoir si la nuit a été bonne, vu la situation de la veille. J'ai donc demandé si les âmes étaient bien toutes parties... La dame me dit : « Enfin !!! On a bien dormi, la maison nous paraît tellement vide. Nous n'entendons plus les âmes. Nous ne les voyons plus non plus ! ». Ensuite, à plusieurs reprises elle m'a remerciée.

Suite à notre conversation, je compris le message que j'avais reçu à travers mon rêve. L'Être de Lumière était venu avec toutes les âmes pour me remercier de les avoir accompagnées au paradis. Je remercie le Ciel de me faire vivre de belles expériences.

La petite voix et l'intuition

Dans notre éducation, les parents ne nous apprennent pas à écouter notre soi intérieur, d'agir en fonction de nos ressentis, à écouter son Cœur qui est notre meilleur guide.

Dans mes expériences de vie, j'ai appris à lâcher prise, à vivre dans le détachement et à écouter mon âme qui me parle. Ma façon de vivre me permet d'être plus sereine et de me faire confiance.

Ma citation : *« Lorsque tu écoutes ton Cœur, il te répond avec Amour ».*

Comment entendre la voix de son Cœur ?

La petite voix de votre Cœur, elle vous parle avec Amour, elle est votre meilleur guide et vous accompagne quotidiennement avec douceur. La seule voix à qui vous pouvez faire confiance est uniquement votre voix intérieure. Elle ne veut que votre bien, vous pouvez y avoir accès en étant dans le silence.

Est-ce si difficile d'écouter la divinité, la source qui est en vous ?

Dans la vie, vous devez prendre des décisions mais vous ne savez pas toujours si vous faites les bons choix. Alors oui, il est difficile pour vous d'écouter votre âme. Par manque de confiance, vous demandez l'avis de vos amis en pensant qu'ils auront la solution. Finalement il arrive que vous soyez encore plus perdus, le doute et la peur s'installent.

Il n'y a pas de mauvais choix, car dans chaque chose que vous entreprenez, il y a un enseignement, une leçon à comprendre qui va permettre de faire grandir votre âme.

Lorsque l'on doit faire des choix ou prendre une décision, nous devons écouter nos ressentis, notre intuition. On dit souvent que la première idée qui nous vient en tête est fréquemment la bonne ! Faisons ce qui est le mieux pour nous.

Apprenons à ressentir avec notre cœur. Nous ne devons jamais nous sentir obligé de faire les choses. Nos décisions prises en conscience doivent nous apporter un bien-être intérieur, notre âme doit sourire, ressentir de la joie.

Cette voix du cœur nous murmure les meilleurs choix à faire. En prenant l'habitude de l'écouter, nous pourrons davantage faire confiance à notre intuition.

Comment entendre votre petite voix qui vous parle quotidiennement ?

La meilleure façon de communiquer avec votre cœur s'établit dans le silence. Il vous permettra de vous retrouver avec vous-même. Ces moments de pause sont importants pour ressourcer votre corps, votre âme et votre esprit. Faites-vous ce cadeau régulièrement. Respectez votre corps, écoutez-le en prenant soin de votre âme.

Comment ? En pratiquant la relaxation, la méditation. Savoir se détendre dans la nature par exemple, sortir avec des amis. Le fait de se changer les idées, vous permet de faire le vide, de lâcher prise. C'est souvent dans des moments de plaisir où l'esprit est distrait, qu'une réponse ou une solution peut apparaître, comme une évidence.

« La Voix de ton âme est la voix de la Divinité. Prends le temps de m'écouter, je suis là pour te guider. Seul le cœur connaît la vérité. Aie confiance en moi, laisse-toi guider par mon énergie d'amour. Ne sois pas influencée par le monde extérieur mais par l'énergie de ton cœur. Lorsque tu l'écoutes, il te répond avec amour. Nourris ton esprit et l'intérieur de ton cœur de Lumière pour ressentir le bonheur. En écoutant ta petite voix, elle te fera avancer, évoluer sur le chemin de Lumière » *Cathy Divine*

Laissez-vous guider par la divinité.

Personnellement, je suis convaincue qu'il y a quelque chose de supérieur à moi, et qui me guide. J'ai toujours cru aux anges, à la force divine et au pouvoir de l 'amour. Je reste convaincue qu'il n'y a pas de hasard dans la Vie. La divinité est amour, nous sommes des Êtres d'Amour, et notre Cœur contient des énergies d'amour qui nous guident vers la Lumière. Je dirai même que la divinité est en nous, je communique avec mon cœur, mon âme, mon guide.

La Divinité comprend :

Les Anges, les Archanges, les Guides. Ce sont des Êtres de Lumière, des Êtres supérieurs qui communiquent avec vous avec amour en passant par notre cœur. Lorsque vous ouvrez votre cœur, un canal s'ouvre pour que la communication s'établisse avec votre Moi Supérieur, votre guide.

Du moment où vous êtes conscients que vous n'êtes pas seuls, il suffit de demander de l'aide. Ainsi vous verrez que vous recevrez des réponses par synchronicité, par intuition. Il faut Savoir se laisser bercer par son cœur, par les énergies d'amour.

Je vous assure que lorsque vous aurez compris que vous n'êtes pas seuls, que vous êtes aidés et aimés par ce monde invisible qui nous veut que du bien, vous verrez la vie autrement. Elle est juste magnifique. Les Êtres de lumière nous aident à faire évoluer notre âme vers cet amour inconditionnel. Chaque jour, je remercie la puissance divine pour m'accompagner dans l'évolution de mon âme.

Faites confiance en votre intuition, et vos réponses vous apparaîtront sous plusieurs formes.

L'intuition sait ce qui est juste pour vous.

Soyez attentif aux signes que vous pouvez recevoir ! il se peut que vous ayez une idée qui vous vienne en tête. Et si c'était un message de votre guide pour éclairer votre chemin ? Votre âme vous parle, écoutez-là. Des réponses peuvent apparaître par des images ou à travers les rêves. Elle peut se manifester par l'intermédiaire d'une personne ou de la musique. Bien d'autres signes encore, comme une pièce de monnaie, une plume, un papillon, un rouge gorge ou des instants de synchronicités, peuvent être des signes de l'Univers.

Il vous appartient d'ouvrir votre cœur à ce

monde Divin qui se manifeste, pour vous dire qu'ils sont là, tout près de vous. N'ayez aucun doute, ayez confiance aux Êtres de Lumière. Ils vous guident dans votre vie.

Savez-vous faire la différence entre la voix de votre cœur et celle de votre mental ? Par qui vous laissez-vous guider ?

Pour laisser place à votre intuition, il est important d'avoir l'esprit calme et se débarrasser des pensées mentales, des idées reçues qui polluent le cerveau. Certaines activités vous apporteront un bien-être tels que le yoga, la sophrologie, la méditation en vous concentrant sur la respiration. Vous serez alors en mesure d'écouter l'intérieur de votre Être.

En allant au-delà de votre mental et de votre intellect, laissez parler votre cœur le plus souvent possible ! Vous y arriverez en évitant les bavardages personnels, en évitant que votre mental vous raconte des tas d'histoires. Tant qu'il occupe votre esprit, et, d'une certaine manière votre cerveau, votre conscience analytique vous empêche de ressentir avec votre cœur !

Quelques messages de ma petite voix du Cœur

« Lorsque tu as des doutes, des peurs, sache que tu n'es pas connecté à ton cœur. Apprends à calmer ton mental, à lâcher-prise, écoute-moi, écoute ton intuition, je t'insuffle les réponses dans ton cœur. Il suffit de l'écouter et de lui faire confiance. Le mental sèmera toujours le doute, la peur et la souffrance. L'amour ne ment jamais, il apporte le bonheur dans le cœur. Par qui veux-tu te laisser guider ? »

« Écoute ta petite voix. Nous te parlons avec Amour, pour t'insuffler et te guider vers la Lumière. Écoute ton intuition, elle vient de ton Cœur, de la Source, car la Divinité et la vérité sont en toi. Aie confiance en tes capacités, confiance en nous qui t'amenons la Lumière dans ton Cœur.

Ta petite Voix est Amour. Écoute-nous. Gratitude »

« Pas besoin d'avoir peur. En se laissant bercer et guider par les Énergies Divines qui sont à l'intérieur de ton Cœur, tu sauras lire la Divinité.

Savoir lâcher prise et apprendre à ressentir avec son âme, c'est ce qu'il y a de mieux pour Soi, pour son évolution. Tout est à l'intérieur et non à l'extérieur.

Écoute ton cœur, écoute-nous. La Lumière est en toi, elle est en nous. Fais confiance en l'Amour Divin. Connecte-toi à ton cœur pour ressentir cette vibration et avance en ayant un regard positif dans toutes choses. Ne baisse jamais les bras, les Êtres de Lumière sont toujours là pour te relever en t'entourant de leurs ailes, de leur Amour, pour continuer à avancer sur le chemin que tu t'es choisis : la Paix, l'Amour et la Lumière. Gratitude »

De la nuit vers ma lumière

Le lâcher-prise

Avant d'arriver au lâcher prise, il y a bien un travail à faire sur soi pour accepter de se laisser guider avec confiance et foi, par la puissance divine que vous pouvez invoquer comme vous le souhaitez : Dieu, Allah, Marie, Jehova, Bouddha … Tout cela reste lié à votre éducation dans une religion donnée. Il vous appartient de savoir que la véritable information a toujours été donnée, dans toutes les religions.

En lâchant prise, vos pensées ne sont pas dirigées dans le passé ou le futur. Vous n'êtes plus dans l'attente mais vous savourez chaque jour, l'instant présent sans être contrôlé par votre mental qui vous fait souvent souffrir, ou à ruminer sans cesse des situations.

« Tu es un Être heureux, du moment où tu lâches prise, tu n'attends plus rien de personne, tu as choisi en conscience de te laisser bercer par les Énergies Divines et tu n'es jamais seul. En lâchant prise, tu ne mentalises plus. Tu es un Être Heureux lorsque tu es connecté à Ton Cœur, à l'Amour.

Savoir accueillir les situations qui sont là pour faire évoluer ton âme vers la Lumière, le Pardon et la Paix.

Plus tu es dans l'attente et le manque, plus ton cœur souffre. Plus tu lâches prise, plus l'Univers t'ouvre les portes de Lumière pour mettre de la magie dans ta Vie. Vis l'instant présent, ta Vie, dans la légèreté du Cœur. Il est là le Bonheur. Gratitude »

« Lâcher-prise c'est ne plus s'agripper au passé, mais s'ouvrir à l'instant présent. Ce n'est ni craindre, ni espérer en l'avenir, mais construire celui-ci au présent. Lâcher-prise, c'est dénouer le

fil de la peur. C'est dénouer le fil de toutes les peurs.

C'est accepter de faire confiance, faire confiance à la vie et se faire confiance.

Lâcher-prise, c'est apprendre à agir et non à réagir. C'est apprendre à aimer sans rien attendre et s'ouvrir à ce qu'il y a de meilleur en l'autre.

C'est savoir accepter que l'autre soit différent et l'aimer tel qu'il est.

Lâcher-prise, c'est apprendre à pardonner, et à se pardonner. C'est aller au-delà des apparences, et s'ouvrir à ce qu'il y a de meilleur en soi-même.

Lâcher-prise, c'est naître et renaître à chaque inspiration. C'est apprivoiser le détachement à chaque expiration. C'est porter un regard sans cesse renouvelé sur tout ce qui nous entoure. Lâcher prise, c'est savoir écouter sans se croire obligé de conseiller ou de diriger. C'est respecter l'autre et se respecter.

Lâcher-prise, c'est savoir se taire pour vivre le silence. C'est apprivoiser le silence pour que naisse la paix. Souviens-toi : Quand tu pardonnes, Tu guéris.

Et quand tu lâches prise, Tu grandis. »

Lâcher-prise (Auteur inconnu)

La prière

Prier, est-ce que c'est quelque chose que vous faites tous les jours ? Priez-vous quand vous êtes seulement en difficulté ? Peut-être que vous ne priez pas du tout ? Peu importe, l'Être humain est libre de faire ou de ne pas faire. Il est important de respecter le choix de chacun.

Certaines personnes que je rencontre me disent ne pas savoir prier. Un conseil que je pourrai vous donner, « ouvrez votre Cœur au Tout-Puissant, aux Anges dont leur amour est inconditionnel pour chacun d'entre vous ». Laissez parler votre cœur, confier vos soucis. Les Anges sont là pour vous écouter, vous aider. Leur mission est de vous protéger et de vous guider. Soyez sincère dans vos demandes, soyez dans l'amour, dans l'intention de vouloir faire du bien autour de vous. Une prière est efficace lorsqu'on y met tout son cœur. Vous avez le choix de prier en récitant une prière, sinon, les mots choisis par votre âme sont aussi efficaces.

J'ai le souvenir qu'étant petite fille, je lisais une prière tous les soirs dans mon lit. Je parlais toute seule. Je savais qu'on m'entendait. C'était ma façon de prier, de demander avec mon cœur. A ce jour, la prière continue à faire partie de ma vie. Je ne passe pas un jour sans prier, je peux me retrouver dans la voiture, ou n'importe où, et avoir tout simplement des pensées lumineuses envers les êtres ou le monde. Ce qui me paraît important aussi, c'est de remercier le ciel d'être à mes côtés, de m'envoyer des signes, pour me montrer que je ne suis pas seule, d'exaucer mes vœux et de me faire vivre mes expériences sur terre pour faire évoluer mon âme. Alors oui je prie, et je suis dans la Gratitude tous les jours.

Lorsque tu pries, un Ange est près de toi pour amener de la douceur et la lumière dans ton Cœur. Gratitude.

L'Archange Raphaël, l'Archange Michaël

Mon amie médium Malorie m'a dit que j'étais accompagnée par plusieurs guides durant les soins en magnétisme ainsi que par les archanges Raphaël et Michaël. Etant donné les résultats positifs de mes soins, j'ai voulu m'informer sur ces deux archanges. Quelle aide apportent-ils durant le soin énergétique ?

L'archange Raphaël est le médecin chirurgien du ciel, il contribue également à guider les guérisseurs pour alléger vos souffrances. Il est un puissant guérisseur, les êtres humains et même les animaux retrouvent rapidement la santé. En effet, étant magnétiseuse, je canalise l'énergie de cet archange pour la transmettre à la personne que je soigne. Il intervient pour faire disparaître le stress et les différents maux. Durant le soin je visualise la couleur verte qui se dégage de cet archange. Elle favorise la guérison.

Je vous offre ici la demande que j'effectue auprès de lui : *« Archange Raphaël, envoyez votre lumière curative Vert émeraude dans mon cœur, pour que mon âme soit apaisée et que je puisse avancer sereinement dans ma vie, avec foi et confiance. Gratitude. »*

L'archange Michaël est l'ange protecteur, le plus puissant du ciel.

Vous pouvez demander son aide pour nettoyer votre maison ou tout autre lieu, et qui aurait des mauvaises énergies qui seraient à l'origine de conflits. En faisant votre demande avec Amour, l'archange Michaël interviendra pour chasser les basses vibrations et y déposer la Lumière.

Voici ma manière de faire appel à lui :

« Archange Michaël, merci de bien vouloir chasser toutes mauvaises énergies pour que ma maison vibre de Lumière, d'Amour et de Joie. Gratitude »

Prières inspires de ma petite voix intérieure

- « *Merci Archange Michaël de me protéger, de m'entourer de ton Amour Divin.*

Donne-moi la force pour me relever de mes épreuves difficiles. Merci de me guider pour avancer sur le chemin de la paix. Reçois l'Amour de mon cœur, je t'aime. »

- « *Merci l'Archange Raphaël de libérer mon Être de toutes les mauvaises énergies, de mes tensions, de mes douleurs physiques et morales. Merci l'Archange Raphaël d'apporter la Lumière à mon âme, de faire circuler l'énergie de Guérison dans mon corps pour retrouver la santé parfaite. Merci pour ton aide Divine, je t'aime.* »

- « *Je demande aux Forces Divines de déposer sur mon cœur l'énergie d'amour, de libérer mon cœur de toutes souffrances, d'apaiser mon âme pour retrouver la paix intérieure. Gratitude. Je t'aime.* »

Mes citations de pensées positives, se traduisant par un sentiment de paix et de calme

- « *J'ai confiance en moi, je suis guidée par mon cœur, le meilleur est devant moi, j'aime la vie et la vie m'aime. Je suis un être lumineux, je rayonne l'amour, la divinité est en moi. Gratitude* »

- « *Je choisis de suivre mon cœur. Lui seul sait me guider vers la lumière. J'ai confiance en mon cœur, lui seul me procure le bonheur. Je crée ma vie de façon positive. Tout rayonne autour de moi. Gratitude* »

- « *J'entretiens des pensées positives pour attirer la lumière, j'avance avec légèreté, je me laisse guider, je suis protégé(e) par la divinité, je suis un Être de Lumière, je tends toujours ma main pour diffuser l'amour autour de moi. Mon âme vibre de paix, d'amour et de lumière. Gratitude* »

- « *Pour connaître le bonheur, chaque jour, j'ai un regard optimiste sur ma vie. Je prends soin de mon cœur par des pensées d'amour, cela me donne la force, le courage. Plus je prends soin de mon âme, plus je suis en paix avec moi-même. Gratitude* »

- « *Je prends soin de mon âme pour qu'elle vibre de Lumière. Ce bien-être que je m'accorde, détend mon être. Je libère les tensions de mon cœur pour retrouver la plénitude. L'énergie diffuse dans chaque partie de mes membres, de mes cellules, je retrouve la vitalité. Gratitude* »

- « *Chacun de nous a la possibilité d'évoluer pour trouver la paix, l'amour dans son cœur, l'âme progresse lorsque je me remets en question, j'évolue à travers les expériences de la vie, j'écoute l'intérieur de mon cœur qui me fait avancer. Merci l'univers de faire évoluer mon âme sur le chemin de lumière. Gratitude* »

- « *Dans la vie tu as le choix de souffrir ou de sourire à la vie. Choisis de nourrir ton âme d'amour pour que ton cœur rayonne l'énergie divine et qu'il soit en paix. Tu mérites le bonheur, à toi de le créer. Ton âme sera en paix, lorsque ton enfant intérieur sera libéré de toutes souffrances, la guérison intérieure apporte la paix, l'amour dans toutes tes cellules, ton âme devient légère, pure, elle peut sourire à nouveau à la vie. Gratitude* »

- « *Le bonheur, c'est vivre l'instant présent en se laissant guider par l'énergie de son cœur. Faire les choses qui nous rendent heureux. Ton âme vibrera d'amour. Sache que le bonheur vient de l'intérieur et non de l'extérieur, suis toujours ton cœur, lui seul t'accompagnera sur le chemin du bonheur. Gratitude.* »

- « *La vie n'est pas facile. Évite de la compliquer par des pensées sombres. Regarde la vie avec les yeux de l'amour. Accepte tes situations difficiles, tu as des leçons à comprendre pour l'évolution de ton âme. Si tu ne les comprends pas, elles se répéteront tant que tu ne les auras pas comprises. Remercie l'univers de ce que tu possèdes, il te donnera ce qui est juste pour toi. Apprécie ce que la vie t'offre, sois dans l'accueil et non dans le contrôle, il est important que tu ouvres ton cœur à l'amour et non à la haine et la colère, tes pensées négatives mettront un frein dans ton évolution, dans ta vie. Apprécie ce que tu as, prends soin de ton âme, fais la paix avec toi même, entretiens des pensées lumineuses, tu attireras à toi des situations favorables. Lâche prise et vis dans l'amour. Apprends à t'aimer, à te respecter. Pour éviter de souffrir, n'attends rien de l'extérieur ainsi tu pourras vivre dans la paix du cœur. Gratitude.*

Ma paix intérieure

(Puissance de la Méditation : Joseph Murphy)

Mon esprit est calme et en paix, je reflète la sagesse et la beauté suprême.

L'esprit de Dieu coule à travers mes pensées, mes paroles et mes actes, je suis en paix. La paix qui passe tout entendement, me remplit.

Je sens et j'ai conscience de la sécurité et de la tranquillité de mon esprit qui est à l'unisson de l'infini. Je me repose dans les bras éternels. Ma vie est la vie de Dieu et elle est parfaite. Je suis unie à mon Père et mon Père est Dieu.

Je suis parfaitement détendue et équilibrée.

Mon esprit est l'esprit de Dieu et il est parfait. Les idées de Dieu s'épanouissent constamment en moi, m'apportant harmonie, santé et paix.

Je prends ma force dans la connaissance que Dieu est, et que tout est Dieu.

J'irradie l'Amour de Dieu. L'amour est

l'accomplissement de la loi et je suis ce que je contemple.

Ma petite voix m'insuffle la Lumière

Je vais vous présenter mes méditations quotidiennes. Je les ai canalisées en écoutant ma petite voix intérieure. Pour commencer la journée dans de bonnes énergies, je vous conseille de lire dans le calme et en conscience, la petite voix de mon cœur qui aura pour but de vous apporter la Paix, l'Amour, la Foi, l'Espoir, et de vous faire avancer positivement dans votre vie.

L'optimisme

Mon cœur voit la vie du bon côté pour vibrer d'amour. Je nourris l'intérieur de mon Être Divin par mes pensées positives, pour que mon âme puisse s'élever et rayonner. La Lumière brille dans mon cœur, elle me remplit de bonheur. Gratitude.

La méditation

Je me détache de mes préoccupations pour apaiser mon mental. Je me relie au divin, à mon âme, pour faire grandir la lumière dans mon Être intérieur. Mon cœur est en paix. Il vibre d'amour. Je retrouve l'harmonie.

Gratitude

La confiance

Aucune peur ne m'empêche d'avancer sur le chemin du bonheur. Je nourris mon cœur d'amour. J'ai confiance en moi, en l'Univers. Il m'apporte tout ce dont j'ai besoin, la paix et l'amour. Ma foi, ma force et mes pensées positives me guident sur le chemin de Lumière.

Gratitude.

La protection Divine

.Je prie avec mon cœur pour augmenter les vibrations d'amour et communiquer avec mon ange gardien, il m'enveloppe de son énergie divine pour

me protéger. Cette lumière brille tout autour de moi. Je suis protégée par l'Univers. Je suis un Être de Lumière.

Gratitude.

L'Amour inconditionnel

Au fond de mon âme, j'ai la racine de l'amour. Chaque jour, je sème l'amour dans les cœurs en envoyant des pensées lumineuses et chaleureuses. Le pardon est la clé qui ouvre la porte de mon cœur pour laisser sortir l'amour inconditionnel. Mon cœur vibre d'amour.

Gratitude.

Mon Cœur rayonne

Je dirige mes pensées vers le meilleur pour apporter de la couleur à mon cœur.

J'écoute ma petite voix intérieure, la réponse est dans mon cœur. Je crois aux forces spirituelles cela m'apporte du bonheur.

Gratitude.

Le lâcher-prise

Je remets mes inquiétudes à l'Univers, j'ai confiance en la vie, elle m'apporte ce qu'il y a de meilleur pour mon cœur. Je lâche prise, je remplis mon cœur de lumière. J'ai la conviction que ma route sera amour. Je décide de vivre le moment présent, d'aimer la vie.

Gratitude.

La gratitude

Je remercie tous les jours l'Univers de tout l'amour qu'il apporte à mon cœur

J'apprécie la simplicité du bonheur quotidien. Merci à la vie pour ses cadeaux qui me permettent de grandir dans l'amour. Merci pour cette force spirituelle qui me permet d'avancer sur le chemin de lumière. J'envoie des pensées d'amour au ciel pour lui dire que je l'aime.

Gratitude.

Ouvrir son Cœur

Avec l'aide divine, mon cœur est inondé de lumière. J'ouvre mon cœur à l'amour pour apprécier la beauté de la vie. Je vis le moment présent dans la joie, mon cœur sourit à la vie, j'ouvre mon cœur au bonheur.

Gratitude

Le monde invisible

Dans chaque situation difficile un ange est près de moi pour m'envelopper de son amour, pour me relever et me guider sur le chemin de la gaieté. Je ne suis jamais seul(e), je prie avec sincérité pour avoir l'aide divine. Mes vœux sont exaucés, je remercie l'Univers d'être à mes côtés pour apporter de la douceur à mon cœur.

Gratitude

La patience

Je ne perds pas patience, l'aide divine est toujours près de moi pour m'offrir l'énergie du bonheur au bon moment, pour retrouver le sourire. Je ne me décourage pas, je garde espoir. La patience m'amène sur le chemin de la réussite. Je patiente en laissant briller la lumière à l'intérieur de mon cœur. Je vis en Paix.

Gratitude.

Les leçons de vie

La vie est une école où j'apprends des leçons. Elles me font grandir dans la lumière et l'amour. Chaque leçon est un enseignement positif pour mon avenir.

Je demande du soutien à mon ange gardien pour recevoir son énergie et sa force. Le soleil est devant moi.

Gratitude.

Le Cœur

Chaque jour, je prends soin de mon cœur pour lui apporter l'énergie du plaisir.

Je le purifie pour que l'énergie circule en

douceur et que mon âme vibre de lumière. Elle s'élève quand je prends soin d'elle. Gratitude.

Donner avec le Cœur

J'ouvre mon cœur pour donner avec amour, sans rien attendre en retour. Tout m'est rendu au centuple. Je donne avec mon cœur. L'énergie du bonheur va vibrer en moi et autour de moi.

Gratitude.

Apprécier la vie

J'apprends à aimer ma vie malgré les difficultés. J'ouvre les yeux de l'amour pour apprécier le moment présent. L'Univers m'envoie des étincelles de bonheur. Cette lumière pure est source de joie pour mon cœur. J'apprécie ma vie. Chaque jour je grandis.

Gratitude.

La guérison

A chaque fois que mon Être Intérieur souffre, je demande humblement à l'Univers de purifier mon corps, d'être inondée de lumière, d'énergie Universelle. Je retrouve la force et l'énergie à l'intérieur de mon cœur. La lumière divine circule en douceur dans mon Être pour retrouver petit à petit le bonheur. J'ai la conviction d'être protégée. Je remercie pour l'énergie d'amour que j'ai reçue par les plans supérieurs.

Gratitude.

Les synchronicités

L'Univers apporte la beauté dans mon cœur pour éclairer mon âme. Les synchronicités se manifestent au bon moment de ma vie. Les cadeaux du ciel me guident vers le chemin qui m'est destiné. Avec tout mon Amour, je remercie la Terre pour apporter de la magie dans ma vie.

Gratitude.

La gentillesse

J'aime les Êtres qui m'entourent, je parle avec le cœur, avec douceur. Je sème l'amour autour de moi. Cette lumière diffuse dans le cœur des Êtres. Cette énergie d'amour est Source de Bonheur pour moi et autour de moi.

Gratitude.

La générosité

Mon âme est généreuse lorsqu'elle prend plaisir à donner. J'ouvre mon cœur avec amour pour donner le meilleur. Ma générosité apporte la sérénité, la paix et la lumière dans tous les cœurs.

Gratitude.

La réussite

J'entretiens dans mon cœur des pensées lumineuses pour que mon âme dégage la douceur, la lumière. Ainsi j'attire à moi des opportunités pour réussir dans ma vie. J'ai le pouvoir de réussir, je m'en donne les moyens. L'univers m'apporte son aide divine pour avancer sur le chemin de la réussite.

Gratitude.

Les rêves

Je réalise mes rêves en écoutant ma petite voix intérieure. Elle sait me guider sur le chemin de la vérité. Je fais confiance en mon âme, l'énergie m'est donnée par l'Univers pour concrétiser mes rêves. J'avance avec sérénité, avec le cœur léger.

Gratitude.

La nature

Chaque jour, je prends le temps de m'occuper de mon âme pour libérer mes pensées négatives, admirer la beauté de la nature pour relancer l'énergie dans mon cœur. La nature nourrit mon âme de lumière.

Gratitude.

La compassion

Je tends la main du cœur vers les Êtres en souffrance pour leur apporter du réconfort. Je transmets ma joie de vivre. Je donne avec amour le soleil à l'intérieur du cœur pour que la lumière éclaire l'âme. L'amour redonne le sourire et la paix dans les cœurs.

Gratitude.

L'harmonie

Je libère mes pensées négatives en y mettant la lumière, pour que l'énergie circule harmonieusement dans mon Être intérieur. Je ressens le silence et la paix au fond de mon âme. Mon cœur est lumineux et heureux.

Gratitude.

L'évolution

Je demande au ciel de m'accompagner pour évoluer dans ma vie. L'Univers met des Êtres lumineux sur ma route pour que j'évolue. J'ai confiance aux plans supérieurs qui est amour. Je me laisse guider par mon âme en toute sérénité qui évolue sur le chemin de lumière. Gratitude.

L'ancrage

J'entoure un arbre de mes bras avec amour, je lui demande sa lumière pour me fortifier et m'ancrer. Je ressens son énergie qui revitalise mon Être intérieur. La Lumière circule dans tout mon corps. Je deviens plus calme. Je remercie l'arbre de m'avoir donné son énergie, sa force.

Gratitude.

La prière

Je prie avec mon cœur. J'envoie des pensées d'amour aux Êtres de lumière, à l'Univers, à mes Anges pour leur dire que je les aime. Je demande à mon guide d'amener l'énergie universelle aux Êtres en souffrance. Leur cœur vibre à nouveau au bonheur. Mes prières, vibrant d'amour, sont entendues. Je remercie le Tout-Puissant.

Gratitude.

L'Âme

Je nourris mon âme de hautes vibrations comme l'amour, la tendresse, la joie, pour que l'énergie circule dans tout mon Être intérieur. Je prends soin de mon âme pour qu'elle rayonne. Mon esprit, mon cœur et mon âme sont en paix.

Gratitude.

L'amour de soi

Je m'aime, j'apprécie ma vie, je me fais plaisir. Je profite de la vie en prenant soin de moi. J'ouvre mon cœur à l'amour. J'accepte l'Être divin que je suis, avec mes qualités et défauts. L'amour de soi est une des clés pour m'épanouir et atteindre le bonheur.

Gratitude.

Le bonheur

Je travaille sur ma pureté intérieure. Chaque jour, j'alimente mon soleil intérieur en ouvrant mon cœur par des pensées lumineuses. Mes pensées positives apaisent mon esprit. Mon âme retrouve l'énergie. Mon cœur retrouve le bonheur. Gratitude.

Le moment présent

Je lâche prise sur les évènements du passé. Je retrouve le calme intérieur. En appréciant le moment présent, je suis sereine. Mon Être divin vibre de lumière en lui apportant l'amour tous les jours. Je suis en harmonie avec moi-même.

Gratitude.

L'intérieur de mon Cœur

Je nourris mon cœur par des pensées d'amour pour qu'il soit apaisé. Je lui apporte la force, le courage, en augmentant les vibrations dans tout mon Être intérieur. La lumière circule dans mon cœur tout en douceur. Je retrouve la paix intérieure.

Gratitude.

Le silence

Chaque jour, je prends soin de mon Être. En m'accordant un moment de silence, j'atténue les bruits intérieurs de mon cœur et j'écoute ma petite voix. Dans le silence, je suis en connexion avec ma Lumière intérieure. Je suis en Paix.

Gratitude.

L'univers

L'Univers, les Anges, les Guides de Lumière sont Amour. Je reçois leur Énergie pour que mon Être intérieur soit lumineux. Cette énergie d'amour apaise mon cœur et me guide sur le chemin de la vérité. Merci l'Univers de m'accompagner et de me protéger.

Gratitude.

Les vibrations

J'entretiens des pensées positives. Je garde espoir, la foi, pour avoir de belles vibrations lumineuses. Elles me donnent la force pour *avancer. Plus mes vibrations sont rayonnantes, plus j'attire à moi de belles choses pour mon cœur.*

Gratitude.

La vérité

A l'intérieur de mon cœur circule la puissance divine qui éclaire mon âme. En silence, j'écoute l'intérieur de mon cœur. Lui seul connaît la vérité. Je lui fais confiance et me laisse guider par l'énergie d'amour, en toute sérénité.

Gratitude.

Les signes

Avec Amour, je demande à recevoir un signe de mon ange, de mon guide, de mon étoile qui veille sur moi. Mes hautes vibrations d'amour me permettent de recevoir un clin d'œil du Ciel : la musique, un papillon, un oiseau, une plume, le prénom de mon ange. Tous ces signes sont souvent des réponses à mes questions. Je remercie l'univers pour les cadeaux qui réchauffent mon cœur. Gratitude.

La vérité

Mon cœur est libre, il ne dépend de personne. Aucun Être ne peut m'empêcher de progresser, d'avancer en toute sérénité. Je me relie à mon cœur, je l'écoute. A chaque pas que je fais, l'énergie divine éclaire ma route.

Gratitude.

Le partage

L'Univers me guide pour recevoir des informations, des messages qui me font évoluer dans ma vie. Ses cadeaux du ciel, je les offre avec mon cœur aux Êtres qui m'entourent, afin de faire progresser leur âme. Je partage avec amour. Je recevrai la lumière.

Gratitude.

L'humilité

Je suis un Être de lumière qui vit en toute simplicité, qui évolue chaque jour. Mon âme est heureuse. Je ne me glorifie pas de mes succès. Je *ne prétends pas être au-dessus des autres. Je remercie le Ciel de m'accompagner à me réaliser.*

Sans lui, je ne suis rien. Gratitude.

La source

Lorsque mon corps manque d'énergie, je me relie à la source pour qu'elle inonde mon âme de lumière. Cette énergie purifie tout mon Être intérieur. Je retrouve la vitalité qui me permet d'avancer. Je remercie du plus profond de mon cœur l'amour que j'ai reçu.

Gratitude.

Le potentiel

Chaque Être vient expérimenter sur terre. J'ai du potentiel et je me fais confiance. J'ai la Foi. J'extériorise la lumière qui est à l'intérieur de mon cœur. J'avance main dans la main avec mon guide qui est toujours là pour m'aider à évoluer et à réussir dans ma Vie.

Gratitude.

<u>Les pensées positives</u>

Chaque pensée positive que j'envoie avec mon cœur, avec sincérité, est une prière qui est entendue par la Source. J'ouvre mon cœur en y déposant des pensées lumineuses. Mes pensées positives éclairent mon âme et me donnent la force d'avancer dans l'harmonie du cœur.

Gratitude.

<u>L'éveil spirituel</u>

La spiritualité est un appel de l'âme. J'accueille les choses à moi sans rien forcer. Je fais confiance. Mon guide intérieur me conduit sur le chemin qui m'est destiné. Je laisse le soleil briller dans mon cœur au lieu de m'inquiéter. Je donne avec sincérité l'énergie d'amour sans rien attendre en retour. La lumière que j'ai dans mon cœur fait vibrer mon âme. Je ressens de la joie et la paix dans mon corps, je suis un être qui rayonne.

Gratitude.

La lumière

Au fond de mon cœur, il y a une partie sombre. Chaque matin, j'inspire en conscience la Lumière. Je la visualise pour la faire circuler dans tout mon Être.

J'expire la partie sombre qui encombre mon cœur pour retrouver l'harmonie et le sourire dans mon quotidien.

Gratitude.

Mon guide intérieur

Tout Être qui se relie à son guide, trouvera les réponses en ayant un regard à l'intérieur de son cœur et non à l'extérieur. J'apporte l'énergie de la Paix à mon âme par la méditation. L'étincelle divine me guide vers ce qui est le plus juste pour mon évolution, pour faire les bons choix. Je lui fais confiance. Gratitude.

Un moment de bien-être

Il est nécessaire de prendre soin de son âme,

pour qu'elle garde sa lumière intérieure. Ce bien - être que je m'accorde, détend mon corps. Je libère les tensions de mon cœur pour retrouver la plénitude. L'énergie diffuse dans chaque partie de mes membres, de mes cellules. Je retrouve la vitalité.

Gratitude.

Respirer l'Amour

Je suis un Être lumineux. Pour conserver cette énergie qui éclaire mon âme, je demande à mes anges de m'envelopper de leurs douces ailes, afin de ressentir leurs vibrations. J'inspire leur énergie d'amour qui purifie et apaise mon cœur.

En expirant, je partage cette lumière divine autour de moi avec la pure intention que toutes les âmes en souffrance puissent vibrer d'amour.

Gratitude.

Retrouver l'énergie

Lorsque ma Lumière intérieure est affaiblie

par la négativité de mon entourage, je m'autorise à me recentrer, à me donner de l'amour, à lâcher prise sur des évènements qui sont là pour mon évolution. J'ai le droit de m'entourer des Êtres lumineux, enthousiastes. Ainsi je retrouve l'énergie pour avancer vers la lumière. Mon cœur est en paix.

Gratitude.

Les choix

A chaque proposition qui se présente à moi, je me connecte à mon soi intérieur. Lorsque mon cœur ressent le bonheur, c'est que l'univers m'a guidée pour faire le bon choix. Je remercie le divin d'éclairer mon chemin.

Gratitude.

Le Divin

Chaque matin, mon cœur est relié au divin pour lui dire combien je l'aime. J'envoie l'énergie d'amour à tous les Êtres présents au fond de mon âme sans oublier les étoiles qui brillent pour moi.

Je ne suis pas seule, je suis entourée et guidée par les énergies supérieures. La Lumière est en moi et autour de moi. Gratitude.

La douceur

Chaque jour mon regard est lumière, mes paroles sont amour, elles sont le reflet de mon âme. Mon sourire apporte le soleil, ma tendresse, mes gestes apportent la paix, l'amour. Je choisis d'apporter l'étincelle du bonheur qui vient de mon cœur.

Gratitude.

La guérison intérieure

Je cherche à l'intérieur de mon cœur et non à l'extérieur, la solution, pour trouver la guérison intérieure. La Lumière finit toujours par arriver avec l'aide divine. Je prends soin de mon âme en lui apportant de l'amour. Je retrouve ma joie intérieure qui favorise la guérison. Gratitude.

Un être sur ton chemin

Je prends conscience que chaque Être que je croise sur mon chemin peut déclencher en moi une souffrance intérieure. Il a juste réveillé des mémoires, des anciennes blessures dont je dois me libérer, afin de pouvoir avancer sur mon chemin de lumière, dans la paix et dans l'amour du cœur. Je remercie le ciel d'avoir mis cette personne sur ma route, elle m'a permis de faire évoluer mon âme.

Gratitude.

Protège-toi

Je me protège des cœurs sombres qui souhaitent éteindre ma lumière intérieure. Peu importe ce que pensent les Êtres autour de moi, je n'agis pas en fonction des autres. Mon âme est amour. Je continue à faire briller le soleil intérieur de mon Être, je me laisse simplement guider par la lumière de mon cœur qui me protège.

Gratitude.

La pureté de mon Cœur

De mon cœur émane l'amour en envoyant des pensées chaleureuses. Cette énergie participe à la guérison de la Terre, de tous les Êtres. L'amour absorbe ces mauvaises énergies pour laisser place à la paix et à la lumière, je remercie les plans supérieurs de m'aider à apporter cette chaleur, pour adoucir les cœurs. Gratitude.

Mon Âme progresse

Chacun de nous a la possibilité d'évoluer pour trouver la paix, l'amour dans son Être. L'évolution, je ne l'apprends pas. Mon âme progresse lorsque je me remets en questions. J'évolue à travers les expériences de la vie. J'écoute l'intérieur de mon cœur qui me fait avancer. Merci l'Univers, de faire évoluer mon âme sur mon chemin de lumière. Gratitude.

Un Cœur joyeux

Je relativise sur mes expériences de vie, j'évite d'avoir des pensées de basses vibrations. Mon cœur est heureux quand j'entretiens des pensées de lumière. Je transmets mes vibrations positives autour de moi pour apporter de la joie.

Gratitude.

Aimer

J'apprends à aimer l'Être divin qui est en moi avec mes qualités et mes défauts, sans jugement. Je m'aime, je suis Amour, j'ai confiance en moi, je suis un être de lumière qui vibre l'amour. Je peux aimer inconditionnellement tous les Êtres qui m'entourent et leur apporter l'amour dans leur cœur pour qu'il rayonne. Gratitude.

Chasser mes peurs

A chaque fois que mon Être ressent une peur, une angoisse, j'ouvre mon cœur avec sincérité en demandant de l'aide à mes anges protecteurs. Je reçois leurs douces énergies afin de me nettoyer et apaiser mon âme. Mon cœur retrouve sa lumière intérieure, je remercie d'avoir reçu l'aide divine.

Gratitude.

L'égo

Si mon âme souffre, c'est l'égo qui s'exprime. Je lâche prise, je me relie à mon cœur, lui seul peut m'apporter l'énergie du bonheur, mon âme va retrouver le sourire.

Gratitude.

Fais de ton mieux

Chaque jour j'écoute mon âme, je fais un bilan de ma journée. J'améliore ce qui doit être amélioré pour que mon être soit en totale harmonie. Je fais de mon mieux, pour que mon cœur soit heureux.

Gratitude.

J'écoute mon guide

J'écoute mon guide. Il se trouve à l'intérieur de mon cœur. Je lui fais confiance

Il me guide toujours sur le chemin de l'amour. Il ne veut que mon bonheur. J'ouvre mon cœur, je prends le temps de l'écouter, mon guide aime communiquer avec moi pour m'apporter de la joie, de l'amour au fond de moi.

Gratitude.

Se purifier

Je purifie mon lieu de vie. Je purifie l'intérieur de mon Être pour que la lumière circule, m'apaise et m'éclaire. J'accueille les nouvelles énergies qui m'apportent la gaieté et la sérénité. Mon Être rayonne de Paix, d'amour et de lumière.

Gratitude.

La lumière est devant moi

Mon âme sait que la lumière est devant moi. Chaque jour j'ai des pensées d'amour pour élever les vibrations de mon Être. Je vois le meilleur autour de moi, cela me remplit de joie. Je nourris mon âme de lumière, ainsi je suis en harmonie avec moi-même. Je peux apporter l'aide aux cœurs blessés, l'énergie d'amour cicatrice leurs blessures. Petit à petit, ils retrouvent la sérénité. Chaque Être retrouve le goût à la vie et le bonheur à l'intérieur de leur cœur, l'âme vibre d'amour de paix et de lumière.

Gratitude.

La loi d'attraction

Dans mon quotidien, j'adopte une attitude positive, un état d'esprit lumineux ainsi j'attire à moi la lumière. Je maintiens les bonnes vibrations de mon Être pour ressentir la plénitude, la paix à l'intérieur de mon cœur. Je fais ma demande à l'Univers avec confiance, avec Amour. Je crois, j'ai la foi, j'obtiens !

Gratitude.

La paix intérieure

Je cesse de nourrir des basses vibrations. Dans le silence ou par une musique douce, je me connecte à mon âme, à la Source, pour apporter la lumière à mon Être. Je retrouve la paix intérieure, mon cœur est léger et apaisé. Gratitude.

Quelques canalisations de mes messages inspirés par ma petite voix

Pour ne pas que ton Cœur souffre, offre-lui de l'Amour, de la Lumière, chaque jour, pour qu'il soit en Paix.

Tu es un Être important. Apprends à te respecter.

Donne-toi de l'Amour pour être heureux dans ton Cœur. Le Bonheur est en toi, ici et maintenant. Sache que tu es Maître de ta Vie. Le bonheur ne dépend que de toi. Tu es le seul Être qui peut prendre ta Vie en main. Choisis de suivre l'énergie de ton Cœur où habite la Divinité. Laisse-toi guider par l'Amour.

Gratitude.

Je suis là pour t'accompagner et non te juger. Tu veux des réponses ? Va au plus profond de ton Être, les solutions sont à l'intérieur et non à l'extérieur. Tu es maître de ta Vie, tu as une multitude de possibilités, de choix. Il suffit que tu apprennes à écouter la Divinité qui est en Toi et tout va s'éclairer. Te plaindre ne te fera pas avancer. Si tu entretiens ta Lumière intérieure, le meilleur viendra à toi. Dans la Vie tu as toujours le choix, fais ce qui est le mieux pour ton Âme, pour ton bien-être, ne sois pas matérialiste. Sache que le matériel n'apporte pas l'Amour. Ouvre ton Cœur à l'Amour, tu recevras l'Amour et le Bonheur. Construis ta Vie sans peur et avance dans la Lumière. Ton Âme sera épanouie et en Harmonie.

Gratitude.

Tu sais que je suis toujours près de toi pour t'accompagner, te faire évoluer

Tu peux ressentir tout l'Amour que j'ai pour toi car je déverse dans ton Cœur ma Lumière Céleste pour bercer et réchauffer ton Âme. Écoute-moi, laisse-toi guider par la Divinité et tu sauras où je veux t'amener. Tu es entouré, aimé, par les Êtres de Lumière. Tu ne dois pas douter de notre Amour, de notre Force que nous t'envoyons chaque jour pour avancer sur ce beau chemin étincelant. Ta Vie n'a pas été facile, tu as toujours continué à semer l'Amour autour de toi. Nous sommes fiers de toi car tu as toujours surmonté les difficultés dans la Lumière et la Sagesse. Nous fermons une porte pour en ouvrir une autre. Une porte Lumineuse où ton âme va pouvoir s'épanouir. Nous serons là pour continuer à avancer dans la Lumière, éclairer le monde grâce à l'Amour qui émane de toi. Ton Guide, tous les Êtres Spirituels, sont avec toi.

Avançons ensemble dans l'Amour, pour un monde meilleur. Nous t'aimons. Nous ne faisons qu'un. Gratitude

Tu es un Être libre du moment où l'on ne contrôle pas ton existence. Vole de tes propres Ailes pour vivre et découvrir la douceur et la beauté de la Vie. Le papillon vole en direction de la Lumière. Tu dois en faire de même pour faire évoluer ton Âme. Pour avancer dans cette énergie lumineuse, tu passeras par l'ombre pour en tirer des leçons. Tes prises de conscience te feront grandir pour voler plus haut vers la Lumière. Tu as déployé tes Ailes. Maintenant vole, vole avec Amour. Nous volerons avec toi pour atteindre la Lumière.

Gratitude.

Dans chaque épreuve douloureuse, nous te guidons vers un jour meilleur. Un travail sur soi est important pour retrouver l'harmonie dans ton Cœur. Ton Être devient plus léger pour avancer et évoluer sereinement. Nous sommes là pour t'ouvrir les portes de l'Amour pour continuer à rayonner la

Lumière. Tu es toujours soutenue par la Divinité. Avance, laisse-toi guider par notre Amour, par ton Cœur. Tout finit par s'éclairer. Tu es protégé(e) par l'énergie Universelle. Gratitude.

Quand il y a du soleil dans ton cœur, tu rayonnes la Lumière. Même dans tes moments difficiles, essaie de faire sourire ton Cœur pour entretenir la Lumière, l'Espoir, la Foi. Je suis toujours là pour te guider vers ce qui est le mieux pour toi, pour l'évolution de ton Âme. Elle peut souffrir mais je ne t'abandonnerai jamais. Chaque jour, tu es aidée par la Lumière Céleste. Nous te guidons par synchronicités vers des Êtres Terrestres.

Nous sommes tous Unis pour amener l'énergie de Guérison.

Gratitude.

Apprends à te connecter à ton Être intérieur. Tu as cette capacité à te purifier, pour que ton âme et ton enfant intérieur soient en paix. Nous te demandons de faire un travail en profondeur, d'aller à la Source du problème afin de te libérer. À chaque pas que tu fais pour avancer, nous semons la Lumière de guérison dans tes cellules pour attirer à toi des situations lumineuses. Les Êtres de Lumière sont toujours près de toi pour te guider vers des anges terrestres qui sont là pour éclairer ton âme. Garde la Foi, la Force et l'Amour qui sont en Toi, ils te permettent de t'élever dans de hautes vibrations.

Plus tu prendras soin de ton enfant intérieur, de ton âme, plus tu connaîtras la Paix, le Bonheur, plus la lumière circulera en toi et rayonnera dans ta vie. Ton Cœur s'ouvrira à l'Amour. Tu seras un Être Pur.

Gratitude.

Il n'y a pas de bonne ou de mauvaise personne, nous mettons sur ta route des Êtres ou des situations pour en tirer une leçon pour l'évolution de ton âme. A toi de comprendre ce que nous voulons t'enseigner. Nous souhaitons que tu progresses sur ce chemin de Lumière et d'Amour. Que tu sois dans l'Ouverture du Cœur, malgré les difficultés que tu peux rencontrer. Continue à *semer les graines de l'Amour. En semant l'Amour pour toi et autour de toi, nous serons en mesure de t'ouvrir les portes de Lumière pour que tu puisses vivre le paradis sur Terre. Remercie la Vie de te faire grandir dans l'Amour du Cœur.*

Gratitude.

Si tu veux te comporter comme un adulte et être en harmonie avec toi- même, fais grandir ton enfant intérieur en le libérant de ses blessures. Sois toujours proche de lui, écoute-le. Soyez complice. Rassure-le. Donne-lui de l'Amour. Vous pourrez avancer sereinement. Vous rayonnerez d'Amour, de Lumière et de Paix. Tout vient de l'intérieur. Le Bonheur commence à partir de là. Quand ton Enfant Intérieur est Heureux, tu l'es aussi. Sois conscient(e) que ton enfant intérieur a besoin de toi pour que vous soyez épanouis. Quand tu auras trouvé cette paix en toi, les Portes de Lumière vont s'ouvrir pour Toi avec Amour.

Gratitude.

Pas besoin d'avoir peur. En se laissant bercer

et guider par les Énergies qui sont à l'intérieur de ton Cœur, tu sauras lire la Divinité. Savoir lâcher prise et apprendre à ressentir avec son âme, c'est ce qu'il y a de mieux pour soi, pour son évolution. Tout est à l'intérieur et non à l'extérieur. Écoute ton cœur, écoute- nous. La Lumière est en toi, elle est en nous. Fais confiance en l'Amour Divin. Connecte-toi à ton cœur pour ressentir cette vibration et avance en ayant un regard positif dans toutes choses. Ne baisse jamais les bras, les Êtres de Lumière sont toujours là pour te relever en t'entourant de leurs ailes, de leur Amour, pour continuer à avancer sur le chemin que tu t'es choisis : la Paix, l'Amour et la Lumière. Gratitude

Lorsque les yeux de mon cœur croisent ton regard, j'aperçois la lumière de ton âme. Gratitude.

Sois toujours maître de ta vie. Laisse-toi guider par la voix de ton âme. Déploie tes ailes pour voler vers la Lumière. Tu es un Être libre.

Gratitude.

La route vers ma lumière !

Quand le Cœur est en paix, l'Âme vibre d'Amour. Lorsque tu écoutes ton cœur, il te répond avec Amour.

La vie n'est pas toujours facile, il y a beaucoup de souffrances dans le cœur de chaque Être, souvent lié à un passé douloureux, ce qui peut expliquer les difficultés à surmonter les épreuves et à ne pas être épanoui dans la vie. Suite à mes expériences et un travail personnel, j'ai décidé de partager avec vous ce que ma petite voix m'a insufflée pour réussir à vivre en harmonie. Par ailleurs, je vais partager deux méthodes efficaces, la sophro-analyse des mémoires prénatales de la naissance et de l'enfance puis l'EDMR. Je vous conterais ensuite mon expérience personnelle, le seul outil qui m'a réellement permis de libérer mes souffrances pour faire place à la Paix intérieure.

Comment trouver cette paix intérieure pour vivre sereinement, après des expériences de vie difficiles

Je vais vous présenter ce que mon âme m'a insufflée pour vivre dans la paix du cœur.

- Apprends à pardonner ton prochain avec ton cœur, pour ne pas ressentir de rancune envers l'Être qui t'a fait du mal. Ainsi tu arriveras à vivre en paix avec toi-même. Le pardon est un acte d'amour, lorsque tu arriveras à pardonner, tu ne ressentiras plus aucune colère à l'intérieur de ton corps, mais juste de la paix et de la joie.

- Il faut apprendre à se protéger des personnes négatives ou qui t'ont fait souffrir, en y mettant de la distance pour éviter de revivre les mêmes erreurs, les mêmes conflits. Vois le côté positif de chaque expérience pour ton évolution personnelle.

- Pour vivre en paix, respecte-toi et fais-toi respecter. Aie ton propre arbitre, sois à l'écoute de ton âme, tu auras toujours la réponse car elle vient du cœur. Pense à toi avant de penser aux autres, c'est savoir se respecter et s'occuper de son âme afin qu'elle puisse vibrer de paix et d'amour.

- Tu es maître de ta vie. Mets les choses en place pour ressentir la joie dans ton cœur. Tu seras toujours bien servi par toi-même car tout est fait avec l'énergie de ton cœur. Lui seul sait ce qui est bon pour toi.

Il se peut que tu sois parfois déstabilisé par les pensées ou conseils extérieurs de certains, ce qui engendre le doute, la peur et donc la perte de confiance. En écoutant ta petite voix intérieure, elle te guidera sur le bon chemin. Tout conseil positif qui te sera transmis, ne sera pas forcément bon pour toi, sois toujours maître de tes propres idées.

- Lorsque tu auras compris que chaque expérience négative est là pour t'enseigner quelque chose de positif dans ta vie, pour te faire évoluer, essaie de t'améliorer chaque jour, à devenir un Être bon et généreux. Ouvre ton cœur à l'amour.

- Essaie de vivre en harmonie avec toi-même, en libérant les pensées négatives et en y mettant la lumière pour retrouver la paix intérieure. Il est important d'entretenir des pensées positives. Tu auras ainsi plus de chance d'attirer le meilleur à toi. Aie la Foi, aie confiance en l'Univers, aie confiance en toi.

- Sur ton chemin de vie, tu vas rencontrer des personnes négatives qui te feront culpabiliser. Ne t'entoure pas des Êtres qui polluent ton existence, ils mettront un frein dans ton évolution.

- Entoure-toi de personnes lumineuses, ton cœur sera rempli de joie. Est-ce que tu as besoin du monde extérieur pour combler ce vide ou ce manque qui est en toi pour être heureux ? Le bonheur et la paix sont à l'intérieur de toi, tu dois le créer.

- Apprends à t'aimer, à t'apporter l'amour, chaque jour, en prenant soin de ton âme, à écouter le silence pour être en connexion avec ton cœur. Pour cela, promène-toi dans la forêt, cela va te permettre de te ressourcer. Lorsque tu réaliseras que tu apprécies ta propre compagnie, tu seras un être heureux. Tu ressentiras la paix et le bonheur dans ton cœur, où que tu ailles.

- Apprécie ta vie malgré les difficultés. Lâche prise sur les évènements du passé, il faut s'en détacher pour pouvoir avancer sereinement. Le passé t'a permis d'être la personne que tu es devenue. Sois fière de ton chemin parcouru et remercie l'Univers de t'avoir accompagné à surmonter tes épreuves, tes leçons de vie.

- Apprends à vivre dans le moment présent et à faire en sorte que chaque jour que tu vis se déroule dans l'amour, la joie. Ainsi tu vivras en paix. Lorsque tes vibrations sont élevées, ton cœur est en paix, elles te donnent la force pour avancer et tu attires le bonheur dans le cœur. Aime la vie et la vie t'aimera.

Prière de guérison par Edgar Cayce[3]

- « Par le pouvoir de ma pensée, je demande à mon énergie d'éliminer les poisons dans chacun de mes corps afin de laisser place à l'influence et à la force christique.

Je demande à toutes mes énergies de se remettre en mouvement et à un corps de se connecter sur l'onde de guérison la plus parfaite pour moi.

Je demande à mon corps physique et à tous mes corps subtils de coopérer et d'harmoniser leurs programmes afin de me régénérer, de me libérer et de me guérir.

Amen »

---

[3] Edgar Cayce – Philosophe Christique

Messages inspirés par ma petite voix

Mon Cœur, j'ai appris à t'aimer, j'ai appris à t'écouter, j'ai appris à avoir confiance en toi, j'ai appris à te laisser me guider, j'ai appris à ressentir, à transmettre l'énergie d'amour qui circule dans mon cœur. Tu es mon meilleur ami qui sait me conseiller. Le Bonheur est dans mon cœur.

Tu fais partie de ma vie, Gratitude.

Ne cesse jamais d'espérer dans la vie. Tout peut arriver. Il suffit de garder la foi. De lâcher prise. Avoir confiance en l'Univers. Il sait ce qui est bon pour toi, afin que ton âme puisse évoluer. Dans la vie, tu as parfois des décisions à prendre, n'aie pas peur du regard des autres. Agis en te laissant guider par ton cœur. Il t'amènera sur le chemin qui t'es destiné pour vivre dans la sérénité.

Gratitude.

Pour aimer la vie, apprends à lui sourire. Pour être heureux, donne-toi de l'amour. Le bonheur ne se trouve pas à l'extérieur. Tout est à l'intérieur de ton Être. Ton Cœur est rempli de richesse. Fais lui confiance, va à sa rencontre. Tu y découvriras cette Lumière qui va t'aider à évoluer dans la paix et dans l'Amour. La divinité est dans ton cœur.

Gratitude.

Dans le silence, reçois en conscience la lumière qui est devant toi. Cette énergie diffuse en douceur au plus profond de ton Être pour que ton âme baigne dans l'amour, maintenant écoute ton cœur. Ton âme te parle avec Amour.

Gratitude.

Parle toujours avec ton âme, tes paroles doivent être le reflet de ton cœur. Parle avec douceur pour transmettre l'énergie d'amour autour de toi, pour que chaque Être vibre de joie. Garde la lumière, l'amour et la foi au fond de ton cœur. Ton chemin vibrera de bonheur.

Gratitude.

Le bonheur est une énergie d'amour qui doit circuler tous les jours à l'intérieur de ton Être. A toi de faire vibrer ton cœur pour connaître le bonheur.

Gratitude.

Le soleil est une énergie d'amour qui réchauffe le cœur de tous les Êtres. Ouvre le tien à l'amour. Aie de la compassion. Aime davantage ton prochain, pour que, dans le regard des Êtres, on retrouve cette étincelle d'amour. Lorsque tu as des doutes, des peurs, sache que tu n'es pas connecté à ton cœur, apprends à l'écouter. Les belles vibrations d'amour t'amèneront toujours sur le chemin de lumière. Relies toi à la divinité, à ton cœur, pour vivre en paix et dans la sérénité.

Gratitude.

Continue à avancer, même si tu rencontres des difficultés. Prends la vie du bon côté en ouvrant ton cœur vers le soleil. La lumière viendra à toi si tu désires l'accueillir.

N'abandonne pas. Avance en ayant confiance

et en écoutant ton cœur.

Gratitude.

La liberté :

Ne sois pas dans l'attachement. Ton cœur souffrira. Sois un Être libre dans ton cœur, tu connaîtras le bonheur. Crée ta vie comme ton âme le souhaite, en appréciant le moment présent. Vole de tes propres ailes dans les vibrations d'amour sans rien attendre en retour, tu verras comme la vie est belle, tu seras un Être libre et en harmonie, vole, vole, aime la vie, et la vie va te sourire !

Gratitude.

Tu es Unique. Chaque Être doit chercher à l'intérieur de son cœur, la clé pour vivre dans la sérénité. Plus tu as confiance en toi, plus tu rayonneras. Plus tu as confiance en l'univers, plus les portes de lumière s'ouvriront à toi.

Gratitude.

Tu es le créateur de ta vie. Tout est à l'intérieur de toi pour que ta vie vibre d'amour et de joie. Écoute ton âme en réalisant tes rêves qui t'apportent le bonheur dans ton cœur. Prends conscience que l'amour est partout. Reconnecte-toi à la nature pour ressentir les bienfaits : le lâcher prise, la paix intérieure. De ton Être divin émane la Lumière. Continue à rayonner comme un soleil, continue à donner avec ton cœur, continue à aimer sans juger, continue à prier pour que le monde vibre d'amour, de paix et de lumière.

Gratitude.

Apprends à être heureux avec toi-même. Ainsi tu pourras être heureux n'importe où et avec n'importe qui. Gratitude.

Dans la Vie, tu as toujours le choix :

De regarder ton passé qui te fait souffrir et t'empêche de t'épanouir ou d'ouvrir ton cœur, en te donnant la chance de connaître le bonheur.

Gratitude.

Choisis de vivre et non de souffrir. Choisis de vivre et abandonne tes peurs. Accepte chaque expérience douloureuse qui est là pour faire évoluer ton âme.

Choisis de vivre et d'être heureux. Choisis de vivre et d'être libre. Choisis de vivre et de t'aimer. Choisis de vivre et de faire confiance à la divinité, cette énergie pure qui émane de ton cœur. Choisis de créer ta vie avec des sourires.

Choisis de vivre en harmonie. Choisis de vivre en ouvrant ton cœur à l'amour.

Choisis d'aimer la vie et la vie t'aimera.

Gratitude.

Apprendre à se détacher

- Il est important de savoir que personne ne nous appartient, comme les ami(e)s, la famille, les collègues. Nous rencontrons des Êtres qui sont destinés à faire un bout de chemin avec nous ou toute une vie.

- Chaque personne qui se présente à nous est là pour faire évoluer notre âme. Alors apprenons à vivre dans le détachement de tout jugement. Ce dernier engendre des peurs, de la souffrance. Nous devons vivre sans posséder l'autre, le laisser vivre en toute liberté.

- Lorsque nous vivons dans le détachement, nous ne sommes plus dans le contrôle d'une situation. Nous retrouvons une certaine liberté dans notre cœur, nous laissons l'autre libre de ses actes. Laissons agir l'univers, laissons-nous guider sans rien forcer, apprenons à être dans le lâcher prise.

- Lorsque quelque chose ne se réalise pas comme nous le souhaitons, il serait bien de penser que l'univers nous prépare quelque chose de mieux pour notre évolution, qu'une opportunité va se présenter prochainement.

- Il nous faut être dans l'acceptation de tout ce qui se présente à nous, que ce soit positif ou négatif. Dans chaque situation négative, il faut apprendre à se remettre en question, pour y voir le côté positif. Ainsi nous attirerons la lumière, si notre regard se porte vers le positif.

Ce que nous avons, c'est un cadeau de l'univers. Nous obtenons toujours les choses au bon moment. Tout est juste et parfait pour notre évolution.

- Il faut apprendre à se détacher de toute chose pour éviter d'être dans l'attente et de souffrir. Quand nous souffrons, nos vibrations ne sont plus lumineuses.

Chaque pensée négative, les peurs entre autre, font baisser nos vibrations. Nous devons transformer les pensées sombres en lumière, pour que notre cœur soit en paix.

Nous devons apprendre à augmenter nos vibrations d'amour, à travailler la joie, la paix, la confiance et aimer les Êtres. Savoir être généreux à travers une parole, une aide quelconque pour ceux qui en ont besoin.

Le fait d'aider son prochain nous apportera la

joie intérieure, mais aussi chez celui que nous allons aider. L'amour vibrera en nous et autour de nous. Pour entretenir cette belle énergie, nous devons lâcher prise, relativiser les situations vécues, tout en sachant que chaque épreuve nous rend plus fort. Il est nécessaire de prendre du temps pour soi, afin d'offrir à notre âme cet amour, et de la partager autour de nous.

Citations inspirées:

- *« Lorsque tu seras dans l'acceptation de chaque expérience, dans le lâcher prise, à l'écoute de ton cœur et non de ton égo, tu retrouveras la paix intérieure. Fais rentrer la lumière dans ton Être pour que ton âme vibre d'amour.*
Gratitude. »

- *« La Lumière est à l'intérieur de toi. Va à sa rencontre pour que ton âme puisse t'éclairer. Ton cœur verra des synchronicités envoyées par la divinité. Laisse rayonner l'énergie d'amour en toi, et autour de toi, pour transmettre la paix et la joie.*
Gratitude. »

Apprendre à écouter son Cœur

- Il faut savoir écouter en conscience ce que vous dicte votre âme. Elle est la seule à savoir ce qui est bon pour vous. Il nous faut agir sans mettre des barrières, par peur d'être jugé.

- La vérité se trouve à l'intérieur de votre cœur alors écoutez-le !

- Personne ne doit diriger votre existence, elle vous appartient, vous êtes le créateur de votre vie. Vous êtes capable de savoir ce qui est bien pour vous. Ayez confiance en votre petite voix intérieure. Elle est là pour vous guider.

Pour être connecté à votre cœur, il suffit de vivre dans le détachement, être à l'écoute de vos ressentis, et qui vibre à l'intérieur de votre cœur. Il vous faut faire les choses qui vous rendent heureux, et non pas par obligation.

- Apprenez à relativiser sur vos expériences qui vous paraissent insurmontables. Sachez que vous n'êtes jamais seul, mais guidés par des Êtres de lumière, les anges gardiens. N'hésitez pas à allumer une bougie pour faire votre demande avec sincérité. Reliez-vous à eux pour ressentir leur amour et l'apaisement. Vous serez toujours entendu car vous êtes aimé par ce monde invisible.

- La vie est belle pour celui qui veut l'apprécier. Celui qui aime la vie est dans l'acceptation de ses propres expériences sur terre. Il sait que le meilleur est devant lui. Il faut apprendre à apprécier le moment présent, et faire chaque jour ce qui vous rend heureux.

- Vous pouvez connaître le bonheur en mettant en place des actions, en conscience en écoutant votre âme. Vous ressentirez alors, de la joie à l'intérieur de votre Être.

Comment libérer ses souffrances intérieures.

En libérant votre cœur des souffrances, puis en vivant dans le détachement, vous serez en mesure de vous laisser guider par votre cœur et d'être en paix dans le quotidien.

Cela demande un certain travail personnel. Vous passerez sûrement par des moments difficiles, par beaucoup de pleurs. Mais au final vous vous sentirez transformé, libéré intérieurement. Il est important de savoir, qu'il existe des thérapeutes qui sont compétents pour nous aider, nous accompagner pour réussir à trouver la paix intérieure. J'ai un jour, rencontré Nathalie, une praticienne de sophro-analyse des mémoires prénatales, de la naissance et de l'enfance.

Qu'est-ce que la sophro-analyse des mémoires prénatales et de l'enfance ?

La sophro-analyse des mémoires prénatales de la naissance et de l'enfance est une thérapie brève d'une vingtaine d'heures environ.

Cette méthode psycho thérapeutique complète et non dirigiste, permet en toute sécurité, par une simple relaxation guidée, d'aller libérer l'origine des souffrances telles que des périodes de dévalorisation ou non estime de soi.

Cette méthode va permettre de nous libérer de tous ces scénarios de souffrances psychiques, de croyances limitantes, d'auto sabotage, qui entraîne des comportements particuliers, et qui pourrissent la vie, même si la personne a « tout pour être heureuse ».

C'est un outil extraordinaire qui nous aide à rayer définitivement ces scénarios répétitifs. Ceux-ci sont très souvent mis en place pendant la petite enfance ou durant la vie intra – utérine. Ils se sont littéralement « gravés » dans notre psyché à ce moment-là. Ces empreintes vont alors rester actives à l'intérieur de l'adulte et prendre une importance de plus en plus grande dans la vie, y installant le mal-être et souvent des maladies.

La thérapie commence après une anamnèse et une détermination d'objectifs : « ce pourquoi le patient est venu ».

A chaque séance, le client, par simple relaxation se relie à son âme en quelques minutes. Cette partie de lui, qui va le guider en fonction de ses capacités émotionnelles, de son niveau de conscience, va l'amener exactement là où c'est juste, là où c'est bon pour lui. Elle va le guider là où il y a les ressources pour gérer, là où c'est prêt ! C'est à chaque fois un parcours sur mesure pour la personne.

L'âme retourne au moment où ces croyances limitantes se sont mises en place dans la vie du client, soit quand il était enfant, où lorsqu'il était dans le ventre de sa mère. Rappelons que la conscience s'incarne dès la première cellule créée.

Quand le client réalise à quel moment de sa vie il a été ramené, le thérapeute intervient pour recadrer, changer l'interprétation. Il s'emploiera à donner un nouveau sens à la situation, afin qu'émerge une nouvelle compréhension de ce qui a été vécu, une nouvelle prise de conscience, libératoire. Une réconciliation avec l'amour, au-delà des apparences pourra alors naître : « non je ne suis pas coupable », « oui mon père et /ou ma mère m'aiment », « oui j'ai été désirée » etc.

Au fil des séances, la colère, les culpabilités, les souffrances sont libérées. Le regard que l'on porte sur soi et sur les autres s'apaise et devient plus serein. La paix intérieure s'installe. La personne retrouve aussi son potentiel, le manifeste dans sa vie. Il peut enfin se réaliser, trouver sa place et donner un sens dans la vie. L'énergie de vie est retrouvée !

Cette nouvelle conscience porte la guérison à son plus haut niveau, dans l'acceptation de toutes les expériences ombre-lumière.

La sophro-analyse est une thérapie basée sur l'amour, la compassion, la bienveillance et l'ouverture du cœur.

Cette méthode a été initiée par Claude Imbert[4], écrivain, éditrice, conférencière internationale, thérapeute et formatrice. Ses découvertes avant-gardistes sur la psychologie prénatale, les mémoires et la fréquence des « jumeaux nés seuls », ont contribué à effectuer un pas de géant en psychothérapie. Elle est l'auteure de plusieurs essais et livres sur ce sujet.

---

[4] Claude Imbert : Chercheur en médecine – Ecrivain-Conférencière. - www.claude-imbert.com

Elle fut reprise et améliorée par le Docteur Christine Louveau[5] qui, malgré un doctorat en biologie et 10 années de recherche en laboratoire pharmaceutique, n'arrivait pas à s'épanouir dans cette voie, ni dans sa vie. Un jour, elle découvrit un des livres de Claude Imbert [6]. Sa vie bascula dès lors. Elle fit une thérapie avec elle, puis se format en Allemagne pendant deux ans à la programmation neuro-linguistique (PNL), en analyse transactionnelle et en constellation familiale. Elle travailla avec Claude Imbert pendant quelques années et reprit le centre de formation au départ de Claude. Plus tard, elle décida de partir vers d'autres voies de réalisation.

Rencontre avec Nathalie

J'ai rencontré Nathalie, la thérapeute en sophro-analyse, un peu par hasard, en août 2016. J'ai immédiatement eu le pressentiment que nous allions travailler ensemble. Ce fut le cas quelques mois plus tard. Je ne pouvais imaginer cela en

---

[5]Christine Louveau : Docteur en Neurobiologie – Chercheur-Auteur conférencière- www.sophro-analyse.org
[6] Claude Imbert : « l'avenir se joue avec la naissance » 1999 Editions Visualisation

commençant cette thérapie.

Nathalie m'a fait prendre conscience que ce n'était pas Cathy qui était en mal-être, mais cette petite fille intérieure qui se cachait en moi. Sa souffrance était liée à mon passé douloureux. Alors j'ai décidé de suivre cette thérapie afin de guérir de mes blessures intérieures pour que cette petite fille retrouve la paix et que je puisse continuer ma route en toute sérénité.

A chaque séance et en toute confiance, je me suis laissée guider par ma thérapeute et par mon âme. Elles ont su m'accompagner à la source de mes souffrances par rapport à une situation qui a tendance, parfois même, à se répéter dans ma vie, à mes peurs, mes doutes, mon manque de confiance…

Comment savoir que mon âme a su aller à la source du problème ?

Tout est dans le ressenti. Lorsque mon âme a su m'accompagner à la source (avec l'aide de Nathalie), j'ai toujours éclaté en sanglots. Quelque chose d'incroyable et d'incontrôlable, se produisait. Les pleurs sortaient de mes tripes. C'était des instants très forts et libérateurs.

Cette méthode est très efficace. J'ai pu en ressentir immédiatement les bienfaits, en portant un autre regard sur la situation qui me rongeait intérieurement.

A ce jour, mon cœur est libéré de toutes souffrances, j'avance sereinement et en harmonie.

C'est un vrai bonheur de ressentir cette énergie de paix qui circule à l'intérieur de mon cœur. Je n'avais jamais ressenti ce bien-être auparavant. Aujourd'hui, mon âme est calme, et cette petite fille intérieure est en paix.

Nathalie m'a permis de me libérer de mes souffrances, puis en comprendre le sens pour retrouver la paix intérieure.

Une période encore difficile

A partir de juillet 2017, l'Univers m'a testée en mettant sur ma route une situation pour me montrer finalement que mon cœur n'était pas guéri.

Un jour, j'ai fait la connaissance d'une personne qui m'a donné les coordonnées de Christel, thérapeute en sophro-énergétique demeurant dans la région Toulousaine.

J'ai consulté Christel pour des blessures d'abandons, le manque d'amour de mes parents et d'autres soucis personnels liés à mon enfance.

Nous avons commencé l'accompagnement par des séances en EMDR (Eye Movement Desensitization and Reprocessing), technique qui permet de travailler sur les traumatismes du passé et d'enlever les stress.

Tout vécu, dans une connotation trop stressante, reste dans la mémoire périphérique de notre cerveau.

Monsieur Edison et Monsieur Einstein ont démontré que notre cerveau est un émetteur-récepteur très puissant. Tant que ces expériences douloureuses ne sont pas digérées, rangées, classées, elles restent présentes et attirent à nouveau des expériences similaires.

Le travail de Christel est de mettre en lumière, de faire prendre conscience de ces répétitions. Grace à la technique de l'EMDR (mouvements oculaires et clapping au niveau des mains), elle permet d'enlever le stress et offre la possibilité de ranger les souvenirs.

Ainsi nous retrouvons cette paix à l'intérieur de nous, en nous ouvrant à de nouvelles expériences.

J'ai fait trois séances d'EMDR. J'ai beaucoup pleuré à chaque fin de séance, mais j'ai pu retrouver le calme intérieur. En alternance, j'ai reçu des soins corporels, des massages énergétiques, cette pratique permet de nettoyer, au niveau corporel, les stress et mémoires engrammés.

À ce niveau de l'accompagnement, Christel travaille sur le plan spirituel avec les mémoires de l'âme ainsi que sur les douleurs corporelles. À la fin du soin, la personne se sent reconnectée à elle-même.

Témoignage de ma thérapeute Christel :

« Cathy est venue le cœur ouvert avec une réelle détermination de déposer ses armes, ses souffrances. Elle est allée à la rencontre de son enfant intérieur afin de s'accueillir en toute vérité. Elle a construit en elle des piliers forts en remplacement des vécus de souffrances en lien avec ses parents. Sans victimisation et en profonde compréhension des limites de l'autre, elle a positionné ses parents intérieurs remplie de douceur, de nourriture affective et son adulte intérieur, ce qui lui permet de se sécuriser. »

Grâce aux magnifiques soins de Christel, j'ai réussi à me libérer de deux expériences karmiques qui maintenaient de fortes relations en émotions négatives. Par cette libération je laisse rentrer dans ma vie des rapports plus simples et apaisés.

Est-ce que cette technique a été efficace dans le temps ?

Je vous en parlerais un peu plus tard, mais pour l'instant, mon Cœur est en paix.

Il n'y a pas de hasard

J'ai assisté à des conférences médiumniques près de chez moi, en juillet 2016. J'y ai reçu le message d'une médium qui me disait qu'elle me voyait faire des conférences. Je lui ai répondu qu'honnêtement, que je ne me sentais pas du tout prête à faire cela. Parler devant un public n'est pas quelque chose qui m'attire.

Le temps passe, l'été 2017, une amie m'invite à sortir et me présente Lydie, avec qui je fais plus ample connaissance.

Nous nous rencontrons à plusieurs reprises pour nous rendre compte que nous avons beaucoup de points en commun. Elle est praticienne en médecine traditionnelle chinoise. Son souhait était d'évoluer dans son métier.

En septembre 2017, je revois mon amie

médium, Malorie, avec qui je fais un échange de soin. Mon guide me dit que ma place n'est plus derrière mon bureau mais que je dois partager ma lumière à l'extérieur de chez moi, ce qui veut dire faire des conférences ! Ahaaa ce mot qui revient dans mes oreilles ! Je ne voulais surtout pas l'entendre !! C'était certainement dû à ma peur d'être jugée, au manque de confiance en moi. Je n'avais jamais parlé devant un public. Cela paraît si simple mais pas pour moi. "Eh oui Cathy tu dois sortir de ta zone de confort et aller de l'avant ! "

Malorie m'avait bien rassurée par les messages médiumniques, en me disant que je ne serai pas seule et que je serai bien entourée par mes guides. J'ai bien retenu les beaux messages que je garde au chaud dans mon cœur. Quelques jours après avoir vu Malorie, j'ai revu Lydie qui me conseilla de contacter l'association "Artmonyl", celle-ci proposant des stages de bien-être à Saint-Félix du Lauragais.

Je contacte alors Stéphanie, la responsable de

l'association. Nous nous présentons mutuellement, puis elle m'explique qu'elle a une salle où l'on peut faire des conférences à titre personnel. A partir de là, j'ai compris ce qui allait se passer prochainement, c'était une évidence.

Il n'y a vraiment pas de hasard dans les rencontres. Tout s'emboîte comme il se doit, par synchronicités. J'ai tout simplement été guidée pour faire ces rencontres, dans le but de faire mes premières conférences avec Lydie dans cette association. Dix personnes s'étaient inscrites pour ma première. A la deuxième, il n'y avait qu'une quinzaine de personnes. Cela peut paraître peu, mais pour moi c'était déjà beaucoup pour parler en public. Pour tout vous dire, à la fin de la conférence, j'étais heureuse d'avoir dépassé mes peurs. Je me suis sentie grandie intérieurement, malgré un peu de stress. J'ai été capable de faire ces conférences, j'étais fière de moi ! Tout s'était fait naturellement. J'avais bien senti la présence du monde invisible, leur amour. Ce fut des moments magiques, divins.

Suis-je prête à en faire d'autres ?

Je me laisse guider par ce que ressent mon cœur et ce dont il a envie de faire. C'est le plus important. Je ne veux pas m'éparpiller. Je souhaite faire les choses les unes après les autres. J'ai un projet que je vais mettre en place prochainement, faire un atelier ou une conférence pour présenter une méditation guidée. J'en ai déjà parlé à une thérapeute qui souhaite que je la présente dans sa salle destinée aux conférences. Je ne m'inquiète pas, les choses se feront si elles doivent se faire ! J'envisage de créer ma chaîne Youtube, de me procurer un tambour chamanique que j'utiliserai pendant les soins. Je me laisse porter, et tout se fera au bon moment.

Un nouveau projet va se réaliser en mars 2018, un documentaire « 5 min pour vous dire » qui m'a été proposée par Edmond GIROU[7], auteur de plusieurs livres sur les phénomènes inexpliqués et les mondes invisibles. Edmond va venir m'enregistrer et me filmer dans le but de présenter mon activité de magnétiseuse. Mon amie Anne sera présente pour faire la patiente. Ce documentaire sera mis sur la chaine You tube et sur mon site.

---

[7] Edmond Girou : Chercheur - Auteur- Conférencier

Edmond, une belle âme que l'Univers a mise sur ma route dans le but de me faire avancer vers la Lumière. Je ne pouvais pas refuser sa proposition car là aussi j'ai compris que c'était un cadeau du Ciel. Oui, mon âme est heureuse de pouvoir réaliser cette nouvelle expérience avec mes deux amis de Cœur, Edmond et Anne, une journée inoubliable qui sera gravée dans mon cœur. Gratitude.

La libération définitive de mes souffrances

Vous le savez, j'avais consulté Nathalie et Christel pour faire un travail en profondeur. Ces deux personnes très compétentes ont su m'aider à retrouver l'harmonie.

Malgré leur aide, il m'arrivait, de temps en temps, de ressentir un mal-être. J'avais envie de pleurer. Le problème était toujours lié à mon passé, à mes parents. Même si je me sentais beaucoup mieux intérieurement, je devais continuer à faire ce travail personnel. Il n'était pas encore terminé. Je sentais au fond de moi que j'étais proche de la guérison. Je suis une battante, et je sais que j'arriverais très bientôt à me libérer de ce poids qui m'empêche d'être sereine. Un jour, mon cœur sera entièrement guéri.

J'ai pris les choses en main pour essayer moi-même de continuer à libérer mes blessures d'âmes, notamment en faisant un exercice qui m'a permis de retrouver la paix, de vivre dans le lâcher prise. Je ne verse plus une larme. Enfin mon cœur est guéri !

Oui, mon cœur n'est plus vide, car j'y ai mis de la lumière et de l'amour. Mon cœur est heureux car je n'attends plus rien de personne. L'amour que je n'ai pas eu, j'ai appris à me le donner et je me le donne tous les jours. J'ai tourné une page de ma vie pour continuer à avancer vers la Lumière avec le sourire.

Voici ma petite expérience que je pratique à chaque fois que j'en ressentais le besoin.

Un jour, j'ai décidé de prendre une feuille et un stylo. J'ai allumé une bougie et me suis installée sur une chaise pour écrire. J'ai commencé par demander de l'aide à mes guides pour m'aider à me libérer de mon passé et trouver définitivement cette paix intérieure.

J'ai commencé à écrire tout ce qui me dérangeait vis à vis « de mon père, de ma mère, de ma belle-mère… », de mon passé douloureux qui était toujours présent dans mes cellules.

Oui j'ai pleuré, lorsque j'ai écrit toutes ces pages. Une fois terminé, j'ai relu en pleurant tout ce que j'avais écrit, et je l'ai relu jusqu'à ce que je ne pleure plus. Je me suis sentie vidée et apaisée à la fois, une grande fatigue s'est fait ressentir.

Le fait d'écrire permet de libérer ses émotions de souffrance et révèle en conscience nos qualités élévatrices de notre âme.

J'ai ensuite décidé de brûler mes écrits, en demandant à mon guide de recevoir les énergies de guérison dans mon cœur. Il m'est venu à l'esprit de dire : je te pardonne pour le mal que tu m'as fait. A partir de là, j'ai prononcé à haute voix et avec mon cœur : « je te pardonne papa pour tout le mal que tu m'as fait ». Ce fut un moment assez douloureux car j'ai beaucoup pleuré sans pouvoir m'arrêter, tellement l'instant était puissant. J'ai prononcé autant de fois qu'il fallut « je te pardonne papa » jusqu'à ce que je ne pleure plus. Du moment où je n'ai plus pleuré, je savais que j'étais libérée de mon fardeau et que mon cœur avait réellement pardonné aux personnes qui m'avaient blessée.

J'avoue que cet outil a été très efficace pour moi. Il fut libérateur, et que je ne peux que vous le conseiller, comme je le fais à toutes les personnes que je vois pour un soin.

Le fait de brûler ces écrits permet d'accueillir les véritables qualités de notre âme.

Nathalie et Christel avaient été là pour m'accompagner mais la seule personne qui a su me guérir, c'est moi. J'ai su pardonner à mes parents et surtout je l'ai fait avec mon cœur, avec amour. Personne d'autre que moi ne pouvait guérir mon Cœur. Malgré tout ce que j'ai vécu, j'aime toujours mes parents.

Ainsi, j'ai retrouvé la paix intérieure. Mon cœur sourit. Je vis l'instant présent avec bonheur. Je vis enfin dans le lâcher-prise. Je me laisse guider par les synchronicités. La vie est tout simplement magnifique. J'ai toujours aimé la vie mais je l'aime encore plus chaque jour. J'ai appris à accueillir ce que la vie nous offre, savoir se remettre en question, travailler sur soi pour pouvoir avancer dans l'harmonie.

Suite à cette purification « aux feuilles brûlées » mon amie Maud, thérapeute en art thérapie, m'a conseillée d'écrire un mantra.

La lecture quotidienne d'un mantra permet d'ouvrir notre cœur et de nous révéler avec authenticité.

Ce mantra, je l'ai lu à haute voix, pour que toutes mes cellules s'en imprègnent, dans le but que tout se transforme à l'intérieur de moi et autour de moi. Ce mantra, je vous le livre ici. Il pourra éventuellement vous permettre d'écrire le vôtre.

MON MANTRA :

JE SUIS UNE FEMME LIBRE

JE RAYONNE DANS L'AMOUR, DANS L'HARMONIE AVEC TOUS LES ÊTRES

JE SUIS UN ÊTRE DE LUMIÈRE

JE SUIS HEUREUSE ET JE SOURIS A LA VIE

J'AVANCE AVEC CONFIANCE DANS LA LUMIÈRE ET DANS LA PAIX DU CŒUR

JE SUIS UNE FEMME AFFIRMÉE, INDÉPENDANTE REMPLIE D'AMOUR

JE M'AIME PROFONDÉMENT

JE SUIS UN ÊTRE DE LUMIÈRE QUI RAYONNE LE BONHEUR

JE ME RÉALISE EN TANT QUE FEMME LIBRE.

Je souhaite terminer ce livre par une partie importante de mon cheminement vers la Lumière. Je désire vous montrer que nous sommes maîtres de notre vie et ce, malgré les souffrances que nous possédons. Nous avons ce pouvoir de nous en libérer par différentes techniques pour vivre quotidiennement en paix.

Nous avons toujours le choix de vivre avec le cœur en souffrance, ou avec le cœur qui sourit. Mon choix est de vivre en toute liberté dans l'harmonie de mon Cœur. J'ai pu me libérer de mes souffrances à partir du moment où j'ai pardonné avec mon âme. Je suis en train de renaître et de nouvelles portes s'ouvrent à moi, la Lumière est là.

En tant que thérapeute, il est important pour moi de travailler avec un cœur guéri plutôt qu'avec un cœur en souffrance.

A ce jour, je suis heureuse de pouvoir partager l'énergie d'amour et de guérison autour de moi. Paix, Amour et Lumière.

« Savoir aimer et pardonner avec son cœur pour transmettre la lumière.

Savoir aimer chaque Être en toute liberté sans rien attendre en retour. Tu verras le soleil briller dans ton cœur.

Sur ta route, tu rencontreras des âmes pures qui sauront te tendre la main.

Elles te seront envoyées par la Divinité pour ouvrir une porte dans ta Vie.

Quand tu acceptes de découvrir l'inconnu, tu ressens cette lumière envahir ton cœur, pour ressentir le bonheur et tout l'amour que nous t'envoyons.

La Source te guide à chaque pas que tu fais pour avancer dans l'ouverture du cœur.

Entretiens toujours la Lumière pour faire le bien autour de toi.

Laisse-toi guider par l'énergie de ton âme pour transmettre l'Amour.

Nous souhaitons un monde meilleur, tout cela

dépend de vous.

Soyez bon envers vous-même pour être bon envers les autres. Ainsi le monde vibrera de belles énergies de Paix, d'Amour et de Lumière. »

Cathy Divine

Remerciements

Baptiste, Antoine, Mathieu C : Mes chers enfants, je vous dédie ce livre avec Amour. Lorsque vous serez plus grands, vous pourrez découvrir mon chemin parcouru. Il est important d'écouter son cœur et d'avoir un regard positif sur la vie malgré les difficultés que l'on peut rencontrer. Je vous aime.

Edmond Girou : Merci pour ta présence, ton soutien et ta Lumière. Elle me fait avancer un peu plus chaque jour. Merci de m'avoir tendue la main pour réaliser de beaux projets qui me comblent de joie. Tu es un cadeau du Ciel, je remercie la Divinité pour t'avoir mis sur ma route.

Mon cœur t'envoie plein d'amour pour la réussite de tes projets.

Anne L : Merci pour ton amitié, ta fidélité, ta douceur. Merci pour ton aide précieuse, ton investissement dans mes projets, pour ta présence au quotidien et ta confiance. Tu es un ange !

Yves Eleuthéria : Merci d'avoir croisé mon chemin, pour ton amitié, pour tes encouragements, de ton aide et nos échanges quotidiens. Je te souhaite le meilleur.

Yves Eleuthéria, auteur du livre « Journal d'un éveillé. »

Malorie L : Ton guide a tout fait pour nous rencontrer, quel bonheur ! Merci de faire partie de ma vie, grâce aux messages spirituels des guides, j'ai pu me lancer avec confiance vers de nouvelles expériences. Merci belle âme, continue à éclairer les cœurs par ta Lumière.

A toutes fins utiles, je vous donne le numéro de mon amie médium : 06.11.91.18.91

Guy B : Pas de hasard dans notre rencontre. Je te remercie pour ton amitié, ton soutien, pour ta présence. Merci pour ta Lumière, je te souhaite une belle évolution et la réussite dans tes projets.

Doriane B : Heureuse que tu ais croisé ma route. Merci pour nos partages dans la Lumière. Je te souhaite une belle réussite.

Christel V : Ma thérapeute lumineuse et exceptionnelle qui a su m'accompagner, à guérir mon Cœur. Je suis heureuse que l'Univers m'ait guidée vers toi.

Contact : 06.23.62.08.17

Maud M : Merci ma sœur de cœur pour ton soutien, pour ton amitié, pour ta confiance, pour ta belle lumière. Je te souhaite le meilleur.

Thérapeute en Art Thérapie. Le Mans : marteau.maud@gmail.com

Son association : l'Art d'Être Soi.

Lydie T : Heureuse d'avoir croisé ta route et d'avoir accepté de faire les deux conférences. Ce fut un moment de bonheur qui restera gravé dans mon cœur.

Je te souhaite la réalisation de tes projets et t'envoie plein de lumière.

Médecine Traditionnelle Chinoise : lydie.thirouard7@gmail.com

Stéphanie de « l'association Artmonyl » : Merci d'avoir accepté que je puisse faire mes deux conférences dans ton association bien chaleureuse. Merci de m'avoir fait grandir. Plein de soleil et d'amour pour ton association.

Contact : 06.58.59.86.20

Nathalie D : Merci Nathalie pour tout le bien que tu m'as apportée par cette thérapie. Je la conseille à tous, afin que votre cœur, votre âme soient libérés de cette charge émotionnelle de souffrances, pour retrouver la joie de vivre.

Son mail : nathalie.desautee@gmail.com

Je remercie mes guides spirituels et tous les Êtres de Lumière qui m'accompagnent pour transmettre l'énergie de guérison aux personnes en souffrance. Gratitude.

Je remercie mes étoiles, mon oncle et ma grand-mère pour leurs signes que je reçois régulièrement, me faisant comprendre qu'ils sont près de moi. Merci pour votre lumière, je vous aime.

Je remercie tous les Êtres qui ont croisé ma route, qui m'ont permis de grandir dans ma vie privée et professionnelle.

Je remercie toutes les personnes qui me soutiennent, pour leur confiance, pour leurs témoignages car sans vous, je n'en serais pas là aujourd'hui.

Cathy Divine

https://sites.google.com/site/cathymagnetisme

GRATITUDE

CreateSpace, Charleston SC

2018